have mercy

a Have a Life Novel

Maddy Wells

Blue Heron Book Works

ISBN 13: 978-0-692-35990-7

ISBN 10: 0692359907

This is a work of fiction. Any similarity to persons living or dead or events past or present is solely and luckily due to the uncanny talent of the author.

Blue Heron Book Works, LLC

www.blueheronbookworks.com

Printed by Createspace, an Amazon.com company

Cover design by Angie Zambrano

TO MAUDE APATOW

ACKNOWLEDGMENTS

As this is my first novel, I have to thank everyone, but especially the people who had to live with me while I wrote it: my husband, Jonah, and my unnamed cat. Any ideas there? Special thanks to my editor, Paul Fuhrman, who made me a better writer. Thanks to Angie Zambrano for the delicious cover. And finally thanks to publisher, Bathsheba Monk, and all the folks at Blue Heron Book Works who helped me bring *have mercy* to you.

1

Tim, my bass player and I wasted an *hour* of practice time arguing about how we were going to present ourselves to The Griffin—a world famous metal rocker and incidentally my dad who was visiting me and my mom in two days. The argument this time was about a gimmick, a device, a *trick* to make us different from the other eight million rock bands out there, of which—according to "Sleep Walker" on Yahoo Answers—seven million, nine hundred and ninety-nine thousand, nine hundred and ninety-nine suck. "Sleep Walker's" humble opinion, but still. Eight million freakin' rock bands. Wikihow says in their excellent article, How to Form a Rock Band, which I refer to on my iPhone at the beginning of the argument: "Try to find something you could do like always wear a certain head band when performing or (if you can) twiddle your ears while singing or playing the instrument you do." Which, honestly, might work if we were a novelty band and sometimes when I'm looking at a Ziggy Stardust video or something, it seems to me that those are the only ones that everyone loves. I mean Bowie's a giant, sure, but still. And what about Lady Gaga? I'm not saying she isn't talented, I mean how could I say that, look where she is, but it doesn't hurt that she dresses like an alien slut and that she cuts Madonna, who is exactly like her when you analyze it except Madonna is old enough to be her grandmother, but they both keep it going like Family Feud or Judge Judy or something and everyone's glued to their fight, which isn't music, it's a *gimmick*. I wish there were a study of the young musicians that started out with just talent and energy and those that started out with a gimmick and the study would tell you what happened to them both in ten years. Which ones were still playing and which ones got jobs in pest control. The thing is, I think we—Tim and I—have enough talent and energy to make it without putting on the clown nose, but then again, we haven't gotten a lot of valuable feedback.

"We're living in a very militaristic world and berets say we're on top,

1

we're winners," I told Tim. "The entire Olympic team is going to wear berets. And we both look good in berets." I'd picked up some berets, epaulets and jackets at Crazy Duffy's Army Navy store and made Tim try a couple of things on before we started practice. "No one's done that since Michael Jackson."

"Yeah, and Michael Jackson's dead. And this shit is wicked hot. It's like a thousand degrees in here. On stage, with all those lights, it'll be even hotter."

I admired Tim's clear-cut vision of us—of himself at least—on a stage with Klieg lights burning our eyeballs out, with him definitely shirtless, or maybe an open leather vest showing off his hairless chest which he flashes every chance he gets and which he is sociopathically proud of. He shrugged off the woolen Russian officer dress coat, checked out his triceps which were nicely pumped from heaving cases of Vitamin Water at his job, picked up his guitar, turned up the amp on his bass, let go an E flat—the key I sing in—on reverb and segued into a riff á la Jimi Hendrix.

I followed him down the scale on my guitar, a Fender that The Griffin gave me for my last birthday. It was much more satisfying playing music than arguing costumes. I mean, what's the point of having a rock band if you spend ten percent of your time on music and ninety percent of your time on packaging? Why don't you just form a marketing company?

But it was stupid to think that someone was just going to be walking by my garage studio, hear our incredible riffs, be rightfully astounded and sign us up for a world tour with a recording contract. That was a fairy tale and at almost-sixteen I was too old to believe in fairy tales. Eight million bands. And those were just the ones with Facebook pages.

Tim unplugged and packed up his guitar. "I gotta go to work."

Tim's job at the Seven-Eleven was becoming a total pain because we had to turn down gigs—okay, one gig—because he had to work on Saturdays which were party days and the only gigs we could get were at parties of kids our age and they always happened on Saturdays when parents were out of town.

"Try to fix your schedule so you can have off on Saturday from now on," I said.

He rode down the driveway on his bicycle with his guitar case flung over his shoulder just as Jane was coming out of the house. Jane was my size exactly which gave me no hope whatsoever for adding more inches to either my height or my chest. The doctor told me last year, when I *finally* got my period and Jane dragged me there so Doctor Frazier could tell me all the things that Jane was disinclined to tell me about being a woman, that sometimes girls had growth spurts, but not to get up my hopes of being the next Beyoncé. The most I could hope for was five seven and breast implants and what's that? You're not an Amazon warrior, but you're not an adorable elfin princess either. The vision I had of myself—six foot tall in leather pants, bustier, and magenta gelled hair—didn't work on five-five unless I wore ten inch platform heels, but then I'd be Lady Gaga, right? With my conventional looks—pretty, no tattoos—yet—I should be a freakin' folk singer playing acoustic, but there's only so much tolerance in the world for sincerity, Jane says, and the world passed that mark without a goodbye party way back in the last century. So five-five with brown hair and hazel eyes is the numbingly average raw material I have to work with. Thanks a lot, Jane.

It doesn't matter to Jane if she looks average, she's just a high school teacher. Jane tries to dress hip and she's always getting in trouble for not wearing the K-Mart formless that the school principal holds up as a mature standard. She brought home the dress-code-for-teachers brochure that Principal Thwaite had printed up and we almost peed our pants laughing at the clothing in it.

Actually, Jane didn't meet *any* mature standard. Jane was the only teacher left on earth—certainly the only mother—who chain smoked right in front of me, showing her total disregard for my health with her second-hand smoke.

She flicked her cigarette butt into the driveway, watched Tim do a wheelie as he turned the corner, muttered "not bad," and opened the car door to the Kia—a Christmas present from The Griffin—before she saw me.

"Oh, hi," she said.

"Where are you going?" I asked.

"School. Proctor senior make-up exams."

Which was a complete joke, because Jane just did not care if students cheated. An upper classman told me she read her iPhone the entire time his class was taking a math final, kids actually moving their desks closer to the smart kids to cheat and she did not even look up at the sound of metal scraping linoleum. "Why should I care?" she'd ask. "The rest of the world doesn't give a damn if kids cheat. Why should I hold the bag?"

Of course, no one was asking her to hold the bag for the whole world's cheating. No one dared ask Jane to hold the bag for anything, which is why, it seemed, I so often ended up holding it for her.

"Close up the Trap before you go out," she said.

Jane calls my practice space in the garage the Trap because she thinks I'm trying to trap my dad, The Griffin, into staying during one of his rare stops at our house, always on his way to somewhere else. The Griffin has *big* gigs: The Wells Fargo Center in Philly, the Toyota Center in Houston, and so on. I keep a record of his whereabouts on Google Tracker. A couple of times I looked at his house in Texas on Google Earth, but it's not like you can see people on Google Earth, so I can't verify that two people named Marjewel and Isak actually *live* there, even though they *do* according to the article on The Griffin in Wikipedia and on Isak's Facebook page—which I checked out, I couldn't help myself—and then sent him a friend request, which he accepted with a cryptic "nice to meet you." I don't know if he even knows who I am: he has more than 2,000 friends. I checked out Isak's clips on YouTube as well and, honestly, he's a seriously good musician and he's only a year older than me.

Anyway, The Griffin's on the road two hundred and sixty-five days of the year and Jane laughed when I asked her what he did on the other one hundred days.

"You're such a control freak," she'd said, "What do you care what he does?"

It's not that I care *per se* but I would like to know why Jane won't talk about The Griffin's house in Texas, or Marjewel, or Isak, who would be, I guess, my half-brother, and I would like to discuss the possibility that that's where The Griffin spends his time. I mean, if he's my father too, why does he spend more time in Texas than he does here? I know he's married to Marjewel and had Isak before he met Jane, but then he met Jane and they had me. And when I ask Jane about our *specific* status she just says, "You and me and The Griffin are a special and talented family, Mercedes. You can't define us the way you can define ordinary families." Here's the thing: in my mind I have this box with all the information about The Griffin in it and I can't shut the lid until I know what he does with those other one hundred days. He rides around in a black windowless band bus with mythological creatures like himself spitting flames painted on the outside. When he visits us, he arrives in the band bus with the other band members who love to use our toilet and shower and sleep on the couch and spare bedroom as if they never saw a motel room. We order Chinese and pizza because god forbid Jane turn on the stove. It isn't like a big happy family or anything with The Griffin and the band and every wannabe in a fifty mile radius who shows up uninvited, but at least there's some sound in our house besides the music I make in the garage and Jane hacking her head off from smoking too much. When they come it's like a tornado, with music and take-out cardboard and Jack Daniels bottles and red plastic cups getting caught in the whirlwind. I grab for a little fun and when the band drives away all that's left is debris from the storm for me to clean up. Anyway, it bothers me that I don't know where his bus is parked when his time isn't accounted for.

"I'm not going anywhere. I'm auditioning drummers," I told her. "I'll be right here."

"Well, if you go out."

"I'm not going anywhere."

"You should, baby. It'll do you good."

I wanted to say, "What good did going out do you, Jane?" but it would've just been mean. When she went out at my age she went backstage to see The Griffin and the result, nine months later, was me and our special and talented family. So, it would've been more than mean, it would have been self-loathing.

"You're too hard on yourself. When you're done with that, take a break, Mercedes. "

Jane is the only one who calls me Mercedes and it's one of the few things she does that reminds me she is my mom. She says if she wanted to call me Mercy like everyone else does, she would have named me Mercy.

"I'm having fun," I said. "I don't need to go out."

I had one drummer come for an audition this morning, Ruth Shilogh. I had toyed for a while with the idea of having an all-girl band because I philosophically agree with the concept and I have a poster of Patti Smith in the Trap and everything, but the fact is that more than two girls in the Trap at one time becomes something other than a rock band. Boys are much easier to control because their motives are clear-cut. Girls end up talking about everything except the subject at hand—music, hello! —which is actually what Tim accuses me of—talking about a marketing gimmick for example—and he's probably right. But it's my Trap and I control the number and sex of whoever I decide to let in.

Anyway, it was a relief that Ruth couldn't actually keep a beat so I didn't even have to make up an excuse not to let her drum in the band.

"What was that supposed to be?" I asked her after we went through a bare bones *Highway to Heaven*. It wasn't like she was way off, just a quarter beat, but a narrow miss in the rhythm section throws the whole band off.

"I know, I know," she whined, "But my mom thought being in a band would help. And I bought this jacket just so I could be in the band."

Ruth actually wanted to be a ballet dancer, but since she couldn't keep time she was going to have a tough road there. Sometimes it seemed to me that there are so many people who are born excellent at what *you* want to do that you are disqualified before the race even begins. Like, Ruth. She has everything she needs to be a ballerina—she's medium height and skinny and has incredible energy and poise and that *tragic* look dancers always have—but she can't keep time. And you know there are thousands of medium height, skinny, energetic, *tragic* girls out there who *can* feel a beat. I feel sorry for Ruth in that regard, I really do. But I'm not about to be her freakin' teacher. I have other things to do. Her leather biker jacket really did look cool, but it didn't help her drumming. Music goes in one box and fashion goes in another. And how is that any different from my berets and fake military jackets? No different at all, if I'm honest. I hate that.

2

Here's the thing I need to tell The Griffin: When I turn sixteen in January I am going to drop out of school and move to Houston where there is a terrific music scene. Everything is on the internet so please tell me what I'm doing riding in a yellow bus like a prisoner going to highway cleanup or en route to pluck chickens with illegals at the Turbo Chicken Processing Plant behind South Mountain? Riding a school bus is just demeaning. And it's not as if I have actually learned anything in school in the last year. The teachers spend three quarters of class time trying to keep the *Gitanos Reyes* from killing the *Nuestros Barrios* or the other way around and the rest of the time stressing out about the PSAA tests, which, if a significant number of students don't pass, the teachers will lose their pathetic jobs. I think, but don't know for a fact, that teachers get demerits every time they send a kid to the principal's office because once a kid goes to the principal's office a lawyer gets involved in making sure the kid doesn't get his right to an education—a right he clearly doesn't want to exercise which is the funny part—trampled on. That's probably why Jane doesn't even pretend to care about her students' moral compass, which Principal Thwaite is always harping on. The first day of school and every Monday in assembly she lectured us on how finding her moral compass saved her and if anybody knew what she was talking about you couldn't tell because half of us were sleeping and the other half were texting "wtf is thwaite talking about?"

Anyway, everything of value that you learn in school is on the internet: TED lectures, the Khan Academy, whose tutorials saved my ass more than once in trig class when I fell asleep during Miss Horvath's endless talk on how her surveyor husband uses trig for scoping out building lots for new McDonalds or whatever. Everything is on the net and you don't have to pity the teachers for their pathetic lives and unbelievably sad fashion choices—like Miss Horvath who is, Jane says, an old hippie who had too many abortions and couldn't have kids when she finally wanted them and wears this thing over her shoulders that's supposed to be a poncho, but it

6

looks, I swear to god, like a table cloth with a hole for her head cut in the middle of it. I mean, what's that supposed to be? I want to cry every time I look at her—because, unlike her, the TED people are smart and well dressed and don't have to teach gang members for a living. Maybe that's the difference.

So everything I could possibly want to know is on websites and files and easily accessible anytime I need to learn something. Google "How to Write a Song" and a zillion entries come up. I must have looked at half of them. So, considering that I am not stupid, it amazes me that my lyrics suck and I always feel like I've heard them before. Maybe it's because I was raised around music, riding inside Jane who rode the band bus and sang to me through the umbilical cord or something until I was born. Maybe I'm a plagiarist and don't even know it. If I unconsciously steal someone's song, does that make me a plagiarist or am I just tripping on the zeitgeist? That's the one thing The Griffin gets on me for, not being original. Jane, too, now that I think about it, is always harping about being original. They both think you're nothing if you're not original. And my lyric box is empty.

Tim, on the other hand, starts humming when I play a new tune and all of a sudden words shoot out of his mouth that are not only seriously moving but they are original, by which I mean they are not trite or full of emotions that he read about somewhere but you can tell that all this stuff is happening inside him or happened to someone else somewhere but he is so empathetic that the vibes find their way into his lyric box. That's where I need to get.

Writing songs is the only thing I can actually see myself doing for the rest of my life, so, if I can't learn how to write lyrics in school, I don't see the point. I'm dropping out if I can get The Griffin to sign my release and give me a little cash to get me started in Houston. Jane says if The Griffin will sign she will, too. She doesn't want to hold the bag for my potentially disastrous decision or my tantrums if I don't get my way. "There's more to an education than just facts," she says. "You have to learn how to get along with the human race and how are you going to find out how to do that looking at a screen?" but I seriously think she's wrong. She went to college after she had me and look at her: teaching juvenile delinquents she clearly does not give a shit about. And look at The Griffin. He dropped out at sixteen and is the leader of a successful rock band that works all the time.

It's a simple choice made simpler by the fact that The Griffin is coming through Milltown on his way from Toronto to Houston where he will open his first solo tour in ten years. At which time I will get him to sign me up for real life.

"I can always get a GED if I turn out to be a total loser and need to become a teacher," I tell Jane, who pretends not to hear me when I cut her like Lady Gaga cuts Madonna. "I mean, sixteen is not the end of the world," which is an even meaner thing to say because sixteen is exactly when Jane's world ended.

Jane said, "Maybe you should clean out the Trap if you want The Griffin to jam with you."

Two days till The Griffin lands. I open the garage door to the Trap and start sweeping out the crap that gets in under the door and was in the middle of a sneezing fit—I think I have allergies nobody ever bothered testing me for—when Tim pulls up on his bicycle with his guitar over his shoulder. He hops off the bike and pulls the guitar out of its case and starts playing. I put down my broom, pick up the Fender and keep up with him. After about an hour, we stop, spent, breathing like we just climbed Mt. Everest.

"I can't believe The Griffin is actually coming to Milltown," he said.

"He's coming to see me and Jane." I felt it was important to make the distinction.

"He's going to be here, though, right? Right here?"

Here's the thing about being the daughter of a famous person. You're never quite sure why people like you. It's especially problematic when you have a band and your parent is a famous rock star. Until right now, Tim Coles had never said a word about The Griffin and he had moved here six months ago from Black Eddy and we had been playing together for five of those months. So I've had five months of naïve stupidity where I allowed myself to think that news of my juicy endowment didn't matter to him. Look how he fought me on the berets. If he were trying to kiss up, he would have stuck a beret on his head and asked me if I approved of the angle.

"Yes, he's going to be right here," I said.

"We got to get a drummer," he said, excited. "We'll sound much better with a drummer. Do you think Raymond would sit in?"

Raymond, which everyone pronounced with the accent on the second syllable with no d as if he were French or something—Ray*mon* not Raaaaaymond—is The Griffin's bass man. He is from Montreal, which doesn't make him French at all. I'm not trying to be snotty, it's just a fact. But he acts French, that is, he has strong opinions about everything like whether you got fatter since the last time he saw you—"*Cher* Mercy, your *avoirdupois* is looking *très Americain*. No more *pommes frites pour toi!*"—to whether or not the latest song you wrote is worth anything. Since he is the best musician in The Griffin, actually one of the best bass players in the world, his opinion matters and his cuts always hurt.

"We can ask him," I said. "They just usually crash out when they come here, though. They crash and get high. I don't know if The Griffin'll want to hear us play."

"Of course, he will," he said, "You're his daughter, Mercy."

It's a complete waste of time to wonder how things would feel if this or that were different in your life. Like what would it be like to have a mother who gave me helpful tips on my changing body, like why getting my period made me feel like a griffin myself, ready to pounce at the least offence and why it took my body so damned long to change in the first place. Or what it would be like to have a father who thought it was worth his time to pay attention to me when I didn't have a guitar in my hands, although I did notice that every picture of Isak on Facebook featured him playing the guitar, so I'm not the only one *obviously*. All that neglected spawn stuff is in a box called "yeah, right" which I opened once to sample and almost threw up it tasted so bad.

"What should we play?" I asked, humoring Tim.

"You know that tune you were playing yesterday? I gave it some words."

Which we put to the tune, then the tune changed to fit the words and pretty soon we had a real song on our hands. It was so depressing that I couldn't come up with words like Tim could. There *had* to be a website that addressed my deficiency.

Tim put his guitar in its case to get ready to go to his job at the Seven-Eleven. I picked up the broom to continue the clean-up I'd begun. He walked his bike up and stared at me.

"What?" I asked. "What's wrong?"

To my horror, because I should have seen it coming, he leaned over and kissed me on the lips, which I actually really wanted him to do for a long time, but I hated that he did it now. I actually liked his hairless chest and his incredible triceps and I liked him, but I wanted him to like me for myself, not because of The Griffin on my coat of arms.

"Don't forget to find us a drummer," he said as he swung a leg over the bike and coasted down the driveway.

I waited until he turned around to see if I was watching him to lift my sleeve to wipe my mouth, just to prove how little his kiss meant to me, but later, when I remembered it, I licked my lips.

3

It was the end of May and school was almost over. The seniors, except for the idiots who were slogging through remedial reading and writing, had finished classes and were waiting for graduation and the Prom bacchanalia, meanwhile buzzing the school in their cars because they were like dogs who only knew their way from the kennel to home. The halls were mostly empty as most of the underclassmen were on educational field trips to the Franklin Museum in Philly or the Met in New York City. It seemed pointless to put up flyers looking for a drummer at school, but I did anyway.

I printed the flyers on Barbie Girl pink paper and sprinkled glitter on them—girl drummer bait. Girls, myself included, and even girls who wear only black and even girls who have had abortions, have some chemical that makes it impossible to resist pink sparkly shit. Pink brings up girlish happy reminders of innocence or something, which is hilarious because no girl I know is either happy or innocent.

I taped the flyers in all the usual places: the band room, the library, the cafeteria and I had one left so I headed to the gym. I had no sooner taped a flyer to the girls locker room door when a sturdy junior, Janet Kirby, who had been the captain of the field hockey team since she was a sophomore—Captain Kirby they called her—knocked me off balance when she pushed the door open.

"Soooooorrrry," I said, waiting for her to apologize back.

"No problem."

Captain Kirby looked back at the door to see what was so interesting, read the flyer and pulled it off the door. "A drummer. Hey! Unless…you saw it first." She handed the flyer to me with a show of polite sportsmanship. "You go ahead."

"No, no," I said. "I'm already in the band. It's my band, I mean. Do you drum?"

"I dabble," she said.

"We don't need a dabbler, we need a drummer."

"Hehe…hehehe," she said. Her voice was really low. "Sounds like fun."

"We need someone who can actually keep a beat."

"I can keep a beat. What do you think hockey is all about?"

I had no idea what hockey was all about, but I was hoping that a girl drummer would take Tim's attention away from me until he decided what it was he liked about me: the real Mercy or Mercy, daughter of The Griffin. And it didn't seem likely that Captain Kirby was the girl to do it. It wasn't that I was a beauty or something—as I said, average average average—it was just that with a mostly shaved head with bangs in front and a bullish neck Captain Kirby didn't look like a girl to distract Tim from me.

"Well, why don't we find out what drumming and hockey have in common?" I said. "Here, come to the Trap." I wrote the street number down. "Can you come tonight?" It would give us two nights to practice before The Griffin showed up.

"Yeah, I can come tonight." She pocketed the address and patted it.

Right. I could see where she probably didn't need a secretary to keep her social life straight.

"What kind of music do you like?" I asked. "Do you like rock? We're a rock band."

"Doesn't matter," Captain Kirby said. "Whatever. I like everything."

Definitely the wrong answer to give a rocker. She must have seen my disapproving look.

"Drummers, you know," Captain Kirby said, "Can't be particular. We're the dumb blondes—no offence—of a band. No one wants our opinion or they laugh when we give it. They just want us to do our job and keep quiet. So to speak." She did a little air drumming, flicking her wrists expertly enough so I was hopeful she could do what she said she could. At the end of it, she did an impromptu dance and was surprisingly light on her feet considering how big she was.

"Have you played with a band before?" I asked.

"My cousins."

Great. Everyone plays with their cousins or their brothers.

"There are some famous professional musicians coming to the Trap the day after tomorrow. You think you might want to jam? I mean you still have to audition and everything."

"What is this Trap you keep talking about? I never heard of it."

I'm not sure why I thought my Trap was the most famous band practice space in Milltown but clearly news of it hadn't traveled to the girls' locker room so how famous could it be?

"It's just my garage, actually."

"And who are these famous musicians we're going to jam with? I don't care, mind you," Captain Kirby said. "Like I said, it's all the same to me. I just do my job and…" She put her thumb and index finger together and dragged them across her lips.

"Right. Well, it's The Griffin." I peered into her eyes, waiting for that glint of recognition.

"The Grif*fith*?" she asked.

"It doesn't matter," I said. "Just come tonight and audition. We'll see what you can do."

She looked down at the flyer. "Cool flyer." She touched some of the glitter and patted her nose. Even Captain Kirby wasn't immune to glitter and pink. "So you're Mercy? As in Have Mercy, the name of the band?"

"Yeah, that's me. That's the band."

"Cool."

"I'm not saying you're in or anything, I mean it's an audition process," I said. "And the other band members have to approve."

"I totally get it," she said.

"So. See you later?"

"See you later."

I twirled around to leave, thinking it was actually pretty great that Captain Kirby had a shaved head so I could mentally measure her for a beret. It was even greater that she didn't know who The Griffin was.

4

"It's too bad The Griffin is coming on prom night," Jane said. "But, I guess, we get him when we get him."

She was punching the pillows on the sofa, her big skill in housekeeping arts. She thwacked away until she finally got the result she wanted: zig-zag creases down their middle. She actually hired a cleaning lady twice a month on her skimpy salary saying that she was too busy to dust and vacuum. I told her she should hire me. I could use the cash, seeing how I only get some measly walking around money from whatever The Griffin sends from the road—I noticed that the return address was never Houston—and I had to roll up my sleeves before she forked it over so she could go through some mom routine she'd seen on Oprah, checking my forearms for tracks and the base of my back for an upside down cross or whatever. She said it wasn't right to pay me for work around the house, and if I did anything around the house it should be because I wanted to contribute to the common good. Commie talk, definitely. If Jane ever watched the news, she would know that Commies were a giant threat, and I told her I hoped she wasn't talking like that in the teachers' lounge. "You're a funny kid," she'd said. "Where do you get this stuff?"

"Well, who cares if it's prom night?" I told her now. "That just means there will be fewer groupies to buy take-out for."

"I'm a chaperone so I have to stay till it's over," Jane sighed, as if she hated chaperone duty. "It's too late to back out." It pleased her that students requested her more often than any other teacher so she was always chaperoning some lame-o student festivity or field trip. She kept a purse full of rubbers to pass out in violation of official school district think that high school students didn't sprout genitals until after graduation, and a flask full of vodka which she disguised with orange soda in the bathroom when the fun got a little too boring even for her.

"So don't go," I said. "Proms are lame."

"You've never been to one, so how would you know?"

"It's not that I haven't been asked," I lied.

"Somebody asked you to the prom? Why didn't you tell me?"

"I'm not going. I'm only a freshman. I think people should act their age."

I followed her upstairs and helped her put some clean sheets on the guestroom beds then she went outside for a smoke break and I had an idea for a song, so I went to the Trap and turned on the amp.

Da da da, something something something Jane... Jane Jane Jane.

Mother's Day was a couple of weeks ago and I forgot it. It gets hard when you're older to remember holidays because teachers don't have you making Popsicle stick art a week in advance and the whole time "Mother's Day Mother's Day Mother's Day" is dangling from the ceiling in big red cut out letters. You're on your own in the holiday department in high school so my freshman year I forgot every holiday that didn't involve me getting a present. Jane didn't say anything about my lapse until we were riding around—she actually let me get some driving time in—that Sunday night looking for a place to eat and I saw a big sign on Friday's that said "Moms Eat Half Price," and I said "Why do Moms get to eat half price. That's discrimination." or something equally wise-ass and Jane said, quietly, "It's Mother's Day."

"Oh, shit, I forgot!" I said, and Jane smiled and said, "That's okay. It's just a Hallmark Holiday. We're cooler than that. *Really*. Aren't we the Two Cool Society?" She patted my hand and I felt *really really* awful even though we were cooler than Hallmark and I wanted to make it up to her with a song just about her but I couldn't think of anything to say until just now. There was something about her karate chopping those pillows that I found...I don't know....lonely, I guess. Like it was just her and me and neither of us, but especially her, had any idea how to do things. She didn't even know how to balance a checkbook: that was one of my chores the last day of the month, writing out checks for our bills. I mean she didn't even have a Facebook page like every other mom in Milltown who used Facebook to spy on their kids—I don't think she even realized that was an *option*—and she only used a computer for grading papers.

Jane Jane Jane da da da la dee da... I played some chords but no words came.

"Hey, that's pretty good."

I looked up to see Captain Kirby backlit in the driveway. A size 14. At least. Big. Really big. If she wasn't stronger than every other girl at school she would have been beaten up every day of her life for that girth.

"I brought my sticks," she said.

"Great," I said. "I have a set up right here."

14

"So I see." She got behind the Pearl ePro Live EPLX205P/C464 Electronic Drum Kit, which came in Quilted Maple Fade which I had special ordered in Quilted *Pink* Fade since The Griffin, changing the subject when I asked him if Jane and I could visit Isak and Marjewel the next summer, had volunteered to buy them for me.

Captain Kirby pulled her sticks out of the case and *rat a tat tat* and a foot pedal *boom* then *bada bing* on the cymbal.

"Sweet," she said. She touched the rims of the smaller drums lovingly.

"My dad bought them for me."

"They're so *cool*."

"My dad is The Griffin. I guess I should have told you."

"Your *dad* is the famous rocker you were telling me about?" She had a funny look on her face and for a second I thought she was going to cry or something, but then she perked up.

"You okay?" I asked.

She hit the cymbal. "Never better."

Jane walked in and stared at Captain Kirby for a second before telling me "I'm going to get some liquor for the gang. I won't have time tomorrow."

"This is Captain Kirby," I said.

"I know you, don't I? Janet, right? Fifth period study hall?"

"Yes ma'am, Mrs. O'Reilly." Kirby gave her a big smile. "Except I won't be in school tomorrow."

"That's okay," Jane said.

"I have to go with my mom somewhere. I have a note and all if you want to see it."

"That's okay."

If there was one thing Jane couldn't stand, it was keeping track of student excuses. I knew for a fact that she never did roll call, so she wouldn't even notice if Captain Kirby didn't show.

"I'll be there next time, though," Captain Kirby said.

"Great," Jane said, looking at me funny. "Where's Tim?"

"He'll be here soon. He's at work."

Jane left and Captain Kirby and I started to see if we were simpatico musically and we definitely were and we were taking a break when she said, "Your mom is really hot." I felt like throwing up but instead I got out my cell phone to order a pepperoni pizza so we could eat when Tim showed up.

5

Captain Kirby grabbed the cell phone out of my hand before I could give Papa Johns the delivery address.

"You can't eat that shit," she said. "Pepperoni is full of nitrates and the cheese doesn't even come from cows and the dough is loaded with gluten and the tomato sauce is corn syrup and red dye. Technically it's not food. I can't believe your mom lets you eat that stuff."

"She doesn't know. She would beat me if she did," I lied.

She put the cell to her ear. "Sorry. That was my kid. No internet tonight for you, Dorothy," she scolded and pushed end call.

"Hey," I said. "If they have caller ID, I'll never be able to order from them again."

"I'll cook us something. What do you have in the fridge?"

Before I could stop her, she was taking the stairs two at a time and opening the refrigerator. It was pretty gross in there: a lot of Chinese take-out, a six-pack of Yuengling, and an uncovered dish of something that had morphed into a science project. "This looks like a frat house refrigerator," she said and before I could come up with an appropriate response to her foodie pronouncements or ask her how she knew what the inside of a frat house looked like, we were in a bashed up VW van—a definite advantage of hanging with a junior is wheels—and she was explaining how her mom—out of nostalgia for the good old days she had been born too late to participate in—had bought the junker on eBay and we were pulling into the Wegman's parking lot.

"Just a second," she said, reaching behind the drivers' seat and pulling out a maroon sweatshirt with Captain Janet Kirby, number 77, Regional Champions 2011 in big gold letters on the back.

"It's kind of hot for that, isn't it?" I said.

"We're gonna need it."

First stop was the fish counter where Kirby picked out some wild red Alaskan salmon.

"You like fish, right? Well, this wild stuff is a little gamey, isn't it…Ralph," she said reading the fish clerk's nameplate, "but it's better for you than that pink stuff, which is just coloring. The fish are actually grey. Not the fish's fault. Not your fault either, Ralph. Just saying."

The wild salmon was $23.00 a pound and she bought two pounds of it.

"Forty-six bucks for some lousy fish!" I said.

"We'll put some meat on your bones, Mercy." she said and winked at Ralph.

I started to feel uneasy. She made me push the cart while she wandered through the produce aisles picking out tomatoes, showing me how to tell which were ripe and what would have to sit in a brown paper bag for a couple of days, a couple heads of lettuce, and some mushrooms.

"None of this is organic," she said. "I'll take to you the farmers' market out in Berks County when we have some time."

Then we were in the water aisle and grabbed two gallons of distilled water—Milltown water is polluted, she said, mercury from the old mills, not to mention the dentist offices which dump the stuff unhindered down the drain—then the soup aisle, two cans of broth, a box of brown rice, and a small bottle of olive oil. Kirby seemed to be looking for something as we continued on our pilgrimage. Wegmans was a beehive mess. They were re-designing the layout of the whole store: carts of inventory blockading the aisles, blue shirted employees huddling with supervisors in gold shirts, drop ceiling panels missing, the kind of chaos that comes when something that's been fixed in place for a long time is being uprooted. We stopped beside a scaffold in the detergent aisle.

"This is good," Kirby said. She plucked the salmon from the cart, looked left and right, tore the price tag off, balled it up and dropped it on the floor then shoved the salmon into the hand muff on the front of her sweatshirt. "Sometimes it's pretty cold when the season starts," she explained. "Let's walk to the end checkout counter. I know the cashier there. Stop staring, breath and smile and nod your head like I just told you a joke. Hi, Tawana."

"Hello Cap," the six foot tall black checkout girl answered.

"Meet my friend, Mercy O'Reilly. She's a composer just like you. Tawana composed our fight song," Kirby explained. "Not the official one. The one we sing on the field where the coaches can't hear us."

Kirby reached over the counter and put her arms around Tawana's neck.

Urethane will shatter glass
We always win, you bet your ass
Watch us do our victory dance
Run while you've still got a chance

They sing-songed, did an elaborate handshake and bumped heads.

A couple of bald guys in line behind us laughed. One was wearing a Milltown letter jacket—Springsteen's Glory Days come to life—"How's it looking for next year Kirby?" he asked.

"The best again, sir."

"Can I bet money on it?"

"All the juniors are coming back."

"You play sports, Mercy?" Tawana asked as she bagged our goods.

Do mind games count? I tried to say, but nothing came out.

"She's recovering from a spring flu," Kirby said. She paid for the food—the food she decided to pay for that is—with two rolls of quarters and we walked along the line of checkout counters where someone in every checkout line seemed to know her. Apparently Kirby, unlike me, was already famous. I was so scared the security guard was going to stop us, I was beet red and waterfalls of sweat were running off my pits and all that was keeping me from fainting was that I had to pee really badly. Kirby stopped in front of the manager's counter—where another security guard was looking suspiciously at Kirby's stomach—and put her palm on my forehead. "May I have a couple pieces of Kleenex, miss," she asked the manager who handed her a wad of tissues. She walked slowly to the exit and she pulled the back of my shirt when it was obvious I wanted to break into a run.

I looked at her from the corner of my eyes on the way home, totally intimidated. You know when you think you're really cool and you're all puffed up about yourself because you just know you won't sweat it when they blind-side you? Well that attitude comes from watching too many cop shows. In reality, you cave.

"You were good in there," Kirby said. "Pretending like you had the flu. Fooled me. Hungry? I am."

Captain Kirby, it turns out, was going to be a chef. "Actually, I already am," she said. "But you know, it doesn't hurt to learn some basics from the masters." The masters being chefs at a culinary arts camp she was going to this summer. "Always learning, that's like my theme song."

"I'm going to drop out, too," I told her.

"I'm not dropping out. I never said I was dropping out. You're thinking about dropping out? That's the stupidest thing I ever heard of."

"There's nothing I can't learn on-line," I said, feeling, well, stupid for the first time since I started saying it out loud.

"That's bullshit."

"What do you think you're going to learn in school? How to make cheesecake? It sounds like you can already do that."

"I don't know what I'm going to learn. But that's just it. I don't know yet. What if I miss something big? What if I find out that cooking is just a way into something else that's way cooler?"

"That's a lot of ifs," I said.

I helped her get out some pots and pans—all of which she scrubbed— a good chef always makes sure her tools are clean, she said. She put the salmon in the broiler, the brown rice in a pot, adjusted the temperature for both and began washing the lettuce—telling me about the poisoned food chain—"Michael Pollan is like a *god*. I would marry him right now if he were in the room. Well, if he were a girl"—and how she was going to have her own organic restaurant using vegetables she grew in the back yard.

"Would you raise chickens, too?" I asked. "And cattle?"

"I don't know much about animals. I guess I'll have to learn. But, yeah, why not? Start with chickens, mooooove on from there." She laughed at her joke.

She was telling me about what the big corporations did to chickens— "They cut off their beaks because they keep them in like overcrowded cages and they lose their little minds and would peck each other to death if they could and that's what they feed us."

"No way!"

"Way!"

Jane walked in, carrying a box of booze for tomorrow night's festivities.

"Something smells good," she said.

Tim came upstairs from the Trap where he had been waiting for me. "You having an actual dinner in here?" he asked.

"This is Captain Kirby, our drummer," I said. We were supposed to vote on it, but the reality in any event was that Captain Kirby was the only one who showed up to audition.

"That's cool," he said.

He came over to me and kissed me on the cheek as if he had been doing that forever and I blushed and Jane and Captain Kirby exchanged a look.

Somebody set the table and we sat down to what felt like the first real sit-down homemade dinner we ever had at the house.

"This is different," Jane said.

"Because it's real food," I said.

Tim was the first one up. "Thank you very much Mrs. O'Reilly. We gotta go." He motioned to me and Captain Kirby to follow him down to the Trap, leaving Jane with clean-up.

"You okay with this?" I asked her, loitering on the landing.

"This was fun," she said. "You got to tell me all about your friend later."

"She's not my friend. She's a colleague. My drummer."

I left her with the dishes and went downstairs where Captain Kirby was asking, "So who's this Griffin? I mean, besides Mercy's dad," and Tim was saying, "You don't know *The Griffin*? Well, I guess they're kind of old" and he played a couple of riffs on his bass and Captain Kirby picked up the beat, closing her eyes and feeling it, and I joined in, singing one of The Griffin's songs—Kirby looked at me surprised that she knew the words to it—that he wrote way back when I was riding the bus inside Jane.

Then we did a song that Tim said we should use to showcase our talents to The Griffin.

Captain Kirby said, "I totally get it. I am so into it." Then we had an argument about whether or not to wear the berets.

"Those berets look like circus hats," Tim said.

"We're not a drum and bugle corps," Captain Kirby said.

They both looked at me with such disdain that I took it back and said, "Okay, no berets."

"I loved that song we just did," Captain Kirby said.

"I wrote it," Tim said.

I was going to contradict him, saying the melody came from me, but the truth was it was Tim's song and the reality was that we were his band and as Tim packed his guitar to leave I remembered once that I asked The Griffin how he became the head of the band. I mean he wasn't the best musician, a fact he admitted. Raymond was by far the best musician in the group. "I write the songs, Mercy," he told me. "You write the songs the group belongs to you. Because it's your voice then."

Tim kissed me again, this time on the lips, then so did Captain Kirby—on the cheek—and they walked down the driveway jabbering about our upcoming date with The Griffin and how things couldn't be cooler.

I closed the Trap door and went upstairs. The Griffin's music was blaring in the living room. Jane was conked on the couch. An open Jack Daniels was on the coffee table. The dirty dishes were still on the table. I kicked a kitchen chair. "You couldn't even do a couple of dishes!" I screamed into the music.

Then, of course, I did them.

6

Early the next morning, I was working on my laptop, sitting at the kitchen table bullet pointing my case for quitting school when Tim and Captain Kirby rang the doorbell. They wanted to practice even though I said I couldn't join them for a couple of hours. "Just to get a couple of licks in, Mercy," Tim said. Like, how did they even coordinate to come at the same time? They met twelve hours ago. Were they texting already?

"We'll practice later. I set the schedule," I said, pointing to a schedule on the basement door which I filled in religiously with practice times.

"Yeah, but before that we have a couple of ideas we want to work out," Tim said, not really asking permission as he opened the door to the downstairs while I stared at my laptop.

"Don't worry," Captain Kirby told me. "We're not taking off without you." She looked over my shoulder. "You flunking math? What are you working on?"

I closed the lid on the laptop. "Nothing. Just something for The Griffin."

I used to think that no relationship was more complicated than boyfriend girlfriend—even though my personal experience was nonexistent, I did have a whole high school full of players to observe—but lately it seemed that all my relationships were becoming more nuanced than I could deal with. In the last day, my relationship with my band had turned into a power struggle over how to get The Griffin interested in us and instead of being happy to have allies, I felt like they were usurping my role as daughter. I mean, what if he liked them better?

"I'm presenting my case that I should drop out of school," I told her. "Do you know how many high school dropouts—and I mean high profile entertainers—have become millionaires? Christina Aguilera, Drew Barrymore, Simon Cowell, Mischa Barton, Charlie Sheen…"

"Charlie *Sheen*? He's like an *ad* for institutionalizing slackers."

"He's still a high profile entertainer. Very successful."

"You're a moron if you drop out," Captain Kirby said. "I told you."

"So who are you?"

"I'm two years older than you," Captain Kirby said.

"One."

"Two. I repeated third grade."

"Well, if you couldn't pass third grade, why should I listen to you?"

"Because I'm older, I have more experience."

I opened my computer and went back to making bullet points to accompany the graph of high school dropouts and income. Quentin Tarantino, Hilary Swank, Jessica Simpson, Johnny Depp, Jim Carrey. Okay, I never really got Jim Carrey. Is he supposed to be like a clown reflecting our own ridiculousness, or is he just ridiculous? Even Mr. Dow, my social studies teacher, couldn't answer that. But the point is, Jim Carrey succeeded because he had the whole world telling him it wasn't going to happen. Wouldn't you be more likely to become an artist or whatever if you had the whole culture telling you that you needed to get your educational ticket punched to get ahead? It seemed to me, and I keyed this in as a starred bullet point, that if you allowed yourself to be put to sleep for eight years of high school and college, that you were just a hypnotized troll in a game that had been thought up to make you too numb to think for yourself.

"Look," Captain Kirby said. "Don't get yourself so worked up over this. I know it's hard, your dad coming home only now and then. But this isn't going to get his attention the way you hope."

"You don't know what you're talking about," I said.

"Maybe. Maybe not." Captain Kirby picked up the pencil hanging on a string on a tack on the Trap schedule and wrote in "band practice" in the ten o'clock time slot and drew an arrow straight down to the four o'clock slot I had already booked for us. Then she drew a picture of a dog wearing a beret over it, which made my stomach spaz out seeing how it messed up the whole page. She opened the door and followed the sound of Tim crashing through the head of our new song. *Wanh, wanh, wanh, waaaaaaaaahn.*

I'd decided on a PowerPoint presentation, as usual. Since I had only a limited time with The Griffin I found it was the best way to present my case for whatever I wanted. For example, he upped my walking around money when I showed a graph on escalating snack costs and my stagnant income. I got the idea from Mr. Dow who gave very convincing presentations on the uses and abuses of power using PowerPoint, also nature versus nurture trying to figure out why so many of us were so screwed up "before anything has actually happened to you," he said, scratching his head contemplating our fairy tale innocence, while we scratched ours trying to figure out what planet he lived on. Every kid I knew had something bad going on in their life, even though most kids would never admit their family wasn't a replica of the Family Guy.

I was finishing up when Jane came into the kitchen. "God, what time is it?" she asked, opening the refrigerator and taking out the milk carton. She sniffed it, said, "Ugh," and poured it down the sink. "Did you make coffee?"

"The coffee's cold," I said. "It's late."

She looked at the clock on the stove, which was six hours off because no one bothered to set the time since we bought the stove four years ago.

"Shit," she said. "I have to be at the pre-prom worry session," which was a meeting where the prom committee got together to make sure they didn't forget anything like a streamer of crepe paper or plastic fruit punch cups. "Do you mind? I'm running late." Jane pulled out a cigarette.

"Come on! Outside! The rules."

"Everyone's going to be smoking their heads off in here tonight."

But she dutifully went out to the driveway to have her cigarette, and the music in the basement stopped. I went to the dining room window and saw Tim and Captain Kirby chatting with her. She was laughing and swishing the air with her free hand to keep the smoke out of their faces, which they didn't seem to mind, and when she came back in she said, "I like your friends. They're funny."

"They're not my friends," I said, "They're my colleagues. They're my band."

"And Janet can *cook*, can't she?" Jane opened the fridge, hoping for a different outcome. She closed it again.

"Captain Kirby," I said, correcting her.

"What do you mean, 'Captain Kirby'?"

"Don't call her Janet. Call her Captain Kirby. That's what she wants to be called."

"I thought we had some bread around here." Jane opened the breadbox and pulled out some rolls left over from dinner. She held them up, "Ta da!" before slicing one and sticking it on top of the toaster because it was too thick to fit down the slots. "I'm in a good mood," she said, leaning against the counter with her arms crossed over her chest. "You?"

"Splendid."

"Your friends are jumping out of their skins, they're so excited to meet The Griffin. I guess none of your friends—your band, I mean—are going to the prom."

"No, none of us." I guess we could have gone as a group, which would've been an awesome gimmick. As the band's leader it was my responsibility to schedule stuff, but I never seem to think of stuff outside the Trap in time.

23

"Well, you're lucky. I hate that this is all on the same night. I'd rather hang out with you guys and the Griffin."

"No kidding."

"But it doesn't last all night, thank God. I'll be back before two probably." She buttered her roll, took a bite, wrapped it in a napkin and went back upstairs.

"Are you coming back from pre-prom to help get stuff ready?" I asked her.

"Absolutely. I won't be long, sweetie. I won't stick you with everything. You know that."

I knew nothing like that, but it sounded normal to hear her say it—yes, The Griffin, the male progenitor of our family unit was coming back from foreign wars bearing mortgage money and expensive baubles for Mummy and perhaps some affection for me, and we, mostly Mummy of course because she was the Mom, would order a cornucopia of takeout in honor of his triumphant return—and I smiled in spite of myself.

7

Tim hadn't tried to change his Saturday schedule at the Seven-Eleven like I'd asked him to. His plan was to go in, and after an hour claim severe stomach cramps from eating one of the charred hot dogs that roll around for days on the Seven-Eleven rotisserie and are part of the Seven-Eleven mystique, then pedal home to change into his cool clothes, then race back to the Trap to await the arrival of The Griffin. I was left with Captain Kirby to get the Trap ready for the onslaught.

"You can come back later," I told her. "There's no reason both of us should be tied up doing maid duty."

"Clean-up and prep are just as important as the main event," she said. "It's like the first thing you learn in cooking school."

"There isn't going to be any actual cooking going on here," I said. "Just to be clear."

"Oh, I know," she said. "It's like a rock and roll road show. Beer and pizza. I'm totally cool with that." She had brought rolls of black, cobalt blue, and orange crepe paper and was festooning the Trap with them.

"That looks really good," I said. "It's The Griffin's colors exactly."

Captain Kirby smiled. "I Googled your dad. I mean I knew the words to the song we sang the other day without knowing I knew them, but I didn't know who he was. You know how it is."

"That's okay.'

"But he's like *famous.*"

"I'm just surprised you're so anxious to meet him when you don't even know his band."

"Hand me the staple gun," Captain Kirby said. She was on a ladder making an elaborate creation that looked, I swear to god, like a crepe paper eagle—she pulled out a roll of white for the head and chest—which she hung off the ceiling of the garage.

"He's going to love it," I said. "That's awesome."

"You know, cooking school isn't like just making a roast. You have to know how to make a presentation. Like ice sculptures for the shrimp bar and chocolate fountains and stuff."

"I never thought about that," which was true because I had never seen a shrimp bar or chocolate fountain. I wondered what her family must be like if she knew about stuff like that.

"Even how the table's set. There's so much more to it than people think. That's why I love it. It brings out a part of me I like, the creative part. Like writing music must do for you."

So, Tim hadn't told her that my songs were, at best, grids for him to fill in. If he hadn't come along five months ago, we wouldn't have anything worth playing for The Griffin tonight. It made me feel kindly towards him, as if maybe he liked making music for me not for my parent.

"You don't have to hang around. The action won't start until later," I told her.

She climbed down the ladder and we went outside and sat down together on the front steps.

"I'll just wait for some of your friends to come so you're not alone."

Which startled me for the simple reason that I don't have any friends. This was a big event, so of course my friends should be crowding around me but I don't remember who my last friend was. I didn't want the scrutiny that a friend would subject my life to. Like: Why's your daddy never around? Why's your *mommy* dressed like that anyway? When the questions start, I pick up the Fender and turn on the amps. Captain Kirby was acting like a friend is supposed to, though, and she didn't pry.

"You might be waiting for a long time," I told her. "Really, you don't have to stay."

"Do you *mind* if I stay?"

"No. No, I don't. I just thought you might have other things to do. Your mom might want you to do something."

"No."

Three Goth girls came down the street looking at all the houses when one of them spotted our number on the mailbox and nodded to the other two. They kept walking, more quickly now, mighty interested in their shoes, pretending not to see Captain Kirby and me on the stoop.

"And so it begins," I said.

"Groupies?"

"Probably."

"You psyched?" Captain Kirby asked.

"As a daughter or as a musician?"

"Either one. Both."

The Griffin came by on Christmas Eve last time. He didn't give us any advance warning and I thought my heart would jump out of my body I was so happy to see him. He put on his full regalia—eagle head, lion's tail—before he opened the bus door and I thought Jane was going to expire on the spot she was so excited. "Come in, Griffin," she begged. "I won't talk about anything you don't want to. I promise." But the thing about The Griffin, he never came in anymore. He stayed in his bus and we came to him and he doled out his presents as if he were some sort of black magic Santa, the low watt lighting in the bus softening our edges, making us agreeable and happy to accept his presents in lieu of him. A Fender for me "'cause I know you got the blood, I smell it!" and a Kia for Jane because her old heap of a Honda Civic was running on will power, even though I don't think she ever complained about her car, but that was The Griffin. He just *knew* what you needed.

"I listened to his stuff last night on-line," Captain Kirby said. "He's good."

"Think you want to jam with him?"

"Isn't that what you want to do?"

I shrugged. I wanted to blow him away with my songs. I wanted to play something so freakin' awesome he would tilt back in his orange Barca Lounger that was anchored to the bus floor and tip his eagle head to me. I wanted to see that involuntary nod of appreciation that wasn't fake dad stuff cooked up to make you feel good about yourself. Anyway, what does anyone want from their father, especially one that came with a mythology? To vanquish him? He had never said anything to me that indicated he really thought I had talent. But then why did he give me the Fender and the Pink Fade drum set? And wasn't I part of him? Something of him had to have rubbed off on me somewhere.

It was only four o'clock but couples and three and foursomes strolled—trying to seem casual—back and forth in front of our house then went and stood across the street or on the corner waiting for the cry to go up on Twitter that The Griffin's chariot had pulled into town.

"I find it very hard to imagine that The Griffin is even my father," I told Captain Kirby, which is more than I had ever told anybody about The Griffin and probably more than I should have told her, because I didn't know if I could trust her yet. People will always take what you tell them and use it against you when you least expect it. "I don't mean it like that," I said. "I mean because he wears a costume and everything."

"That's okay," Captain Kirby said.

"I think you should go home and change into something cool," I told her.

"Isn't this cool?" She stood up and vogued her baggy black chinos and tee. "How about you?"

I was dressed basically the same, although I had definite plans to debut my Michael Jackson military look that night. If Tim and Captain Kirby didn't want to go along with me, I would go without them.

Captain Kirby did a pirouette and we laughed. We were startled by a guy laughing louder, walking up the driveway, which I thought was kind of weird, because who did he think he was.

"You waiting for The Griffin?" he asked.

I didn't answer which should have told him go away.

"Me too," he said and plopped down on the lawn and lay back with his hands over his head. "This is like the biggest thing to happen to Milltown."

"It's happened before," I told him. "He has a wife and daughter who just happen to live where you're sitting."

"I just moved here," he said. He sat up and looked at me closely. "So I didn't know that."

He typed something into his phone.

"What are you doing?" Captain Kirby asked.

"Tweeting that I'm waitin' for The Griffin."

"Do you go to school around here?" Captain Kirby asked.

"No," he said, and by the way he said it I figured he was lying. People who are lying always look you in the eye to see if you're buying. And boy was he making big eye contact. "I graduated two years ago from St. Albans," which was the private boarding school in the next township that lawyers and doctors sent their kids to. I didn't know anybody who went there. "I'm a musician. Lead guitar."

"No kidding," Captain Kirby said. "St. Albans? They have a great field hockey team. We beat them in overtime in the finals. "

"Yeah. They're awesome." He stood up and walked over to us. "I'm Rob." He extended his hand and we shook and had a chance to see how good looking he was, which was VERY. "I guess I shouldn't impose, though, on who lives here until The Griffin actually shows up."

"That would be a good idea," Captain Kirby said. "You should at least ask permission."

"Are you," Rob said, pointing at Captain Kirby and looking a little astonished, "The Griffin's daughter?"

"I am," I said.

"What's your name?"

"Mercy."

"No kidding. What a great name." He started typing on his phone again.

There were kids who Tweeted their every bite of a sandwich and there were those who didn't. I was about to ask him to move when Jane drove up in her Kia apologizing like mad as she ran across the lawn for being late and making me do all the work to get ready.

She walked into the Trap which was lousy with crepe. "That eagle is magnificent! Who did that?" Her gaze swept past me and Captain Kirby and landed on Rob. "You?"

He smiled. He didn't deny it. Pants on fire.

"Why don't you come to the gym and work some of your magic there?"

She was flirting with him, like so openly, and I felt embarrassed for her, but he seemed to not mind. She swept into the house.

Rob looked after her. "And that is….?"

"The Griffin's *wife*, Jane. Also my mother," I said. "You going to Tweet that?"

"Absolutely," he said.

8

"Your mom left the door open," Rob said.

He stepped between me and Captain Kirby. I thought to close the door, but instead he went into the house and closed the door behind him. I was going to get up and follow him, because like *wtf*, when it was like a dam opened. Kids stampeded across the lawn led by the three Goth girls who'd been the first to arrive. They planted their Doc Martens an inch from my toes and were giving me and Captain Kirby a death stare that said move over bitches until Captain Kirby stood up with her game face on and made them think again. Other kids were jockeying for position by the curb and clusters of three and four parked themselves in the middle of the lawn and a couple wearing orange and blue leggings so tight fitting that they seemed to be painted on were rehearsing a song in the driveway they were going to burst into to let The Griffin know they were ready for prime time. The afternoon was dry and still and the air was suddenly full of little geodesic floaters of white dandelion seeds that had gone airborne from the trampling and were drifting over the fence to Mr. Henning's next door who was drinking a beer on his porch scratching his belly and watching, and across the street to the Tudesco's, neat freaks who owned four runny-nosed Pomeranians and whose lawn looked like Astroturf, and for a minute I forgot about Jane.

Here's the truth: Our lawn was a dandelion patch. In the early spring you could kid yourself that the yellow flowers were pretty and you could make dandelion salads and dandelion wine if you didn't have a life. I mean a lawn tells you a lot about the people in the house behind it, right? A normal lawn equals a normal family leading a normal existence which we prided ourselves on not leading, and I was thinking that on Monday the Tudescos would call the code enforcers on us and I'd have to mow, but Jane wouldn't be ashamed of that. She would see it as evidence that we were a special and talented family who had better things to do than mow a lawn and douse it with herbicide. It was definitely unlike Marjewel's and Isak's lawn which looked like it was painted on. They probably had a fleet of illegals working on it. Very ordinary.

Captain Kirby elbowed me in the ribs and jerked her head toward the house. "Do you want me to throw that asshole out?" she said.

"Rob?"

"He's a bullshiter."

"So?"

"He's hitting on your mom."

"He's probably asking her to introduce him to The Griffin. Jane can take care of herself." Like yeah right, look at our lawn.

Captain Kirby looked mournfully at the front door. "He said he graduated from St. Albans."

"So?"

"When I said we beat their field hockey team in the finals, he said yeah."

"And?"

"They don't even have a field hockey team. St. Albans was an all-boys school till a couple of years ago and they don't have eleven girls in the whole school."

Captain Kirby had a crush on Jane. Well, get in line, I thought. Jane wore a helpless halo like Marilyn Monroe that brought out the Sir Galahad in certain types, and Captain Kirby was one of them. When I asked The Griffin once if that was what attracted him to her, he laughed and said, "You think she's *helpless*? Jesus, no. *Hell* no. You're one hundred and eighty degrees wrong. Your mom's a wild child." Which I put away in a box I call "Figure Out Later."

Tim peddled up on his bike. He had left his guitar in the Trap and he jumped off the bike while it was still moving and trotted it into the Trap to make sure his guitar was secure and then he came out and ran over to me. "You okay?"

"Sure I'm okay. Why not?"

"There's no crowd control here."

I was in a really bad mood because I'd been sitting on the steps watching dandelion floaters instead of taking charge. "It's not a crowd," I said.

"Fifty people? I would call that a crowd."

"I've seen more."

Tim jerked me up from the steps and led me into the garage. He handed me my guitar then he uncased his and turned up the amps and ran up and the down the scales. He pointed for me to join him and Captain Kirby got behind the Pink Fade and started hitting her sticks. We sounded good and the kids packed into the driveway and were digging us and we nodded to one another because we were *nailing* it and Tim broke into the riff that opened the song we were going to do for The Griffin when a horn started honking out a deafening version of *Jump Naked*, The Griffin's song that Judas Priest covered and took into the top fifty. The Griffin's black windowless bus made a laborious turn onto Walnut Street like our playing had summoned it and drove slowly towards us like a scary mythological beast. The Griffin himself was painted on the side, his giant wings spreading up and over the top of the bus, Raymond lurking under one wing wearing a beret looking very French in an iridescent orange tee and sneering a Cheshire Cat grin, his teeth like shiny piano keys higher than the bus tires, and the drummer, Bang, was depicted as a sinister leering man-in-the-moon, his round pocked face filling the front grill. There was a ghostly outline of another figure on the back. I didn't know who that was supposed to be. A new member? Anyway, the bus looked like a creature from the underworld come to swallow up the good people of Milltown and Have Mercy was forgotten as the metal head mob made a run for the bus screaming and singing along because the horn had stopped honking and speakers mounted in the grill were blaring out *Hotter Than Hell*, The Griffin's new release.

The bus crawled into the driveway with groupies hanging onto it, moaned as the driver shut off the engine and lowered its air suspension, and the doors opened to reveal The Griffin.

9

The Griffin was in full mufti: eagle head, tan suede chaps and a lion's tail. He pawed the bus steps, the crowd went berserk, so he did it again. He turned around so we could see the cool lion's tail, which seemed to have a life of its own, curling around his neck then between his legs then patting his ass, then faced around again, came down a step and allowed people to shove things at him to sign.

"There's plenty of room, plenty of room, love, don't shove," he commanded. He stepped down into the ecstatic horde and the other band members came out after him.

"Ray*mon*!" a girl screamed as if she saw an apparition. There are girls who think Raymond is the coolest—it's that disdainful French thing—but I am not one of them. He ignores them in any event, going after girls who think he's a jerk. He saw me and came over. Case in point.

"*Cheri*, you've gotten…." I braced myself. "Taller, much *much* taller. Can it be *vrai?*"

"Really? You think so?"

"*Non, non, non*, I was wrong. It was just the angle. You are still the little shrimp."

Why I couldn't stand Raymond.

"Hey, man," Tim was right behind me sticking out his paw to Raymond. "Love your work."

"Of course you do."

Tim slipped his hand around my waist.

"He is your lover?"

"No!" I blushed, "He's not my *lover*. I swear."

"I know," Raymond said, "You are waiting for a mature man with technique. Ah, but *quell dommage*, it cannot be. You are your papa's little bo peep."

Okay, so I was a virgin.

"We want to show you a couple of things," Tim said, ignoring that Raymond was putting the moves on the girl he felt comfortable kissing on the lips.

"There will be plenty of time for that later, *ami*," Raymond said, patting Tim on the shoulder. "We have to drink to cement our friendship. But first we must pee."

Raymond wandered into the house.

Tim said, "Did he say we must pee?"

"That's what he said."

"Man, that is so cool."

Bang, the drummer, came up to me en route to the house. "You get prettier every time I see you," he said. He kissed the top of my head.

Jane had told me that Bang's round moon face was a result of prednisone. He had wicked asthma and he used the steroid to control it but because steroids give you a physical bang, Bang upped his dosage until his doctor refused to write him prescriptions. Now, Jane said, he was getting his prednisone on-line from Bangladesh. Captain Kirby intercepted him and put her arm through his and they walked arm in arm into the house.

Which left, of course, The Griffin. The crowd parted as The Griffin made his way toward me. Everyone was looking at me and my heart was ready to burst out of my chest. What could go wrong with The Griffin around? For god's sake, he was a superhero right out of a legend. When I was eight years old, The Griffin stayed with us for a whole month while he was trying to get sober. He rode his Harley all the way from Detroit, where he had grown up and my grandfather still lived, and every day he would arrive on his Harley to pick me up at school. He didn't wear his costume, it was just him in jeans and a leather jacket, and he was so handsome, smiling as if something very cool was on his mind, and all the girls would ask me, "Is that your *father*?" I would put my plaid book bag in the studded leather pouch behind his leg and wrap my arms around my dad and when we rode away, the other kids looking with their jaws down to their knees, I was so happy I thought I would have to pick bugs out of my teeth when we got home.

And now The Griffin strode across our dandelion carpet, and when he spotted me he opened his wings and what could I do but run into them and allow myself to sink into a world where nothing bad could happen to me because The Griffin lived there.

"How's my favorite girl?" he whispered into my hair and when I looked up smiling, "Is that a tear? Cut it out!" he said, and "Where's your mum? Why isn't she out here?"

Those five seconds were the only time I would have alone with The Griffin, of course. As soon as he opened his wings to release me, a gazillion groupies and wannabes descended on him, some pushing CDs on him, which he accepted, handing the overflow to me and promising to listen later.

"It's so great to be here in *Milltown*," he shouted, and at first my heart sang, but then I realized it was what bands shout from whatever stage they're on. "It's so great to be here in Detroit! In Dallas! In Dumbledorf! In whatever the name of this freakin' place is."

I tugged on his wing. "I have to talk to you soon," I said. "Before the party starts."

"Sure, sure," he said and was immediately waylaid by a pretty Goth girl who didn't look much older than me.

"I mean this is serious," I said, which, as soon as I said it I realized it was exactly the wrong thing to say. Nothing would put off The Griffin in his homecoming mode more than a serious discussion. But I needed his signature to drop out of school and a little cash to put my plan in motion and that's all there was to it.

"Of course! That's what I'm here for. To take care of business."

The pretty Goth girl slipped him a piece of paper which he opened, read the message and put his head back and roared. "Don't go too far," he told her.

A Papa John's Delivery truck pulled up, the driver and a helper carrying stacked boxes of pizza into the house, then a House of Han van pulled up and the driver made a couple of round trips carrying shopping bags of take-out in both hands, tiny containers of duck sauce and mustard spilling onto the lawn that I would find all over the house in the morning. The party had officially begun and it was exactly like it always was. I don't know why I felt disappointed. And I can't explain why I felt that something really really bad was going to happen.

10

Tim was leaning against the kitchen sink, discussing the peculiarities of bass playing with Raymond, an empty pizza box between them and a plastic cup filled with what I assumed was Jim Beam in his hand. Raymond was swigging from the bottle.

"You're not old enough," I told Tim.

"He is under my supervision," Raymond said. They laughed.

Whatever. Last year, for the first time—our neighborhood isn't exactly upscale—the cops came, sirens wailing, bubble lights twirling, but somehow all the underage kids disappeared into the bus and it turned out that the police chief was a metal head and the only penalty The Griffin had to pay was a bus stop at the chief's house on his way out of town.

"Have you seen Jane?" I asked.

Raymond jerked a thumb and I followed its direction into the living room where Jane was nose to nose on the sofa with St. Alban's non-graduate Rob.

"Don't you have a date tonight?" I asked her, interrupting Rob's fascinating philosophical monologue about whatever.

Her face got red. "What?"

"The prom? Aren't they expecting you?"

"Oh," she said. "I don't have to be there for another hour. I do have to change those ridiculous decorations on the stage, so I should go now, you're right. Where's The Griffin?"

He was, in fact, right behind me and he said, plaintively, "You're making me come to you, now, love? I've always loved your sadism." They laughed hysterically.

Here's the thing about my parents: I have no idea what's going on between them. I mean obviously they did it once to get me, but I haven't seen any evidence since that they're in love or anything. The only time The Griffin ever stays here longer than a few days is when he needs to dry out—which has actually been three times that I can remember—but no one acts regular then. I mean, Jane doesn't invite the neighbors for potluck and The Griffin doesn't mow the lawn. He spends a lot of time sitting in the dandelion patch in a yoga position humming. Maybe this is how he composes or something, because, he told me, the regular thing that alcoholics in recovery are supposed do—go to church to talk to Jesus—he just can't bring himself to do. One time I caught him blowing on the white dandelions heads, laughing as the seeds floated out over the neighborhood like he just didn't give a damn that me and Jane had to live here the rest of the time and listen to the neighbors bitch about our yard.

"You look good, babe," The Griffin said.

"You too. Look, I have to go to the prom…" and before she finished saying what she wanted to say, he said, "I'm too old to be your prom date, honey, you should have asked me sooner," and they started laughing hysterically again.

The Griffin squeezed in next to her on the sofa, carefully rearranging his tail. He didn't seem a bit phased that Rob was pressed against her other side. "Are you going to tell me again all the things I stopped you from doing?"

"I never said *you* stopped me from doing anything, I only said…." And then I guess she remembered I was there and what she was going to say, so she shut up. "I promised that I would chaperone. You should have given us notice."

The pretty Goth girl had come up behind the sofa and was digging her black fingernails into The Griffin's neck. She'd unzipped her studded jacket to make clear that she had something The Griffin would probably want to see. The Griffin looked back at her and smiled. "Don't worry about us," he said. "We know where everything is."

"I guess you do," Jane said. She took Rob's hand and got up from the sofa. "Why don't you come help me redecorate the gym?"

The Goth girl bent and whispered something in The Griffin's ear. Rob looked at The Griffin, obviously weighing what the chances were if he left that he would get to show The Griffin how he could make a guitar talk. "Sure, sure," he said to Jane, running his hand through his hair.

"Do you have a car?" Jane asked.

"I rode my bike."

Jane laughed and glared at the pretty Goth girl. For a moment Jane looked really sad and I wanted to punch the Goth, but then Jane shook herself and smiled. "This younger generation. And there's always a younger one, isn't there, Grif? They ride bikes instead of cars. We'll take my car. It's a present from The Griffin," she said directly to the Goth girl.

Rob kind of bowed to The Griffin. "You'll be here later, right?"

I was stuffing what was happening into my Figure Out Later box as fast as I could because a lot was going on that needed figuring out when Captain Kirby pounded me on the back. "Oh, my god! Wait till you see the trick Bang showed me on the drums. I'm a thousand per cent better already. Come on! Everyone's in the Trap. We're waiting for you."

And everyone *was* in the Trap and the place exploded with applause when The Griffin tugging the Goth girl behind him and I came down the stairs. Kids were texting like mad about *us* and I felt famous and I know fame is shallow and fleeting and everything, but the great thing about fame that people who *aren't* famous can't know is this: you can actually *feel* adoration pouring all over you from people who don't even *know* you and I don't care who you are, having a crowd of people pour love all over you is the most delicious feeling in the world.

11

The Griffin and Bang and Raymond played a couple of songs to ear-splitting applause from the kids packed into the Trap and the late arrivals in the driveway, then Raymond with a big grin introduced us, saying *Have Mercy* was a group that was going to be big one day *peut etre*, and Tim jumped up and motioned for me and Captain Kirby to take the stage. Raymond joined The Griffin and Bang at the front of the crowd and we played *Hole in the Sky*, the song Tim wrote for the occasion and The Griffin actually paid attention in spite of the Goth girl's pawing because the song was really cool. When it was over, he asked me if I wrote it and it took every bit of integrity I had not to lie and say yes.

"You should talk to my man," The Griffin said to Tim, by which he meant his manager who was meeting them in Houston in a couple of days. "Send him a demo."

"Can I call him or what?" Tim asked.

"No, I'll have him call you," The Griffin said.

And I watched Tim enter that twilight zone where everything is possible as he wrote down the chords for The Griffin and repeated the lyrics, and I was jealous that it wasn't me as The Griffin nodded his approval and patted Tim's shoulder. If only I could be free of school and move to Houston where I just *knew* songs would pour out of me.

"I have to talk to you," I told The Griffin. "It's important. I have a presentation which will explain everything," which I felt kind of ridiculous saying in a garage full of people high on music and alcohol and pot. Like I was Mr. Dow bullet pointing in the Dark Ages to an audience of irate villagers. Boy, would Mr. Dow have a fit when he found out I was dropping out of school.

"Sure, babe. What's this about?"

"It's about school."

"Sure, let's see what you got."

The Griffin always smiled like he was proud of me when I gave him printouts. See, this is the thing about The Griffin. When he's noticing you with his huge blue eyes and he has this half smile on his face reacting to what you're saying, he's *with* you, like you're the only thing in the world that matters to him.

"Let me get my laptop," I said, and by the time I ran up to my room to get my laptop and returned to the basement, the Goth girl, whose name I found out from one of her friends was Evelyn—like *who* is named *Evelyn* who hasn't been *dead* for a hundred years?—was leading The Griffin to the bus where the bus driver, a skinny old guy who's been with The Griffin since I was ten and who wasn't allowed to leave his post, closed the door behind them.

It was two o'clock in the morning. Jane would be home soon from the prom. A couple of people had brought their own guitars and set up with Tim and Raymond and Bang and the music had an air of exhilaration that you get when musicians, previously unknown to one another, discover each other though music. It's an un-reproducible sound, the music of discovery, trading fours, the language of one soul, two souls, three having a conversation without words.

There must have been seventy people in the garage and the driveway grooving and dancing and spilling across the street and the lights were on in all the houses around us and I was wondering when the cops would arrive when Captain Kirby found me. "This is like the best party ever!" she said. Captain Kirby had never told me where she lived or who she lived with. We had only known each other for two days, true, but all of a sudden it seemed like a giant omission. "Don't you have to tell your mom or dad or somebody where you are?"

"My mom's working."

"*Now?*"

"*Your* mom is working, too."

Somehow I never thought of chaperoning as work.

"See," Captain Kirby said, "This is what I want when I'm on my own. A house where people can feel they can come and hang out. With music and food."

"I thought you hated pizza and Chinese take-out. That you thought it wasn't really food."

"I do. I mean, I hate it as a regular diet. But it's great for a party."

"Maybe you can help Jane with a whole food menu the next time the band comes."

She grimaced.

I didn't approve of Captain Kirby backing down on her food ideals. I would have to expand my opinion of Captain Kirby to include this profoundly contradictory information.

"Why don't we bring your mom some food?" I asked, suddenly wanting to be away from the scene which didn't seem to involve me now that The Griffin was in the bus with that girl. "Does she eat pizza?" A

Papa John's delivery van had made the third delivery of the night a half hour ago—Jane must have told them to time their drop offs—and the pizza was still warm.

Captain Kirby considered this as she looked around the best party she ever attended. "She wouldn't mind, I guess."

Her mother had the VW van and Captain Kirby didn't have a bike. I told her she could take Tim's who was high as a kite on himself and was jamming with Raymond and Bang and talking to them like he was their freakin equal—which I guess they thought he was because they were tweaking his song so they must have thought it was worth something—and he didn't even notice we were going. I kept my eyes straight ahead as we pedaled past the bus and into the damp early morning air. The box of pizza was strapped to the carrier on my rear fender. We rode about two miles into town when I shouted to her, "Where are we going?" and she pointed straight ahead to a row of big mansions that used to house the steel magnates in the last century, but were now mostly broken up into doctor offices, a couple were apartment buildings, and one was Kulick's Funeral Home which is where we turned into the circular driveway.

12

"Your mom works *here?*" I asked.

"My mom isn't a people person," Captain Kirby said. She hopped off her bike and put her index finger up to her lips.

"I don't think anyone in here can hear us," I said.

"The owners are very light sleepers."

We walked our bikes around back. The VW van was parked in the lot. Captain Kirby pushed Tim's bike out of sight behind a rhododendron bush and after unstrapping the pizza box I did the same, then we went down a wrought iron stairway and she tugged on a chain hanging from a bell which rang really loudly with each pull and after what seemed like an hour, a woman in a white lab coat, goggles, face mask, paper hair net and rubber gloves opened the door. She looked at us over her goggles which she had pushed down her nose.

"Oh, Janet, it's you," the woman said. "Who's this?"

"My friend, Mercy."

"Well, come in, but you have to be really quiet."

We followed her through two rooms—she had to unlock both their doors—until we arrived at a room lit by florescent lights with a table in the middle with a dead body lying on it covered with a paper blanket. I'd only seen dead bodies before in movies. The place stank like the sulfur kids put on at night to dry up their zits. It was all pretty creepy and I felt a little nauseous. I handed Mrs. Kirby the box of pizza. "Janet said you might be hungry."

"Isn't that thoughtful," she said, putting the box on the dead body's stomach, then changing her mind and putting it on a chair. It was a woman. "I'm almost finished with this one. I'm waiting for the pancake to dry."

She pushed her goggles back over her eyes and applied nail polish to the fingernails of the dead woman's hands which looked like they were a thousand years old.

"Frosted shell pink," Captain Kirby said. "Everyone looks good in frosted shell pink. Especially if they have ridges in their nails from being sick a long time." She obviously had strong opinions about her mother's work, but I thought she was definitely wrong about the frosted shell pink. Jane would die—or something—before she would be seen in frosted shell pink.

"My mom does their make-up," Captain Kirby said, answering the question I wasn't sure how to ask.

A metal make-up case was open on a stainless stand next to the corpse table. For someone's mother—and despite the frosted nail polish—Mrs. Kirby had very hip taste in cosmetics: Urban Decay, Mac, Tarte. She finished the woman's nails—no need to warn her to let them dry for an hour—and started on her hair. She pulled a blue-gray extension out of a drawer in the stainless stand and attached it to the woman's head—cutting it so it fit in with the woman's bob. I had stopped feeling nauseous and was thinking that this was like being in a beauty parlor where you didn't have to make small talk.

"If you're going to watch so closely put on a mask," Mrs. Kirby said. She pulled one out her lab coat and handed it to me.

I had never seen a *real* dead person—two of my grandparents had died but I didn't go to their funerals because one lived in Akron and the other in Detroit—and I was surprised at how unmoved I felt. I thought I should be crying my eyes out. Maybe it was the total stillness of the body—I mean no one alive is that still even when they're sleeping—that made me feel the woman wasn't real. I wanted to touch her forehead to see how it felt, but I knew that would be disrespectful.

"If you're going to touch, you need gloves." Mrs. Kirby was obviously a mind-reader. "But I wouldn't. You have to get used to it like Janet or you'll have nightmares."

"Do you know who she is?"

"Mrs. Joseph McGouldrick is her name," Mrs. Kirby answered me. "She had eleven children and thirty-nine grandchildren." She finished up with eyebrow pencil and lipstick and blush. The blush was the only weird note. "That's who she *was*."

Captain Kirby came up next to us and looked at her mother's handiwork. "Gorgeous, Mom. As usual."

Mrs. Kirby washed up and took off her lab coat and goggles, putting them in a locker. She tossed her hairnet and gloves and mask, gesturing for me to give her mine, in a trash can, then pulled the paper blanket over the woman's face and turned out the lights. "Let's go," she said.

We walked back through the two locked rooms—Mrs. Kirby told me that it was a tradition to keep bodies under double lock because bodies were regularly stolen in the Middle Ages when medical students wanted to study cadavers—I wondered if Mr. Dow knew about *that*, how we haven't advanced in that regard since the Middle Ages—and we went outside and climbed into the beat-up VW van. The back seats had been taken out and two living room chairs were in their place. Captain Kirby indicated that I should take one "Please, you're our guest" while she sat on the floor and her mother sat in the other chair.

"A long day," Mrs. Kirby said. "I did a boy who'd been in a car accident this afternoon. Very messy."

Without her protective gear on, Mrs. Kirby looked like a normal woman, probably prettier than most of the mothers I knew, except Jane of course.

"Mom used to do make-up in Los Angeles, for Vanna White," Captain Kirby said. She waited for me to acknowledge that I knew Vanna White, but I didn't. "It doesn't matter. She was just this bitch on a game show."

"She wasn't a bitch," Mrs. Kirby said, seeming alarmed at her daughter's harsh assessment of Vanna White. "We just didn't see eye to eye." She had brought the box of pizza with her and she opened it now. "This looks lovely," she said.

"Maybe we could go to your house and eat it there," I said. It seemed so weird to be sitting in someone's van, pretending it was a house. But that's what it was it seemed like. The easy chairs. Pictures were taped to the windows which were covered in black privacy shields. Two TV trays were folded up against the back of the driver's seat.

"Or we could go to your house," Mrs. Kirby said.

"We're having a party there. It's just a bunch of kids. I don't think you would like it." I was surprised that Captain Kirby hadn't told her mother about it.

"Well this is fine with me," Mrs. Kirby said. "And the pizza is scrumptious. Yum." It was fake Mom Talk.

"We have to get back to the party, Mom," Captain Kirby said. "You all right here?"

"I'm fine."

We said good-night-nice-to-meetcha etcetera and as Captain Kirby slid the side door closed I noticed two sleeping bags rolled up against the passenger seat. I had mistaken them for pillows in the dark. We fetched our bicycles from behind the rhododendrons and rode silently for a couple of minutes.

"Mom wants me to go back to culinary arts summer camp so I can become a chef and all. She traded our housing vouchers to pay for it. This'll be my second year."

"Okay," I said.

"I think that's very cool of her, don't you?"

"Very cool," I said.

"She's a great mom, like yours."

I actually didn't know what to say, and while I was dithering to myself about where to store the fact that Captain Kirby was basically *homeless*, my phone vibrated. I'm not a big texter. As I said, there are people who live on their phones and then there are the rest of us. So getting a text was a big deal. I thought maybe Jane needed something.

"Wait a minute," I yelled to Captain Kirby who'd pulled ahead of me. I coasted to the curb and read the text, which was from Tim. He said that it was all over the net that some student from another high school was bragging that he bedded a teacher from the senior prom. He thought I should know.

Captain Kirby had turned her bike around. My hands were shaking as I reread the message. "Do you feel sick?" she asked. "Hey, you okay?"

Why did Tim think I should know? Did he think it was *Jane?* He didn't say he thought it was Jane or that anyone had said it was Jane. It *couldn't* be Jane. I mentally pictured the teachers who I knew were chaperones at the prom. It had to be Jane. Who else?

"Actually," I said, "I'm not okay."

13

I sat down on the curb and told Captain Kirby I didn't feel like going home any more.

She sat down next to me and coaxed Tim's message out of me.

"Sonofabitch! I knew that Rob was a phony!"

"You don't know it was Rob! And you don't know it was Jane."

"Of course it was Rob and your ma. They were all over each other."

"He told us he graduated two *years* ago. So it can't be him. And Jane would never do something like that." Something so creepy and weird. I heard actual alarm bells going off in my head, and I put my hands over my ears.

"He's a liar! I told you," she said. "Only a professional liar would say *two* years ago, not *last* year or *this* year."

We pedaled to the twenty-four hour Dunkin Donuts and Captain Kirby ordered a box of Munchkins and two Coffee Coolatas.

"Do you have a couple of bucks?" she asked me, fishing around her giant pants and coming up empty. "I'm out of quarters."

"Let's eat them in the parking lot," I said.

I couldn't look at nice Mr. Rajeet who owned the Dunkin Donuts. After he saw me carrying my guitar once, he always told me "I can see you are going to be a famous musician," and I would correct him by saying "not a musician, a famous rock and roll star," and he would say, "Okay, then, a famous rock and roll star! Even better. Don't forget to practice today." He was always telling anyone who would listen about his two sons in college and how he was working so hard so they wouldn't have to operate a doughnut shop, so they could operate on *brains* or something instead and have a sparkly and clean and pure future loaded with nice people doing the right thing just like Mr. Rajeet. If Jane had done this, how could I ever talk to Mr. Rajeet again?

"You ought to have a couple of these," Captain Kirby said, pushing the box of Munchkins at me.

"You haven't eaten all day."

"Yes, I have."

"No, you haven't."

"I'm not hungry."

It was five thirty and delivery trucks were on the road and a couple of cars were lined up at the take-out window just like everything was normal. The Coffee Coolata was sickeningly sweet and I felt like barfing.

"Well, what are you going to do?" Captain Kirby asked.

A tractor trailer pulled to the side of the road in front of us and sat there with its motor idling. The driver probably was going to sleep in the cab. Maybe when he woke up I would ask him to take me with him to Arkansas, which was where his license plate said he was from. Weren't the Smokey Mountains there? They sounded dark and hidden and I wanted to hide in them with all the other runaway losers and axe murderers.

"I don't know." The more I thought about Jane sleeping with a high school student the angrier I got. What kind of a mother does *that*? What kind of a *teacher* does that? Why couldn't Jane *ever* do what she was *supposed* to do, like be a mom who *chaperoned* students not partied with them. Why couldn't she stay in her damn Two Cool Society mom box? It was *icky*.

"At least The Griffin is here," I said. "He'll know what to do." Part of me, honest to god, thought that once The Griffin saw what happened because we weren't all together, he would take us away on the bus with him. It would be like it used to be when Jane was riding around on the bus and I was riding inside Jane. Maybe this was a good thing no matter how bad it sounded when you said it out loud. Maybe when the sun came up, it would turn out to be a giant joke. The boy was joking. Bragging about nothing. Like boys do. Or maybe it was some other teacher.

I went through the roster in my head again. Mrs. Horvath? Please. Mrs. Thwaite? Give me a break. My mother was the youngest and prettiest teacher at Milltown High. She wasn't like the others. Part of me had always been proud of that, but now it terrified me.

"You can't go back to how it used to be," Captain Kirby said, reading my thoughts. "Believe me, I know."

"What makes you think I want to go back to anything? You're crazy."

"Maybe I'm crazy but I know what I'm talking about."

"How can you know anything," I said, angrily. "You flunked third grade."

"True enough," Captain Kirby said and she then proceeded to shove Munchkin after Munchkin into her mouth until the box was empty. "You finished with that?" she asked then grabbed my cup and drained the last of the Coffee Coolatta and threw all the trash in the garbage, picking up her bike and waiting for me to do the same.

The sky had become the silver it gets before the sun comes up. I mean, I should at least *ask* Jane what happened. Maybe it was a giant mistake. I mean Jane wasn't an idiot. And no one could prove anything happened. Mr. Dow was always saying that the greatest thing about our country was due process and presumed innocence and a trial by a jury of your peers etcetera etcetera. Yeah right. My peers had already chimed in. And oh my god, what would Mr. Dow say when he heard about this? He was the only teacher I liked and I pictured myself slinking into his class with a paper bag over my head so he wouldn't have to look at the person who made the entire high school dirty and full of dandelions.

I would talk to Jane and find out it was a great big mistake and she would probably punish me—not let me play in the Trap for a month or wash my mouth out with soap or whatever—for being so disloyal by believing it was her. And I wouldn't blame her.

I got on my bike and followed Captain Kirby out of the parking lot when I heard the chimes for another message on my phone. I stopped and pulled it out of my pocket again and looked at the screen. It was a Facebook message from my half-brother, Isak. I rubbed my eyes because like maybe I was dreaming. Then I looked again. The message was still there.

"I saw on Facebook," the message said. "Wow! You okay?"

14

I guess I expected a crowd of irate villagers with torches out of one of Mr. Dow's stories of the Middle Ages to be waiting for me on the lawn. But it was deserted. Pizza boxes were strewn around. Someone had made a pile of them like eight feet tall at the curb and scrawled *THE GRIFFIN RULES* in spray paint on the street in front of them. Beer cans and plastic cups were everywhere. Jane's Kia was parked at the curb in its usual spot. But there was an empty spot where The Griffin's bus was supposed to be.

"Your dad's gone," Captain Kirby said.

"Yeah."

We walked our bikes up the driveway. The Trap was locked, probably by Tim who understood how much the stuff inside cost, and there was a note taped to the garage door. "Will whoever stole my bike, please return it. Thank you, Tim Coles."

"Do you want me to come in?" Captain Kirby asked.

"Nah. I'm okay. I mean if you want to you can. You could sleep in the guest bedroom. In the bed we made up for Bang." I faked a smile.

"I should probably check on my mom."

"Right."

She leaned Tim's bike against the garage door and started down the driveway.

"You can take my bike if you want. It's a pretty long walk."

"No, I want to walk. I'll come back this afternoon."

"You don't have to."

"To see if you're okay and everything."

I looked up at Jane's bedroom. The shades were drawn and the awful thought occurred to me that Rob might be in there with her. I mean, Tim didn't say where it happened. I forced myself to walk across the lawn. The front door was open and when I walked into the house I saw Tim sitting at the kitchen table with my laptop open in front of him.

"There you are! Finally!" he said. "I was going to go looking for you but someone stole my bike. I was worried that maybe you ran away, but then I knew that wasn't like you."

49

"I was on my way to Arkansas," I said, wondering what he thought *was* like me.

"Huh?"

"Nothing."

He turned the laptop so I could see the screen. Someone had posted pictures of Jane and Rob (Rob!) dancing at the prom...which wasn't so unusual, lots of times guys asked chaperones to dance, they feel sophisticated or something because they're wearing dinner jackets. But a couple of pictures later Rob's hand was on Jane's ass.

"He's a senior at Black Eddy," Tim said. "He got a girl pregnant there. You should see what *she's* saying about all this. She busted him to his mother."

"He has a girlfriend?"

"*And* she's *pregnant.*"

"I heard you."

"Yeah, look at this." He started keying into her page.

"What do I care what some girl I don't even know has to say about anything," I said. I felt calm for a second. I mean if I didn't look then maybe everything that had happened and was going to happen would only be real inside the internet which was like a pawn shop or something for the real world but then I felt like barfing again. "Where's Jane?" I asked.

"She came home around three and she banged like hell on the band bus, yelling for The Griffin to come out, and when he did he was just in his underpants. He said something to her that he must have thought would make her laugh because he laughed, but she didn't and then they started fighting. Wow, can they fight."

I nodded.

"And then someone in the crowd showed The Griffin something on their iPhone—I guess it was about what happened—and they fought some more. Then The Griffin came into the Trap and told Bang and Raymond to pack it in. 'I don't need this bullshit right before a tour,' he said, and that Goth girl came flying out of the bus half undressed and Bang and Raymond got on, and the bus backed out of the driveway with the Goth girl banging on the grill yelling that she wanted her jacket that she's paid a hundred bucks for, and Jane laughed and walked up to her and gave her the finger and stormed into the house, and then they were gone and everyone else left."

"Did The Griffin say anything for me?" I closed my eyes. "Never mind."

"Do you think this means they won't buy our song? The Griffin said his manager was going to call me."

I wanted to be mean and tell him they never intended to buy his song, that they were just toying with him to amuse themselves like they always did whenever they visited. "I don't know what it means. It'll blow over. It always does."

"This happened before?"

"No. Nothing like this. But almost." My laptop had reverted to my Power Point Presentation on why I should be allowed to drop out of school. When was Jane going to stop getting all the attention and get out of my way so I could stop living her life and start living mine? The Griffin would have understood what I needed. He would have signed and probably given me some get-started money, but because of Jane he left. She was always ruining everything for me, like a kid kicking a smaller kid's sandcastle on the beach. "I guess I want you to go."

"Some asshole stole my bike," he said.

"They returned it. I saw it when I came home."

"No kidding. Wow. You going to be okay?" I let him kiss me. I mean, who gets to decide when I'm grown up? I do. My first decision in my new role was: I kissed him back. I didn't want to miss out on kissing which I actually really *really* liked. He looked surprised then he hugged me.

"It's going to be okay," he said, stroking my hair. "It's just a guy bragging about something that probably didn't happen. Everyone will be talking about something else by tomorrow."

"You think so?"

He hugged me again and it felt like everything was okay, at least until he rode away on his bike. I went outside and sat on the steps and thought about how long it was going to take me clean up the mess by myself.

15

Garbage pickup happens Monday mornings so by seven o'clock I'd collected fifteen garbage bags of trash and lined them up neatly on the curb. The pizza boxes were recyclable so I stacked them together next to the blue paper recycling bin. I rinsed the beer cans and booze bottles out so they wouldn't attract hornets and put them out on the curb in the two blue bins for glass and aluminum stuff. Then I got the hand mower out of the shed—the motorized lawn mower was out of gas, gee, surprise—and mowed down the dandelions. I sat down on the front steps out of breath and surveyed my work. We looked like every other house on the street, sort of. I was trying to think of what else I could do that seemed normal—maybe ask the Tudescos if I could walk their dogs—when Jane came out the door and sat down next to me.

"It's bright," she said, shielding her eyes. She started to light a cigarette then put it in her bathrobe pocket and smiled at me.

"What are you so happy about?"

"I didn't say I was happy."

"You're smiling."

"I thought I'd try it. Jesus, Mercedes, lighten up. You are such a downer to be around sometimes."

"Did you have fun last night?"

She stood up, walked a few steps—"Far enough?" she asked—lit her cigarette and squinted at me through the smoke. "I was working."

"Oh, is that what you call it?"

And all of a sudden she was holding her bathrobe closed with one hand and slapping me a good one with the other. "That's enough!" she said. "What I do is my business. I'm the mother, remember?"

My cheek burned and it felt like steam was rising off the tears that were streaming down my cheeks.

"Sorry, *Jane*," I said, "But it seems that what you do is everyone's business." I ran to the Trap door, grabbed my bike and pedaled away as fast as I could. I'll go to the funeral home, I thought, and move in with Captain Kirby and her mom. Of course, Kulick wouldn't let the Kirby's beat up old van stay parked there during the day when they had viewings and stuff. Tim, I thought. He had an older brother who worked summers for an uncle in Scranton so there'd be an extra bed at his house, but he'd told me he didn't get along so well with his dad who was always looking for reasons to ground him and they were all probably still asleep. I rode to the Seven-Eleven and asked for him, I knew he had a Sunday morning shift there, but the manager said he called in sick. "You look hungry," he said, "here." He handed me a hot dog slathered in mustard. I told him I didn't have any money. "It's okay. You're a friend of Tim's, right? I'll take it out of his pay." I ate the dog and since I had no place to go I walked my bike home and when I got there, Jane was coming down the steps dressed for school.

"I'm glad I caught you," she said, "Principal Thwaite called and wants to see me."

"Now? On Sunday? It's Sunday."

"It's probably about cleaning up the mess from the prom. The post-prom committee probably didn't show up."

"Can't it wait?" I asked, scared that whatever had happened was going to be dragged into the light for everyone to see and then they would start examining everything about us, about me. Jane had always insisted that we weren't like other families. We were way cooler than families who washed their cars every Saturday and put screens in the windows on June 21 and replaced the screens with storm windows on September 21, because they didn't have lives like we did. We were talented and special and we played by different rules. But people only let you play by special rules when you don't break any of their big ones. "Can't someone else clean up? Why can't it wait?" I started to cry again.

"Thwaite said it couldn't wait. I'm sorry about smacking you, honey. You know I have to smoke to wake up. I won't be long. I promise," she said and got in the Kia and drove away.

16

Jane was gone for a very long time and when she came back from her meeting with Principal Thwaite, she was more subdued than I have ever seen her. She said we had to talk and went into the house and came back out with two cans of beer. She cracked one open and handed me the other one, sat down on the steps and gestured for me to sit next to her.

"I don't like beer," I told her.

"You have my permission. You're old enough."

"Actually, no I'm not," I said it snottily and pushed the can away.

She shrugged. "So. Anyway. Thwaite fired me. No, not fired me. I'm suspended. Administrative leave."

"What's the difference?" I asked.

"In my case, none. I'll probably never go back."

"You want that, though, don't you? You always said you hated teaching."

"I never said that! I love teaching. Where did you get that idea?"

"You said it. You said you hated teaching. Remember? When we took that vacation to see The Griffin when I was ten? You asked him to let us live with him and you said you couldn't bear it anymore, that you hated teaching. I re*mem*ber that." My head really hurt, maybe from not sleeping or from the beer, which I was now guzzling, or maybe it was that Seven-Eleven hot dog because I felt like barfing.

"*You're making that up*, Mercedes! You got hysterical when we were leaving."

"I did not get hysterical! I never get hysterical. *You* said your teaching was the only thing keeping us in Pennsylvania. I know! I *remember* that!"

"Okay, okay. Whatever. Well, anyway. Do you want to know why I'm suspended? I guess you have a right to know why I was suspended."

I put my fists over my ears and closed my eyes. "No, no no no," I said. "I don't care why, I don't care!"

"Okay, Mercedes." She looked really sad and I started to really really *really* hate her. I could take care of her when she was happy and we were special and talented, but I couldn't take care of her if we weren't. I mean, I'm the kid, you know, and she's the mother and one of the rules of the Two Cool Society, I made it up and Jane agreed to it, was that being cool made you happy. I didn't *want* to take care of Jane's sadness. I didn't even know *how* to, to be honest. Captain Kirby had said, "You can't go back," but at that moment I wanted Jane to light one of her stupid cigarettes and blow smoke right in my face and leave the dirty dishes in the sink for me to do while she took a nap on the sofa and laugh at the dandelion seeds blowing across the neighborhood and continue not giving a shit what anyone thought like she always did. Here's the thing about Jane: the thing I hated most about her was that she never seemed sad but I was *always* sad. I mean *some*one has to be sad or you aren't a grownup house or something. Maybe, like Mrs. Thwaite said, you *just* need a moral compass. But that's stupid. I mean, who wants a moral compass if you turn out like Mrs. Thwaite?

"I just want you to hear my side of things," Jane said, "Before you hear it from other people. I guess I want you to be on my side." And then she started crying, bawling really, and I was screaming "Shut up shut up shut up, just shut *up!*" but she was telling me anyway that if she didn't turn herself in the sheriff was going to come to the house and arrest her because the DA was pressing charges, he had to, the law was the law, especially for teachers because they were role models, and Rob was seventeen, only eight days from his eighteenth birthday—how was *she* supposed to know *that?* He lied to her!—and she didn't know who she could ask for bail money so once she turned herself in she probably wouldn't be able to make arrangements for *me.* "I'm sorry I messed up, Mercedes, I didn't mean to. I don't know why they're being such pricks about it. I didn't hurt anybody. I was just trying to make The Griffin see…I don't know. I left him a voice message from school. God, I don't know what's going to happen to me."

The beer and the sun baking us and that wrinkled hot dog which I was picturing swarming with bacteria that would multiply in my stomach and travel to my throat en route to my brain was being smothered and choked by a three ton bag of Jane O'Reilly's sorrow which she was trying to ease onto my lap.

"Say you forgive me, Mercedes, for making such a mess. Do you forgive me?"

I couldn't carry the bag of Jane's sorrow and woes, even if I wanted to. It was too heavy this time. Forgive her? Never.

"Excuse me," I said, "I got to go."

"I guess I should call your grandmother in Akron. Come in the house while I do that."

"No," I said, "I really have to go. I have to throw up."

17

At eleven in the morning, when it was becoming pretty clear that Jane—who had driven herself to the courthouse at nine— wasn't coming back, the doorbell rang and I looked through the curtains in the living room to see a large woman on our front porch. She had long straight black hair with an inch of gray roots showing and a weird high forehead. The way she was dressed she looked like Principal Thwaite had done her shopping. She was holding a sheaf of papers and looking at our pathetic lawn with distaste. She rang the bell again and rubbed her index finger down the doorjamb and was examining the dirt on it when she saw me looking at her through the curtains. She walked over to the window, grimacing towards her ears in what I guess was supposed to be a disarming smile.

"Mercedes?" she yelled at the window. "Mercedes O'Reilly? I'm Mrs. Valliere from Orphans and Childrens Court. I'm here to help you." She fished around in her purse and pulled out an ID card which she pushed up against the window but which I couldn't read through the filthy pane.

I stepped away and let the curtains close.

Mrs. Valliere waited for me to let her in and when it became obvious I wasn't going to, she started jerking the knob back and forth and banging on the door. "Mercedes, you have to let me in. I'm here to help you."

Captain Kirby had come over after Jane left. She was standing behind me. "You gotta let her in, Mercy, or it just goes on your record that you're difficult and then it only gets worse."

"Why should I let a stranger in my house? Isn't that what they're always harping on?"

"Just talk to her. She'll tell you how they're going to make everything perfect for you if you do exactly what they say. You can figure out what's next when she leaves."

"My mother will be home soon," I yelled through the door. "Why don't you come back later."

"I'm going to have to call the fire department to let me in if you don't," Mrs. Valliere said loudly.   .

"Can they do that?" I asked Captain Kirby.

"Dunno. Maybe."

Mrs. Valliere began hip checking the door which was making groaning

56

noises. I unlatched it and yanked it open and Mrs. Valliere fell into the house. "Good morning," she said.

"I told you my mother isn't here. She'll be back later."

"You're the one I need to talk to. And you are who exactly?" she asked, narrowing her eyes at Captain Kirby. "Are you Mrs. Tudesco?"

"Janet Kirby, ma'm." Captain Kirby said. "I'm Mercedes' cousin."

"Cousin?" Mrs. Valliere leafed through her papers. "I thought her grandmother was her closest relative."

"My *father* is my closest relative," I said.

"I'm the black sheep of the family," Captain Kirby said. "They pretend I don't exist. I'm not surprised there's nothing about me in your records." She shook her head sadly. "Sometimes I feel like I'm invisible."

"Do you have some identification on you?" Mrs. Valliere asked.

"I can't drive. I have epilepsy. But gosh, I'm glad you came. It would be marvelous if you could help me. With getting a driving license, I mean. Then I can vote, and drink, and do everything you do, m'am."

I thought Captain Kirby was going to have a seizure right then, that's what a good actress she was, and Mrs. Valliere was biting her lip not knowing who to help first. We obviously had enough problems between us for a month of non-stop intervention.

"Well, you'll have to come down to the office tomorrow," she said, finally. "For now, I am here to help Mercedes. Don't you think that should be our priority? To get your cousin with her grandmother? Now, is that *your* grandmother, too?"

"It sure would be great to get a driving license," Captain Kirby said.

"Can we sit down?" Mrs. Valliere asked, as she helped herself to a seat in the kitchen. "Did you have breakfast today?"

"Bacon and scrambled eggs," Captain Kirby said.

"Not you," Mrs. Valliere said, "I mean, I'm glad you had a good breakfast but we're here to discuss Mercedes, aren't we?"

"I had a great breakfast too," I said. "My cousin made it. She's a chef."

Mrs. Valliere looked at Captain Kirby suspiciously. "You look so familiar to me. You don't have any form of ID on you? And it's too bad that Mrs, Tudesco didn't mention you. It's so much easier if there are relatives right in town."

"Whatever you decide is fine with me," Captain Kirby said. "You're the pro. But now, I got to go to work. It was very nice meeting you, m'am."

"Where do you work?" Mrs. Valliere asked.

"At the high school, ma'm. In the kitchen. I haven't been late in five years. Never missed a day. Stuff like that means a lot, right, about your helping me get a driving license, right?"

"I'm sure it will."

"Don't forget to study for your finals, cuz," Kirby admonished me and left.

"It's funny, isn't it?" Mrs. Valliere said, "That she isn't listed here."

I nodded. "Funny."

"That would have made it easier. But she isn't here," she leafed through her papers again, "So Judge Delgado has decided that you'll have to go live with your grandmother in Akron. She's on a plane now and I can tell you, she can hardly wait to see you."

The last time I spoke to my grandmother she had trouble remembering my name. I thought it was because she didn't actually give a shit about me, but Jane said her mother was just distracted. "She has this job she's worried about. Plus she's almost 50." Great. That's just what I needed, a dotty old lady bossing me around.

"What about my father?" I asked. "Why can't I go live with him?"

"Judge Delgado has decided that under the circumstances you should probably have a more wholesome influence. You're a minor, Mercedes. And because your mother is a suspected sex offender, you're a ward of the court. You need adult supervision which Judge Delgado has decided your mother isn't fit to provide and there is a very real possibility your mother is going to jail."

Jane had told me before she left that she might not be coming back and said her mother was on her way, but it was just words like in a story. Now the story was coming to life. It was like a creepy horror movie. A ward of the court sounded like jail. "I didn't do anything wrong," I said.

"We know you didn't, dear. But in case your mother, your sole custodian, is no longer here to care for you, you must go to your next of kin."

"Which is my father," I said. "I can go live with him in Texas. He's on his way there now."

I closed my eyes and could see his house on Google Earth. I had it bookmarked as a favorite and could show it to Mrs. Valliere in a minute. "His house has a swimming pool in the back. That's wholesome."

"Your father travels all the time. He's not a suitable parent for you at this time. You need someone to give you constant supervision. Like your grandmother."

"I don't even *know* my grandmother!" I shouted. "Like I forget her name. Nellie, Jellie, Bellie? I don't remember! See!"

"I know you're going through a hard time," Mrs. Valliere said. "And I wish you could stay with your cousin, Janet, but we have rules for a reason and that is the protection of the child. You, Mercedes."

"The Griffin is a great dad," I said. "I was going to live with him in Houston when I turned sixteen, anyway."

"He said that?" Mrs. Valliere asked.

"Not in those exact words, but I know he wants it too."

"I'm sure he *does*. But for *now*," Mrs. Valliere said, "Your grandmother is your guardian. You have another week of school and she has graciously agreed to stay with you here until school is out. "Then"—she looked down at her papers—"you will go to Ohio to live with her until your mother's trial. Everything's been arranged. You're very lucky that Mrs. Tudesco is such a good neighbor and alerted us to your plight."

"I don't have a *plight*! Why can't I stay here until my mother gets a trial? Mr. Dow says everyone gets a fair trial. Mr. Dow is my social studies teacher. Innocent until proven guilty. Ask him if you don't believe me. He's right at the school."

Mrs. Valliere tapped her pen on the table. "You mother is trying to post bail."

"See. You *have* to talk to The Griffin. He'll post the bail and Jane can come back and everything will be fine. The Griffin is in*cred*ibly wealthy."

"You call your mother *Jane?*" Mrs. Valliere asked, writing it down in her file. *My* file. I was becoming the difficult child Captain Kirby warned me not to become.

"Just talk to The Griffin!"

"Mercedes, this is no longer a suitable environment for you. You can't live unsupervised with a suspected sex offender."

Before this moment, Jane and I had written the official story of our life—The Two Cool Society. To hear our story perverted, to hear Mrs. Valliere matter-of-factly calling Jane a sex offender—a *sex* offender!—made my stomach spaz out which I had the feeling was going to be happening a lot from now on.

"It's not your choice. It's the law's." She clipped her pen on the end of my file as if that settled everything, and stood up. "I'll give you a ride to school. Your grandmother will be here by the time you get out. And we already talked to Mr. Griffin. He told us that he and your mother aren't married and he doesn't want you to come to Texas."

"Of course, my parents are married! Jeez. You misunderstood him. You have to be very specific with The Griffin. So, you asked him that specifically? 'Do you want Mercy to live with you?' Did you ask him *that?* You have to be very specific with The Griffin. He has a lot on his mind."

Mrs. Valliere sneaked a look at her phone and waited for me by the open door. "Are you ready to go? You're already late for school."

I walked slowly to Mrs. Valliere's white SUV which had "Lehigh County Orphans and Children" stenciled in bold black letters on the side doors and hatch over the Pennsylvania Commonwealth Seal. Great. Just in case someone wasn't sure who was in the vehicle. Orphans over here! Orphans!

Mr. Henning was standing on his porch, scratching his belly, shaking his head. Him disapproving of me? That was a joke. I opened the back door because the back windows were tinted black.

"Sit up front with me," Mrs. Valliere said.

I climbed into the passenger seat next to her.

"I'm not going to jump out, if that's what you think."

"I don't think that. Should I think that?"

Mrs. Tudesco was kneeling next to her four Pomeranians who were taking turns at the fire hydrant. She picked up one of her dogs, smootched it and stared—the SUVs front windows weren't tinted—as Mrs. Valliere backed out of the driveway.

On my ninth grade summer reading list was a book called The Scarlet Letter. The way those Puritans made Hester feel so awful had seemed totally ridiculous to me then. I mean, it wasn't even her fault. It was the guy who couldn't control himself. I'd have to ask Jane if she'd ever made it assigned reading.

I turned to put on my seat belt and saw Captain Kirby and Tim hiding behind the overgrown rhododendrons on the side of the house. As we pulled away from the curb I could see them in the side view mirror following us on their bikes. I smiled.

Mrs. Valliere smiled back. "I'm glad you're feeling better. It's going to be okay, see? This is just something to be gotten through. You'll be better off with your grandmother. I spoke with her on the phone. You'll see. A good dose of normal is just what you need."

Whatever that meant. Considering it's their supposed profession, people who are paid to tell you what to do seem to know nothing about what's best for anyone but them.

I asked Mrs. Valliere to stop a block from school so no one would see me getting out of her Orphans and Children limousine, but "No, no," she said, "I'll take you right to the door" as if she were doing me some big favor. I was as inconspicuous as Cinderella getting out of the pumpkin coach. "Your grandmother will pick you up at three thirty," she shouted as I slammed the door and faced the crowd of students waiting for the bell to ring.

Everyone's eyes were on me. I had loved the feeling of being famous when I was with The Griffin at our house and I could feel the love pouring over us when we came down the stairs to the Trap. But this wasn't love. It was blood lust and I felt really scared and I remembered I forgot my books at home. "Oh shit!" I said and closed my eyes. Which made everyone near me laugh and start chanting "Oh shit, oh shit, oh shit." I forced myself through the crowd. "Excuse me," I said. "Excuse me. Excuse me." "Excuse me. Excuse me," the crowd chanted back. When I was halfway to the school steps a senior, Christine Kenealy, a cheerleader who everyone in school knew had the hots for the new football coach, stepped in front of me, blocking my way.

"Hot for teacher," she said, stupidly.

"Get out of my way," I said.

"Hot for teacher," she said again. "Oh yeah, I mean hot for students. What a slut!" Like a mantra, the chant reverberated through the crowd. "Hot for students. What a slut! Hot for students. What a slut!"

The blood had rushed to my head and I was having trouble seeing and my ears were ringing, and I wanted to just sink into the earth because I couldn't move any more when two people hooked their arms through mine.

"Don't let them see you cry," Tim said from the right.

"Cork it till we get you inside," Captain Kirby said from the left.

They lifted me, almost carrying me up the steps. The crowd started booing because their fun was being ruined.

"The men's room," Captain Kirby said, "Nobody will follow us in there."

They put me down gently in front of the mirror where I just stared at myself, not really seeing anything.

"She can't stay in school," Tim said. "They'll tear her apart."

"Well, she can't run away, because then she'll never stop running. She'll have to face it sooner or later."

Tim hugged me and, when I didn't feel his hug, I realized I was actually numb.

The men's room door swung open and Mr. Dow stood there. I searched his face for the hatred I knew he must feel for me. But I saw something in his face that was much worse. He pitied me. I had betrayed everything he had tried to teach us about life. He always said that what he envied about us most was that we were young and to be young meant there was hope. But Mr. Dow was wrong. No hope here.

"I'm sorry, Mr. Dow," I said, finally breaking down and crying.

Mr. Dow came over to me and put his hand out. "This isn't your fault, Mercy," he said. "Come on. You don't have to apologize for anything. I'll take you to the principal's office until someone comes for you. Is there someone Principal Thwaite can call? It'll be in your file. Come on."

"Call my father," I said, suddenly. I pulled The Griffin's number up on my phone and handed it to Mr. Dow.

"We'll do it from the principal's office," he said. "Come on."

19

Mr. Dow led me to the Principal's office where Principal Thwaite gave me a lecture on—surprise!—how the lack of a moral compass will *always* lead you down the wrong road and I found myself yearning to be torn to shreds by the pack of students in the hall rather than listen to her.

"She wants us to call her father," Mr. Dow said, handing my phone to Thwaite who shook her head and motioned him into her office where she probably told him…what? That my father didn't live with me? He already knew that. I'd written a million essays for his class this year.

When he came out of Thwaite's office, he said, "Try to distract yourself by studying for exams, Mercedes. Keep focused on your studies. You have your whole life in front of you and you can't allow this to sink your ship before you even leave the harbor," whatever that meant and he put my phone—with The Griffin's number still blinking on the screen—in my outstretched hand and went to teach his class. What did I expect? Mr. Dow had a pretty wife and a new son and they lived together in a ranch house—somewhere—and I'm sure no one ever called Code on them. So, how could he possibly know what my life was like, or do anything about it?

At lunch I asked Thwaite if I could go to my afternoon classes, but she said I should stay in her office for my own protection.

"Protection from what?" I asked her.

"We don't need another incident, like your mother, Miss O'Reilly," she said.

Tim stopped by with a cheese sandwich and chocolate milk and we shared them on the hard bench in the secretary's office with our free arms draped around one another. "You can stay at my house," he said. "My dad won't even notice."

I knew about Tim's house. His father was a retired Marine and his grandfather who lived with them was a retired Marine. His mother and grandmother had both deserted. So did his older brother who ran away to Scranton the day after his eighteenth birthday. No wonder Tim almost never laughed.

"That's okay," I said. "My grandmother is coming to take care of me. Then I have to go live with her. In O*hi*o." The name sounded like a punishment.

"Why don't you stay with your dad?"

Good question.

"And what's going to happen to *Have Mercy*? Jeez, we were just starting to get good."

"When you graduate, we'll hook up," I said, although I couldn't imagine ever seeing him again.

"But I'm going to miss you in the meantime. *Have Mercy* was the most fun I ever had in my life. In my *life*."

My doubts about Tim's interest in me versus The Griffin dissolved, and I touched his arm and gave him a look that said, "Please kiss me," and he did which was the first comforting thing to happen to me all day when a woman in a navy blue suit, five inch heels, a blond bob and—as Jane would say—"a little work around the jaw" came through the office door. I pulled away from Tim as if he was on fire.

"That's about right," the woman said "Necking in the principal's office."

"Listen lady," Tim said and stood up.

I put an arm in front of him to stop him. "Tim, this is my Granny O'Reilly."

20

"Nice to meet you, Granny," Tim said.

"Puhleez. Call me Judge O'Reilly. And you…" Granny looked at me, probably trying to remember my name. "I have to see what those legal morons are doing for your mother. What is so hard about posting bail? Ah. Why am I asking you? Is the principal in?"

I pointed to the closed door behind which Principal Thwaite had barricaded herself. Before the secretary could stop her, Granny let herself into Thwaite's office and slammed the door behind her.

"Wow," Tim said.

"I know," I said. "She's a judge in Akron. Well, a television judge on a local cable channel. It's not like she went to law school or anything. She was the weather girl until she got too old to tell people it was going to rain."

Granny was back in two minutes. "Are you her boyfriend?" she asked Tim and I was very happy that he nodded yes immediately. "Well, that's very heart warming, but you should go back to class now. I don't want my granddaughter dating a juvenile delinquent. No use everyone losing their footing in this little drama."

Principal Thwaite emerged from her office. She was wringing her hands. "It's not exactly a little drama. A young man, a student, was taken advantage of. His morals were corrupted."

"A young man with a pregnant underage girlfriend," Granny said, "cannot really be said to have had his morals corrupted."

"That's just a rumor."

"Where's there's smoke, there's fire," Granny said. "Has his mother's lawyer named a price yet?"

Tim picked up the remains of our lunch. "I'll see you after school," he said.

"No you won't," Granny said. "We have family matters to resolve. Don't we, Mercedes?   And why aren't you in class?"

"The kids were taunting her," Principal Thwaite said.

Tim signaled with his thumbs that he would text me and slipped out.

"Is that why you're hiding out here? Because you're afraid? Is that how you were raised? To be a coward?"

"I'm not a coward," I said. Although, I thought, maybe I am.

"Well, then get to class."

Principal Thwaite seemed to find some resolve. "I don't think…"

Granny said, "I will try to find out what they did with your mother and I will pick you up at three thirty. Where are your books?"

"In my locker."

"Good." And with that she was gone.

Although Jane made me talk to Granny O'Reilly on the phone on Christmas and Easter our conversations were always short and empty, and this was only the second time I had seen her in person. She was always busy with her television career, well, cable career, and Jane wasn't breaking a leg to visit her and her new husband, Ron, who was a mayor or something. No kidding, I could honestly see why Jane ran away from home when she was sixteen.

"People who don't deal with children think that everything is black and white. If it were only that easy," Principal Thwaite said to me before darting back into her office. Her secretary had gone to the bathroom, so I peeked out into the hall and went down to the girl's locker room to see if Captain Kirby was there.

21

Tim found me and Captain Kirby in the girls' locker room where we had spent a couple of hours lying on the benches, staring at the florescent lights.

"Is the coast clear?" Captain Kirby asked.

"It's in the newspapers and there's already a bunch of blogs about it," Tim said.

"Shit."

I sat up and turned on my phone, which I had refused to look at since the thing began. *The Morning Clarion* ran a blurry lead picture of Jane coming out of the courthouse shielding her face with her hat and another below that of her ducking into a black SUV. I couldn't see who the driver was. The blogs *mommysdirtylittlesecret and adultcybermart* ran pictures of Jane taken from the last three Milltown yearbooks. Another blog named *hototrot* had the shot of Jane dancing with Rob with his hand on her ass. "Hot to Trot Teacher Makes Prom Weekend Something to Remember for 17 Year Old," it blared. *The Morning Clarion* had an accompanying article on The Griffin and his connection, or lack of one, to Jane and to "an alleged fifteen year old minor female."

"I'm almost sixteen," I said.

"At least they didn't put your name in the paper," Tim said.

"Only because they aren't allowed to," Captain Kirby said.

I handed my phone to Captain Kirby and went to the window to watch the students boarding the school buses. I would have given anything to be lining up with them instead of waiting for Granny O'Reilly. And where the hell was Jane? And why wasn't The Griffin calling me? I grabbed my phone back from Captain Kirby and dialed Jane's number. It went right to voice mail. Then I dialed The Griffin who didn't answer. I threw the phone against the wall. Didn't either of them care that I was being passed around like a stale sandwich?

"Hey, hey," Captain Kirby said. "Don't lose your lifeline."

"You don't have a phone so why do you care?"

"I'll get one. One of those pay as you go things."

"They don't take rolls of quarters," I said and began to cry. "I'm sorry,

Kirby. I gotta go wait for my grandmother."

"We'll wait with you," Tim said.

"That's okay," I said. "Why don't you guys come by after Tim gets off of work and we'll jam."

"Awesome," Tim said. "I wanted to do that all day."

I thought how hard it must be to be boy. You never get to cry. You have to hit a ball or play in a grunge band or get into fights to rid yourself of all those feelings that don't fit into any box.

"You'll be okay?" Captain Kirby asked.

"Yeah. Sure. She's my grandmother, not the wicked witch of the west, although that's who she reminds me of."

"You just got to keep that Orphan and Children's lady happy, if she comes back," Captain Kirby said. "Make her think you're thrilled to death that grandma is living with you."

I nodded and picked up my backpack and we wandered down the deserted hallway to the old part of the school then turned to the main entrance. The janitors were already washing the floors. We went outside where a group of band kids were waiting for their parents to pick up them and their tubas and clarinets. Band kids were nerds and if they had heard about Jane's and my problem at least none of them cared enough to say anything to me. Captain Kirby and Tim waved as they walked away and I sat down on the steps beside a tuba until I saw a black SUV pull up and Granny O'Reilly get out. She looked up at the roof of the school like she was reading the school motto Semper something or other then she surveyed the waiting students before she came wearily up the steps, seeming not quite as peppy as she did earlier.

"Oh, there you are," she said, almost tripping over me. She sat down next to me. "You'll be glad to move to Akron. This place is a dump."

"Yeah, I hear stellar things about Akron," I said.

"Really?"

"No. *Not* really. The only reason I've even heard of Akron is because you and Ron live there."

"Oh."

We watched a couple of cars drive up and students unfolding themselves to walk down to meet them. I thought it was funny that only a couple of band kids had ever wanted to join *Have Mercy*—only trumpet players, and I don't like horns mixing with guitars. Pretty soon it was just me and Granny alone on the steps.

Finally she said as if we had been discussing it the whole time, "They kept telling me, 'Imagine if this happened to your sixteen year old granddaughter, how would you feel?' And I kept telling them, 'It *didn't* happen to my sixteen year old granddaughter. My granddaughter is fifteen and it happened to someone's eighteen year old *son.*' That makes all the difference, doesn't it? *Doesn't* it?"

She looked at me, waiting for some teen wisdom I guess to come shooting out of me. But I didn't have any. My teen wisdom box was empty.

"You're fifteen, aren't you? That's what I told them. They found that so interesting that they sent for a clerk to write it down."

"Where's Jane," I asked. "When is she coming home?"

Granny O'Reilly bit her lip. "Don't call your mother, Jane. It's disrespectful."

"She doesn't mind."

"Have you ever asked her?"

Actually, I hadn't. But I thought she figured it made her hip and she never complained.

"What do you think I should call her? *Mommy*?" I snorted.

I didn't expect the slap and it fell short of its mark. "She never said she didn't like it," I whined.

"Well, I don't like it. And I didn't ask to be part of this, but like it or not I am. We're in this together for now."

I followed Granny O'Reilly to the car and we drove all the way home and were parked in front of our house before she said anything. She turned off the ignition and we sat in the car, watching Mr. Hennings suck down a beer. "This is a weird time," she said, finally. "You have real perverts running around and everyone wants to make an example of someone. That's all it is, you know. They need to show they're on top of things."

The way Granny O'Reilly wouldn't look at me scared me. "When is Jane…my mother…coming home? She said she was only going to be charged, and she would be back. Couldn't she get the bail?"

"The bail wasn't the problem," Granny O'Reilly said.

"Where is she? Why won't she call me?"

"It's complicated."

"Complicated how?"

Here's the thing. Of all the things I hate about adults the biggest is their tendency to think that just because someone's not a thousand years old they are too stupid to understand anything.

"She doesn't want the media swarming around. Let it die down a little."

Granny O'Reilly got out of the car and went to the edge of the driveway and kicked a beer can—which had slipped through Mr. Henning's fence onto our driveway—out into the gutter. Mr. Hennings got out of his chair and stood by the porch railing, then let out a huge belch.

"What are you staring at, you old fool," Granny O'Reilly said. "You should be ashamed of yourself."

22

Granny O'Reilly closed herself in Jane's bedroom. I heard her talking on a phone to her husband Ron. I couldn't tell if she was on her cell or the land line by Jane's bed so I ran downstairs and picked up the wall receiver in the kitchen. Dial tone. I ran back upstairs and lay by the crack at the bottom of Jane's door.

"...*unfortunate* incident... in Akron yet?... well thank god for that... a disa*s*ter... worse than you can imagine... the election, yes I know... with her father?... he has a wife and kid down there... why should the wife take her in...puhleese ... a nice enough kid... can't just leave her here... yes, a liability... yes, I'll figure something out..."

She asked him what was going on at Channel 37, the cable station where she was the fake judge. She was worried that someone named Laura was going to take her fake place on the fake bench while she was gone. "I don't care what kind of contract I have," she said. "Once they get used to seeing someone else you know any contract can be broken."

She emerged from the bedroom suddenly—I didn't hear her say goodbye—and almost tripped on me. I was sitting cross-legged by the door but she was so preoccupied it didn't occur to her why I was there.

"Why aren't you doing your homework?" she said.

No one had asked me that question in so long I didn't have an answer.

"Get going," she said. She clapped her hands and went back into Jane's bedroom and turned on the television while I walked to my bedroom in the back of the house and opened my social studies book trying to remember what we were even talking about in class. It seemed so long ago, and since I was a liability what did it matter anyway. In a minute she was at my door.

"How do you access cable in this house?"

"We don't have cable," I said. Jane never got around to ordering cable when we first moved in, and we hardly ever watched television anyway.

"How can you not have cable?" She sat down on the bed next to me. "Every house in America has cable."

"We can still get a couple of stations," I said. "Use the 'seek' button."

"PBS is not technically a television station," she said. "Where's your DVD player? How do you watch *Judge Jen*?"

Judge Jen was, of course, Granny O'Reilly's television show. She sent DVDs of the show every week which Jane threw away without even opening. My face got hot. "I download stuff when I want to see something."

"I see." She stood up and scowled. "What's that noise?"

Tim had let himself into the Trap and was playing some scales.

"That's the guitarist in my band," I said. "We're supposed to be rehearsing."

"You can't rehearse until you've done your homework."

"It's only for an hour. Jane always lets me practice for an hour a night."

"Well, you can do your hour after you've finished your homework."

"He has a job and anyway his father won't let him come later."

"That's because his father cares about him. Is the guitarist that boy?"

I nodded.

"Tell him to go away." And with that, she left.

I mean, could it get any more depressing? I'm almost sixteen years old and suddenly a bunch of *strangers* are telling me what to do. First that witch, Mrs. Valliere, and now my grandmother. I mean, grandmothers are supposed to spoil their grandkids, right? What did they think? That I didn't know how to take care of myself? Who did they think took care of *every*thing when it was just me and Jane?

I took out my phone and called Jane again but pressed end call after the first ring. Then I called The Griffin. It rang a couple of times then went abruptly to voice mail so I knew he'd seen it was from me and pressed *Ignore*. Tears started running down my cheeks. I couldn't help it. "What's that, a *tear*? Cut it out!" The Griffin said when he was here and I was so happy to see him.

Cut it out. Yeah, right.

I marched down to the Trap. Kirby was behind the Pink Fade and did a *bada bing* on the cymbals to greet me. Tim smiled when he saw me then put his head down again to concentrate on his chords. I picked up my Fender, turned up the volume and we began to play his new song, *Hole in the Sky*. After we ran through it twice, I picked up the mike and began to sing:

The world's so black and blue
There's nothing left to say
Words just pass me by
I gotta get away

There's a beam of light
It's blue and bright
It's coming from a hole in the sky

23

Granny O'Reilly came down to the Trap, listened to us finish Hole in the Sky then said, "Okay, everyone out. You have your own homes to go to."

"My band always eats with us," I said.

"They can eat at home. I'm sure their parents have lovely meals waiting for them in their lovely homes. You've had a very stressful day and you need to relax," she said.

"This is it," I said. "This is what I do to relax."

"Who are you?" Granny O'Reilly asked Captain Kirby. "I haven't seen you before."

"Janet Kirby, ma'm," she said.

"Tell her who you are!" I commanded. I couldn't believe Captain Kirby was being so docile. If there was one person who I thought could stand up to Granny O'Reilly, Captain Kirby was it.

Captain Kirby put her sticks in her back pocket. "I gotta go. My ma's waiting for me. 'Good night m'am."

"Me, too," Tim said. "We got finals tomorrow. Don't you have to study, Mercy? Well, you're so smart you probably don't have to. Good night, Your Honor."

I watched them leave with my mouth open. How could they leave me here with this harridan?

Granny O'Reilly smiled with a corner of her mouth and pushed the button to close the Trap door.

"Your friends have manners," she said.

"They're not my friends," I said, woodenly, "They're my band." I didn't remember ever feeling so alone. That hole in the sky looked inviting.

"Be ready to eat dinner in an hour. In the meantime, study for your finals. You didn't tell me you were having final exams. But, of course, it's the end of the year. I should have thought."

She wandered off to the kitchen, yakking about good manners, and I went up to my room to try to study Social Science, the only class I had any hope of acing. And why should I care, I thought, about social studies or anything. I had written off school in bullet points already. Put it and all my classmates in a box to be left in the bathroom of the bus station before I boarded the bus for Houston. Leave it right next to the box for Captain

Kirby and the box for Tim. I shouldn't have trusted them. I couldn't trust anyone. I knew that and let myself be fooled. It wouldn't happen again.

My stomach was spazzing so bad and I felt so sad and I was sweaty for some reason. I went to the window and pushed it all the way open. As I leaned out a stone hit me in the chest.

"Whoops!" Captain Kirby giggled. "Sorry. I meant to hit the window. Out of practice, I guess."

"You okay?" Tim asked, stepping out from behind a bush.

"I thought you deserted me."

"Are you crazy?" Tim said. "We wouldn't leave you alone with the Judge."

"You mean it?" I said then started crying. "You guys are…"

"Shut up," Captain Kirby said. "You're getting your period. Meet us out here at ten o'clock."

24

Granny O'Reilly made some canned soup and sandwiches for dinner and kept apologizing for it. "I'm really a gourmet cook, you know?" she said. "But you have the worst stocked kitchen I've ever been in."

Tell me about it, I thought, although I missed Jane's non-tasty no-hassle non-cooking. We ate out half the time and we never had conversations about the food which was fine by me. "Really, Gran," I said, "It's okay. We usually have nothing in the house."

"What do you mean?"

"Jane shops every day for food, just enough for that day, that's why there's nothing in the fridge."

"Puhleese," she said. Her cell phone rang and she squinted at it. "I have to take this." She went into the living room and I strained to hear her side of the conversation. "Well, I can't afford to be out of the loop for an entire week. I may take her out of school early. Yes, she'll miss her finals but what's going to happen to the girl if I lose my job too? Then what?"

She was talking to Mrs. Valliere.

"Her moron of a father? Puhleese."

She came back to the table and stared at me.

"Everything okay?" I asked.

"Can you get Channel 37 Akron on your computer?"

"We get it all the time," I said. "For your show."

"Bullshit, but it's not your fault. I need to see if they ran a re-run today."

"Sure," I said.

I went to my bedroom, came back with my laptop and googled Channel 37 Akron, because of course we'd never looked at it once in the entire time I've been alive. "Hey, nice website," I said. There was a feature story on a Pennsylvania teacher (Jane! Granny's husband Ron would be calling soon) turning herself in for corrupting the morals of a 17 year old boy. I scrolled down. There was Granny O'Reilly on the left in a black robe looking totally fake judicial. "Judge Jen, Today at 4!" in a banner under her photo. "Hey, look! It's you."

She smiled a little then frowned. "What's that?" She pointed to a hyper-texted headline—"Girl Finds Out Her Aunt Is Her Real Mother"— under her headshot. "Click on that."

74

And as soon as I did, she let out a wail. "That's not my show!"

I started the video and a young blond woman in a black judge's robe was listening thoughtfully to two sisters fight over a girl both claimed to be their daughter.

"Jesus, couldn't they do re-runs for a week?" Granny O'Reilly asked.

"She's pretty," I said.

"Of course she's pretty. She's thirty years younger than me. But she doesn't have wisdom, you know? The reason I'm good, the reason my ratings stay high, is because I've lived a long life and I've seen things, you know, and I've been through a lot. Like your mother. You have no idea what she put me through and look what she's doing to me now! But that's why I can get up on that bench and be smart about people. Laura can't be smart about people, she hasn't lived yet."

I actually didn't know what she was talking about, although she sounded a lot like Mr. Dow, but she was so upset I actually felt sorry for her. It looked like the audience was having a really good time. So were the sisters. Even if Laura wasn't as wise as Granny O'Reilly, she seemed to be a lot funnier. "Look! Oh my god, she's going to let the daughter decide!" Judge Laura brought the daughter out to ask her who she wanted to live with and the daughter kissed both women and the sisters started hugging each other and all three were hugging each other and crying and kissing and the audience was crying and the Judge was dabbing at her eyes and Granny O'Reilly looked like she was going to be sick.

"I can't believe this!" Granny O'Reilly said. "I'm going to lose my show if don't get back to Akron like immediately."

I turned off the computer. "You can go," I said. "I'm finished with exams in two days and the rest of the week is just hanging around for the seniors' commencement which we're all supposed to go to."

"I can't leave you here alone, can I?"

"I'm dropping out of school in January anyway," I told her. "To live with The Griffin in Texas."

"Really? He said it was okay for you to come?"

"Of course. I'm his daughter, aren't I?"

"You can take a plane right to Akron as soon as you're finished with school. I mean, it's not like you're a little kid."

"No," I said, "I'm not a little kid. Definitely not a little kid."

"You seem mature." She looked around the house. "I can't imagine that your mother kept things going around here. I think you probably carried a lot of the load. Knowing her, that is, am I right? What was she thinking going to bed with a seventeen year old? Look at the mess she made for me. How stupid can you get?"

"He told her he was eighteen."

"Why couldn't she be like other mothers? And just have affairs with regular old boring men like everyone else?"

It was what I'd asked myself a lot of times. I'd named us the Two Cool Society, but if cool meant doing things no one else dared to do then it was Jane who was cool not me. I was only along for the ride.

"You mean men like my grandfather?" I asked. I met him once when I was a little kid. Then he died. "Was he boring?"

"No, dear, your grandfather was the coolest."

"The coolest?"

"Yes.

"What about Ron? Is he cool?"

She laughed. "Ron has traits that wouldn't seem appealing when you're fifteen but seem wonderful the older you get. I can't explain."

"That's okay," I said. I would put Ron and Granny O'Reilly in a box marked Open When Fifty-Five.

"You'd better study for your exams, Mercedes," she said. "Things keep getting more complicated. I'll sleep on it and we'll talk about what to do tomorrow. Frankly, I'm not sure how I would explain you in Akron. Reputation is everything in the media. One false step you've lost all credibility. And there's Ron, of course. He's thinking of running for the Senate. Who would I say you are?"

"Your granddaughter?"

"No, I couldn't do that."

We said good-night and I went up to my room and lay on my bed looking up at the ceiling and wondering where Jane was hiding until ten o'clock when I climbed out the window and hopped on my bike to join Tim and Captain Kirby at the corner.

25

"Where did you get the bike, Kirby?" I asked her. She was riding a Fezzari Fore CR5 road bike which I knew for a fact cost five thousand dollars. The guy at Milltown Chain wouldn't even let me touch it when I went in to get the gears on my own bike adjusted.

"Milltown Chain," she said. "Test drive. Are we going to conversate or are we going to make a plan?"

Tim kissed me and we all mounted our bikes and sped out to Sebastian's Pizza on Route 11. Tim, who actually had some money from his job, paid for a pizza with everything and our sodas which we took to an outside table.

"The way I see it," Tim said, "You only have two more days of school, then you can leave. You can tolerate her for two days, can't you?"

"You got to stay to the end," Captain Kirby said, "Or the whole year doesn't count."

"I'm leaving anyway in January, so who cares?"

"You're a moron if you do that."

"But then, I have to go live with her. In Ohio."

"In Ohio?"

"They won't let me live by myself or with Jane without adult supervision."

"'They' being Mrs. Valliere," Captain Kirby said. "She thinks I'm your cousin. That could be helpful."

"She also thinks she knows you from someplace. Does she?"

"Our paths may have crossed," Captain Kirby said, concentrating on getting extra cheese onto her slice of pizza. "I'm in the system."

"Well, the question is," Tim said, "Can you live with it for two days, or are you gonna leave now?"

"I don't think she's going to stick around much longer," I said. "She doesn't want to be with me any more than I want to be with her. I mean, I don't think she even knew what I looked like when she got here. She guessed who I was because I look like Jane. She has this television show she's the star of that she's freaking out about. I think Mrs. Valliere is the problem."

"You've seen the last of her," Captain Kirby said.

I felt my body turn cold. "You didn't do anything….?"

"You're kidding, right?!" She looked from me to Tim. "Look, those social workers are so over-worked, they make the rounds like once a year. You'll be having your own kids before you see her again. She has to visit crack moms and families where the dad locks the kids in a closet, beats his wife, then takes a nap. She thinks you're all snuggly with your grandma. She has a big check by your name: case closed!"

"You think so?"

"I know so."

We picked up our bikes and walked them. Tim held my free hand. "I'll miss you so much if you moved to Ohio," he said.

"I know. We're just getting good," I said.

"No," he said, "I mean I would really miss you."

We got back on our bikes and we rode home. The lights were on in Jane's bedroom, so Granny O'Reilly was still awake.

"I guess I'll go to school tomorrow and take my exams."

"Good girl!" Captain Kirby said.

"I'm a text message away if you need me," Tim said, then he leaned in and whispered, "I'm going to ask my father if you can stay with us." He kissed me and then they pedaled away.

I leaned my bike on the garage door and climbed back through my bedroom window. Granny O'Reilly was sitting on my bed. She had removed her eyebrows and makeup and was wearing a sensible—laughable Jane would say—nightgown. Without the pancake she looked like a sad old lady version of Jane and me.

"You're just like your mother," she said. "Thinking only of yourself. Didn't you think I would be worried about where you'd gone?"

"I didn't want to bother you."

"That's exactly what your mother would say. Having an illegitimate baby with a middle-aged second rate musician. She could at least have picked someone famous like Mike Jagger and gotten a big settlement when he got tired of her."

"I'm not illegitimate," I said. "The Griffin and Jane and I are a special and talented family. We're special. Regular labels don't apply to us."

"Is that what she tells you?" Granny O'Reilly stared out into space. "That's about right. What was she thinking? That she could just come back to Akron where her mother was a TV personality and her father ran a department store? Were we supposed to pretend that that's how we raised her? That we were that kind of people too? Didn't she think other people might suffer the consequences for her actions? She never thought of other people. Where did she get that from?"

I had to reluctantly agree with Granny O'Reilly here. Jane always thought of herself first and I always always felt like I was picking up after whatever she cooked up or neglected to do. But until this moment I always thought it was some defect in Jane. That it was how a free-spirited irresponsible person acted. That it was the price people around you paid for your being cool. It never occurred to me that it was something she learned from her own mother who obviously couldn't think of anything except her stupid washed up career as a fake television judge, who couldn't be bothered thinking about her daughter and granddaughter. No wonder we never visited Ohio. I started to get angry.

"You're just like her," Granny O'Reilly said. "Are you having sexual relations with that boy?"

"That's none of your business," I screamed.

"You are, aren't you? If you come to Akron and you're pregnant, then what? What are we going to tell people?"

"You can tell them whatever you damn please."

"I knew it. You're just like your mother."

"You know what?" I said. "I'm glad I'm like Jane. And Mick Jagger is ten thousand years older than The Griffin. You don't know anything!"

"Really? Your mother is in hiding. She hasn't even tried to contact you, has she? You're glad to be like her? That's how you want to turn out?"

All the anger I had felt since prom night came rushing to my brain. Everything was so screwed up I was angry at everyone. Jane. That shithead, Rob. The Griffin. Mrs. Valliere. How about Captain Kirby, always stealing stuff. She stole that bike she was riding. I knew it. We'd all get in trouble along with her if she got caught. How about Mrs. Kirby? She couldn't manage to get along with living people long enough to earn enough money for her and Captain Kirby so Kirby didn't have to steal.

"You know what?" I shouted. "I don't care how I turn out, as long as I don't turn out like you."

"Perfect." Granny O'Reilly stood up. "There's no chance of that." She left the room.

I was shaking and crying. I took out my phone to text Tim, but thought better of it. He was probably asleep or studying for exams.

I didn't know what to do with what I was feeling. It was all too enormous to stuff it into any of my boxes. It would split them wide open. I lay on my bed trying to figure out what to do for hours I guess because morning was suddenly breaking behind the curtains.

26

I must have fallen back to sleep because it was seven when I got out of bed. I quickly dressed and went downstairs. Granny O'Reilly's purse was on the kitchen table. I opened it and took a twenty dollar bill—she thought I was like Jane so no harm done to our family reputation. To my credit I took out a fifty and put it back—there might be hope for me—and left the house before she woke up.

I rode my bike to Mr. Rajeet's Dunkin Donuts and ordered an iced coffee and a glazed doughnut from a young man. I'd never seen the counter without Mr. Rajeet behind it.

"Where's Mr. Rajeet?" I asked. I plunked two quarters into the tip cup, feeling flush.

The young man said, "He's on vacation."

"Vacation? He never goes on vacation." I couldn't imagine Mr. Rajeet on vacation. Not that I knew much about vacations. Our only vacations had been driving around the country in The Griffin's bus or visiting relatives who clearly didn't want anything to do with us. But, like Mr. Rajeet at the beach or something? I couldn't see it.

I was staring at the young man. "Is Mr. Rajeet okay?" I asked.

"You are a friend of Mr. Rajeet's?"

"Yes, I come here all the time. He told me about his sons in college who are going to be famous doctors." Another young man who looked amazingly like the guy at the counter came out of the kitchen and slid a tray of doughnuts into the display and I finally got it. They were Mr. Rajeet's sons.

"He had a heart attack," the young counter man whispered.

"Oh!" I put my hands over my mouth.

"I think he will be okay, but as you know, it's in God's hands," he said.

"But you aren't in college," I said. "What happened to college?"

He shrugged. "School will have to wait. It's okay, miss. Don't worry. I will tell Mr. Rajeet that you were here and asked about his health. He will be pleased."

"Wait! He doesn't know my name," I said. How would he distinguish me from the zillions of other ordinary looking fifteen year old girls who'd bought his Munchkins? "I know! Tell him the future rock and roll star was asking about him."

The young man smiled. "I'll do that." He put his hands over mine. "Don't worry. He's a very strong man. He may recover."

"Or…." I blurted.

"Or not. Yes." He smiled at me.

"And you might not get back to college," I said as if he hadn't figured that out for himself.

"Or I will. Two things can be possible at one time, future rock and roll star."

Mr. Rajeet's recovery and his sons' scholastic future were suddenly of great concern to me, probably because they allowed me to think about something besides myself for a minute. What I couldn't understand was how Mr. Rajeet's son could feel such uncertainty yet be so calm about it.

I stuffed the rest of my stolen money in the tip cup for his and his brother's tuition.

"Hey, hey, hey!" Captain Kirby nudged me aside. She took the ten I'd dropped in back out of the tip cup. "Mom gave this to both of us," she explained to the young Rajeet who nodded that he took her at her word. "I'll take three Boston Cremes and a large Coffee Coolata with extra sugar," she said then turned to me. "Do you have a brain tumor or something?"

"What are you doing here?"

"I went to your house to convoy you to school and when you weren't there I figured you might be here and here you are. Her honor answered the door."

"Did you talk to her?"

"Of course I talked to her. I am a polite person, although granny should try a semester in charm school. No offense. Just saying."

"I'm hoping that by the time I get home she'll be gone."

We went outside and sat down on the curb, drinking our coffee and inhaling the exhaust from the cars in the takeout line. Between my mornings at Dunkin Donuts and Jane's second hand smoke, my lungs were probably so screwed I probably wouldn't make it to twenty so why was I worried about anything?

"Hey, hands off," Captain Kirby said to a boy who was kneeling in front of her bike. He was wearing a baseball cap backwards and his pants were slung low on his hips, gangsta style.

"A CR5, right?" he said.

"Yep."

"How'd you get it?"

Kirby stood up and wheeled the bike next to me.

"That's what I thought," the boy said and laughed.

"Get out of here," she said. "Before I call the truant officer." And to me, "Aren't you going to ask what me and Granny O'Reilly talked about?

"Okay," I said, "What did you and my grandmother talk about?"

"Your mom is back home."

27

I could hear them fighting before we even got to the front of the house. Jane would scream then Granny O'Reilly would scream. Great.

"You might as well go on to school. I don't think you want to hear this," I told Captain Kirby.

"It's intense," she said. "They were going at it when I left."

I dropped my bike on the front lawn—Kirby stashed the Fezzari behind a bush—and we slowly opened the front door. Jane was sitting on the couch smoking, and Granny O'Reilly was smoking too. They were like two angry dragons, blowing smoke and spitting fire and venom.

"Why do you think this has anything to do with you?" Jane asked. "This has absolutely nothing to do with you. You're such a narcissist."

"Where did you learn such big words? From your therapist?"

"I stopped seeing a therapist years ago."

"Well, obviously you stopped too soon."

"What I don't see, what I really don't see, is how any of this is any of your business," Jane said.

"Really? You know, actually I don't see how this concerns me either. So then why did the Commonwealth of Pennsylvania call me in the middle of the night in the middle of Ohio to come and take care of your bastard?"

Captain Kirby shot me a look.

"You think I'm an unfit parent?" Jane screamed. "Well if I am, I learned at the feet of the master."

"You know," Granny O'Reilly said, "I don't have to put up with this abuse. I have a career that I am putting in jeopardy just by being away, not to mention that my husband's prospects for public office are diminishing with every minute I'm here. What do you think would happen if the media caught wind of my involvement in what was happening here? They would crucify me and I don't blame them. It's filthy and disgusting."

They smashed out their cigarettes in the same ash tray, glaring at each other, then Jane saw us.

"Mercedes," she said, dully. "Captain Kirby."

"Where were you?" I asked.

She lit another cigarette and exhaled loudly. "Your grandmother asked me to stay away while she was here so the media wouldn't connect us and it would all get back to Akron, blah, blah, blah. But it's my house, damn it. And like it or not, she's my mother and I'm yours and it's really messed up, isn't it, that this is how we're acting instead of helping each other."

"You keep talking about messes, but what you don't say is that you caused this mess. It's your responsibility to own up to it and not drag everyone down with you," Granny O'Reilly said.

"Okay, I caused the mess. Okay? I'm a defective human being, okay? But we're family. Shouldn't we stick together?"

"Coming from you, that's the biggest load of crap I've ever heard," Granny O'Reilly said.

Jane looked down at her hand with the cigarette burning in it. She was sitting in the exact same place she was sitting when she was talking to Rob a couple of days ago. Everyone then seemed—if not happy, at least normal and alive. Now everything in the living room seemed dead and completely over. Like the dead lady Captain Kirby's mom was making up the night I met her. There was no way she was ever going to get up off that slab and sing a song, you know?

"I have to go to school," I said.

Jane nodded then she looked up at me. "What are they saying?"

"What do you mean?"

"In school, what are they saying about me?"

Hot for student. What a slut.

"Nothing," I said.

"Really?"

"Not that I know of."

"You kind of keep to yourself," Jane said.

"Let's go," Captain Kirby said, pulling me by the elbow.

"You wouldn't know what anyone was saying, I guess," Jane said.

"Right."

She looked at Captain Kirby for a second opinion.

"I skipped school all week," Kirby said and dragged me out the door.

"Jeez, and I thought my mother was bad."

"She is," I said.

28

I had Trigonometry and Spanish exams in the morning and American Literary Heritage and Plant and Animal Classification in the afternoon. The Plant and Animal Classification exam turned out to be half essay question, "please describe what is meant by evidence of common descent," and I got stuck on that and I wrote something lame-o about me and The Griffin being really alike and everything because I was trying to distance myself from Granny O'Reilly and Jane; to pretend I was born fully formed right out of The Griffin's head or something. Anyway, I was pretty sure I flunked all of the exams because I couldn't focus and couldn't remember any of the questions when Tim asked me later what they were. Junior teachers were proctoring, so I didn't have to endure my own teachers' fake sympathy, although when I turned around to close the door behind me after I finished the Spanish exam, I caught the proctor whispering to a student and looking at me. Or maybe I was turning into a raving paranoid which was very likely on no sleep.

Tim was waiting for me after each session. "You okay?" he asked. "Need something? Anything?"

Which was a funny question to ask because I did need something, but I had no idea what it was. I felt frozen. I certainly didn't want to go home and face the battleground there. I kept calling The Griffin, but he didn't pick up. He was traveling on the bus and probably couldn't even hear it ringing. I knew if I could only see him, talk to him, that he would tell me to come right down. The possibility of that conversation and my escape was the only thing keeping me going.

"I think some music would help," he said, after our last exam.

"Absolutely."

I winced when I saw both Jane's Kia and Granny O'Reilly's rental SUV parked in front of the house. But at least it was quiet. Unless they killed each other. I laughed.

"What's so funny?" Tim asked.

"I was thinking how that social worker Mrs. Valliere thought it was such a hot idea to bring my grandmother in to supervise me."

We opened the Trap and turned everything on. If I moved to Ohio I would have to leave my gear behind. I touched it as if I was saying goodbye to a friend.

"You can have all this stuff," I told Tim.

"I couldn't do that," he said.

"Well, at least keep it safe for me. For when we get back together." The thought that we might never see each other, never play together again was too depressing to think about. I put it in a box to think about at a later date.

"I talked to Raymond today," Tim said.

"Raymond? The Griffin's Raymond?"

"Yeah. We're kind of like buddies. They're in Houston now."

"What do you mean, 'they're in Houston'? Like the whole band?"

"Yeah. They're practicing for the tour. Raymond says your dad is staking everything on this. It's the first time in ten years they played without Aerosmith."

"So, the Griffin is there too?"

"Of course he's there. Hey, listen. I think I have a new song," Tim said. He ran through some chords. "I have most of the words, too."

The Griffin was in Houston and couldn't pick up his freaking phone? "Okay."

Captain Kirby came running up to the Trap and sat behind the drums, pulling out her sticks.

"What happened to your bike?" Tim asked her.

"Sold it."

"You said you were test driving it," I said.

"Yeah, well, I found a chop shop in Harrisburg that does pick-up and delivery. I had to get rid of it quick before too many people saw me on it." Bada boom, bada bing, ya cha cha cha. "What are we on?"

The protocol we developed during the five months Tim and I had been together was to go through all of our old songs before we tried something new. The Griffin had told me, and I verified it on the net, that you have to play a song a hundred times in the woodshed, as musicians call it, before you can take it to the stage. It was our way of getting to a hundred.

We played all ten of them then got to Hole in the Sky.

"We don't have to," Tim said.

"Of course we do. I'm all right," I said.

"You got to stare the griffin in the eye," Captain Kirby said. "So to speak. It's the only way to tame it."

Tim played the intro then raised his finger for us to join him. I picked up the mike and sang, faltering only a little:

If I could, I'd fly away,

There's nothing here to make me stay.
 Sometimes I think I'd like to die
 'cause then I'd fly up
 through that big hole,
 that big hole in the sky

29

We practiced until ten o'clock. If we went a minute past ten, Jane said Mrs. Tudesco would call the cops on us for disturbing the peace, which she actually did once despite the fact that her little yapping dogs had fits in the middle of the night and woke up the whole neighborhood. Anyway, I didn't want to bring any more attention to our house with policemen etcetera.

Tim and Captain Kirby left, promising to meet me in the morning to form a body guard for me in school, and I closed up the Trap and tiptoed up the stairs to the house. Granny O'Reilly was at the kitchen table, smoking, doing a crossword puzzle.

I coughed, hoping she would get the telepathic message. "Where's my mom?"

"Out."

"You know we're not actually allowed to smoke in here. In the house," I said.

She squinted at me through the smoke. "Your dinner is by the microwave. You can heat it up."

"I'm not hungry."

"Of course not. Children are never hungry and you're the most unoriginal child I've ever met."

Even someone as unoriginal as Granny O'Reilly was on me for being unoriginal. There must be something to it. I sat down across from her and started fraying a paper napkin.

"Stop that."

I kept fraying.

"Nervous mannerisms are very unattractive. In women, particularly."

I threw the pieces on the table. "I thought Mom wasn't supposed to go anywhere."

"She can do what she wants until the sentencing. Except see that wretched boy." She peered at me. "Do you know him?"

"Rob?"

"Is that his name?"

"He was here to see The Griffin. That's the first time I met him. Well, I didn't actually meet him or talk to him or anything. There were lots of kids here."

"She shouldn't have allowed it. What was she thinking? I wouldn't have allowed it."

"Well, The Griffin is my father and I never get to see him," I said. "I think Jane…I mean, Mom…just lets him come here so he can see me. He's on the road all the time and when would he get to see me? Only on the band bus when he's going from here to there. It makes perfect sense."

"He isn't on the road half as much as you think he is," Granny O'Reilly said.

"Of course he is," I said, but even as I said it, I saw his house in Texas on Google Earth. I saw the names "Marjewel and Isak" listed as people he might know on People Search. Of course that's where he was. He couldn't be driving around forever.

"What's he like?" she asked. "Rob."

Prom night seemed so long ago. "I don't know. Captain Kirby didn't like him."

"That girl? Your friend?"

"My colleague," I said.

"She has what we call 'street smarts'," Granny O'Reilly said. "You could do worse than her for a friend."

"Hmmm." My street smart friend had stolen a bike that was worth five thousand dollars and had already sold it. I don't know, could they arrest you when your friend does something bad and you know about it but don't say anything? And what if she needed the money for groceries for her mother or something? Could they arrest anyone for that? "Well, she didn't like him, that's all I know."

The front door opened and Jane came bursting through. She seemed in high spirits. "Well, that's taken care of," she said, taking off her trench coat and flinging it on a chair.

"What?" I asked.

"I asked Rob if he lied to me about his age and he said 'yes.' See? I told you."

I moaned.

"You saw … Rob?" Granny O'Reilly asked.

"Of course I did. How else was I supposed to ask him? I knew he wouldn't lie to me again." She looked really pleased with herself.

"Mom," I said, slowly, "That was the one thing you weren't allowed to do: make contact with Rob."

"Well, I don't see how else I could have cleared my name. I don't know why the DA isn't taking that into account. But it's the crux of the matter, isn't it? He lied to me about his age and the only reason I'm being charged is because he wasn't eighteen. So. I think this should be the end of it."

She lit up a cigarette.

"Where did you run into him?" I asked. "Doesn't he live in Nazareth?"

"Well, exactly," Jane said. "I waited for him at his school. Then I gave him a ride home. He was really sweet about the whole thing. He admitted he lied to me about how old he was and how he was still in school and everything. You know, Mom, I know you think that I'm flakey, but you have to admit I'm a very good judge of character. I think this whole thing will just blow over once he tells the judge that he lied."

"So, let me get this straight," Granny O'Reilly said, "You not only talked to him, but you invited him into your car?"

"Just to drive him home. I didn't want people to see us talking."

Granny O'Reilly put her head down on the table, then asked her, "Did you talk to your lawyer before you did this?"

"My lawyer is incompetent. She doesn't think it's an issue, and I keep telling her, it's the only issue and I don't see why no one's bringing it up. Is there any coffee around here?"

Jane zoomed around the kitchen, picking up the covered dish by the microwave and putting it in the wave. "This looks good," she said.

Granny O'Reilly stared at Jane, then at me, in disbelief. I was ashamed to meet her eyes. I had a box for Jane, of course. It was my biggest box because I had known Jane longer than I knew anyone else in my life, but it wasn't big enough to hold what she'd just done.

"I don't see why you two look so depressed," Jane said. "The kid was underage. He lied about it. He admitted he lied. I fixed it. Business as usual."

Which wasn't exactly how the DA saw it. Fifteen minutes later, Jane's lawyer called and I could hear her loud voice through the cell phone.

"But you're not listening to me," Jane said, over and over, then she started to cry.

After she hung up the phone, she stared at the floor.

"What's going on, Mom," I asked her. "What did your lawyer say?"

"Well, at least your grandmother's here," she said.

"I am not going to Akron. If I can't stay here, I'm going to Houston."

And we said stuff like that back and forth for about an hour until Granny O'Reilly finally said, "Actions have consequences, Jane. That's the one thing you could never understand," and went upstairs to bed before Jane could contradict her.

I don't think that Granny O'Reilly went to sleep because I heard noises all night upstairs like she was walking around and going to the bathroom.

Jane and I didn't go to bed either. We were like glued to the sofa in the living room. At one point, Jane said, "I tried to make everything right.

You know that, don't you, Mercedes? That's the only reason I went to see him. Jesus, why else would I go see him? He wasn't that wonderful, you know."

And I nodded like I understood, but the whole thing was so overwhelming to me I just made my mind go blank so it wouldn't explode.

It was noon when the sheriff knocked on the door with another warrant for her arrest. Granny O'Reilly came downstairs fully dressed as soon as the sheriff's car pulled up and said, "I'll meet you there." When the sheriff said he would have to take Jane in himself and escorted her out, Granny O'Reilly went upstairs to get her purse and saw me staring at her. "I'm never going to be free of her, am I?" she said.

And while it sounded mean, it was exactly what I was thinking.

30

I tried to pretend that everything was normal—not that my grandmother was down at the police station trying to get Jane off the hook, again—and opened my social studies book. It was my last exam and passing it was my only hope of not being a complete washout in school. It occurred to me that if I flunked, they'd make me repeat a grade and that would weaken my case for dropping out and being an "autodidact," as I learned that word was for what I wanted to be. I couldn't even learn when people were cramming knowledge into my head, so how could I do it on my own?

Mr. Dow had hinted broadly—okay, he wrote it on the board—the question that was our final exam: Using Your Textbook And Discussions We Have Had In Class On Child Labor And The Draft As Well As The Social Contract, Please Discuss The Pros And Cons Of Teenage Conscription Into The Military. I had copied the question into my notebook, of course, and I had a couple of ideas as soon as I wrote it down, but it made no sense to me now. I didn't think it was even in English. I closed my eyes and was surprised by the silence in our house. I think it was the first time our house was perfectly still and without the noise of Jane hacking her head off from cigarettes, or my jacked up music in the Trap or the commotion of The Griffin's traveling circus, or neighbors yelling at us to turn down the stereo on which we blasted The Griffin because he wasn't here, or the Tudesco's dogs barking their heads off, or Mr. Hennings burping and farting on his porch—which I could actually hear in my bedroom and I wondered if he was aware of that—or me and Jane arguing, or Jane and Granny O'Reilly screaming at each other. Without all that distracting noise, a picture started to come into focus, a picture of me. True, I was pretty ordinary looking which didn't auger well for a career in music, although plain was okay for a normal life. But I didn't want a normal life. I had a talent, I knew it, I could see it, I could feel it burning inside me, and the talent was like the little flame of a Bic lighter that wanted to keep burning till it set the world on fire, but the sound of my songs kept getting drowned out by the noises that surrounded me, that defined me, noises that would never stop as long as I stayed here.

I waited all day for Granny O'Reilly to return, thinking of the new charges that were being heaped on Jane: breaking the terms of her bail, stalking. I could imagine the drama that was being performed at the police station with Jane and Granny O'Reilly and Jane's lawyer and Rob and Rob's mother and Rob's pregnant girlfriend and the judge—a real judge, not a fake television judge, who had to figure out what to do with a problem called Jane O'Reilly—all the yelling and shouting that I decided were no longer part of my personal soundtrack.

When it was ten o'clock at night, I wrote an email to Mr. Dow apologizing for not taking his final exam and disappointing him etcetera, but I said that I would make it up to him. Here's the truth: I didn't really care that I disappointed him anymore, although I didn't put that in the email. There was no reason to be mean. I wrote a note to Granny O'Reilly and put it on the kitchen table under her ashtray, saying it was a real pleasure to finally meet her and I wished her lots of luck with her career, but I didn't think Akron was where I wanted to be and that I was going to go live with my dad. As miserable as Granny O'Reilly was, I could understand why she didn't want to stick around while Jane tried to unload her bag of woes onto her. She had enough to lug around, what with that Laura woman staring her down and being married to Ron, who I didn't know, but if he was a politician I could certainly guess how she had to think about the consequences of every step she took.

At midnight, I got dressed and stuffed my backpack with my shampoo, toothbrush and toothpaste, my learner's permit and my laptop and went down to the Trap. I wanted to take all my amps and speakers, but that was impossible of course. I could only carry one thing on my back besides my backpack and that was naturally the guitar The Griffin gave me. I packed the Fender in its case and strapped it on my back, took a last look at the Trap and kind of said good-bye to my life as I knew it, then got on my bicycle and rode away.

31

The Kirby VW van was parked in the back of Kulick's Funeral Home. I rang the bell and kept ringing it until it finally swung open and Mrs. Kirby was there saying, "Okay, okay, what's the problem? It's so late! Oh, it's you, Mercy," and she let me in. She went through the procedure of unlocking the first door and locking it behind her, then doing the same to the second set of doors, until we were in the room with a cadaver, this time an old man, with a paper blanket pulled up to his chin on the gurney.

"Where's Captain Kirby?" I asked her.

Mrs. Kirby jerked her thumb to a door which I opened and found out was a broom closet with Captain Kirby asleep in her sleeping bag on the floor. I nudged her with my foot.

"Come on," I said. It was odd to see Captain Kirby asleep, not on the attack. "Get up. I'm leaving."

She frowned until she saw it was me. "What are you doing here?"

"I'm leaving. I'm going to Houston."

"That's not a great idea."

"Do you have a better one?" I knew now that Captain Kirby didn't have internet access and went to the public library to get on. She would have had no idea about the latest news on Jane. "I just have to leave."

"What about your last week of school?" she asked. "You got to put in the time."

"I don't care about it. I mean, I do care, but I care about leaving more."

"What if they make you repeat?"

"What's the difference if I'm dropping out?"

"You're a moron. I told you that before, if you drop out."

I sat down next to her. "Stuff happened. I can't tell you about it now. But I have to leave." I told her about the notes I left for Mr. Dow and Granny O'Reilly. "I hope Granny O'Reilly doesn't file a missing persons report."

"If you left a note, you're a runaway, not a missing person," she said, finally rousing herself.

"She doesn't want me to live with her in Akron. I heard her tell Ron that on the phone."

"They won't get the cops after you or anything because you left those notes, there's no foul play. If Granny files a report, they'll send some cops around to your house to see if you're there. Eventually. They're overloaded with runaway and missing person stuff."

"Well, what am I supposed to do in the meantime? Where can I go?"

"You can stay here with my mom until I'm finished my exams then you can go with me to Sunny Vale."

"Sunny Vale?"

"My culinary camp. Remember?"

"Oh, right."

I looked out to where Mrs. Kirby was applying lipstick to the dead old man. From the angle on the floor of the broom closet I could see into the next room where two more bodies on gurneys were waiting for Mrs. Kirby's magic touch to bring them back to seeming life.

"Don't you have to be in school for the rest of the week after exams so the whole year counts?"

Captain Kirby shrugged. "I'll make it up next year."

I was messing up Captain Kirby's life because my own was so screwed up. "Why don't I just go ahead now and meet you at Sunny Vale at the end of the week," I said. "I wouldn't mind learning how to cook."

She considered it. "That would work. How much money do you have?"

None. Talk about poor planning. I was as dumb as Jane.

Captain Kirby reached into her sleeping bag and pulled out a nylon pouch. She opened it and eight hundred dollar bills spilled out.

"Wow! Where did you get all that money?!"

She put her finger to her lips and looked around the door to see if her mom could hear. "That bike I sold."

"You stole that bike."

"Yeah, well, I didn't get full price for it, if it makes you feel any better." She gave me three of the bills. "That'll get you there. I got to give some to my mom to buy groceries and stuff when I'm not here."

"I'll pay it back. I swear."

"I know you will."

"Really.'

"Who cares?" she said.

We discussed what route I should take. We thought a bus would be too risky, they might have flyers or something for missing persons in the bus station and anyway, I'd still have to walk almost five miles from the bus stop to the farm. We decided I should ride my bike.

"But you'll have to wait until later. If you leave now, someone will see you."

"Won't they see you leaving for school?"

"Yeah, but they always see me. They think I bring my mother

breakfast on my way to school."

She stuffed her money pouch into her backpack and got up to leave. She'd been sleeping in her clothes. With her shoes on, too.

"Tell Tim where I am, okay? I didn't get a chance to talk to him."

"My mom will let you out," she said. "But wait until this afternoon, okay"

"Okay."

'You know," Captain Kirby said, "You can't go back. Once you step out, everything changes."

"You think I don't know that?"

"You can know it here," she pointed to her head, "but you don't know it in your gut."

"May I please deal with this tomorrow?"

"I just want you to be aware, that's all. Sometimes I wish I had someone pointing things out to me. Keep it in mind, that's all."

I knew I couldn't go back once I left, but what exactly was I supposed to go back to anyway? I felt like a baby bird who was pushed out of the nest whose mama had destroyed the nest just for emphasis.

I stood the Fender up in the corner and lay down on the sleeping bag which was still warm. "Can I borrow this?" I felt so suddenly tired and before Captain Kirby could answer me I was asleep.

32

I dreamt I was on The Griffin's bus, and I was like his manager or something. I don't know what happened to his regular manager, but it was only a dream so I guess he got a better offer or something. Anyway, The Griffin was asking me, his new manager, if I thought he should ditch Aerosmith and go out on his own and I felt really proud that he was asking me for advice. "I've been opening for them for ten years," he said. "I think it's time to stretch my wings." And he stood up and stretched his fake eagle wings and each wing was like twenty-five feet at least and they kept opening up until they lifted him into the air. "Hey, I didn't know these things worked!" he shouted. "I thought they were just a gimmick. Hey, hey, hey!" He had gone through the sun roof in the bus—I know he wouldn't fit, but it was only a dream—and was hovering above. His lion paws were dangling through the opening, and I grabbed at them trying to go up with him, but he flicked me off. "It's too much weight, babe, back off," he said, then, "Look! I'm way up here! This is so cool!" And I shouted through the sun roof in the bus, "Am I supposed to be happy for you? What about me? What about me?" And he took off into the clear blue sky saying, "You know you're my favorite girl. You know it!" And I shouted after him, "But what does that mean? 'I'm your favorite girl.' What does that mean exactly if I can't be with you?" And I felt really hot and sweaty and I was trying to get out of the bus but the door was jammed and then I woke up.

I climbed out of Captain Kirby's sleeping bag. My neck was sore from the bottle of Clorox I grabbed from the shelf and stuck under my head in my sleep to use as a pillow, and I was massaging it to get the kinks out, when I froze at the sound of voices outside the closet. I peeked out. Mr. Kulick and his daughter, Krista, were dressing one of the cadavers.

Krista Kulick went to my school. She was in my class and I saw her all the time, although I never said anything to her except "Ewww, what are all those black things" when both of our lab partners didn't show up in biology class and we had to dissect an extremely fertile female frog together. She was pretty enough and smart enough and she had a date to the prom (the prom!) with a regular boy who was going off to college in Iowa or somewhere even flatter and maybe she would follow him there in two years—who knew? who cared?—and I just figured she was one of those boring people who would reminisce about our frog experience as a highlight of her pathetic life at class reunions, which I would definitely not attend because I would be famous and reunions—except maybe rock band reunions—are not cool.

Krista had snapped on a pair of latex gloves and pulled some underwear up on the old guy Mrs. Kirby was working on when I came in. She was yammering away to her father and didn't even look at the old guy's junk, which I thought was kind of interesting, because I was craning my neck like crazy to see it although I probably would've puked if I did.

"See," Krista said, "Why does she put this flesh colored polish on men? It doesn't look natural. I told her a million times to use clear."

Mr. Kulick mumbled something and Krista said, "Well, this isn't Hollywood."

Krista moved quickly, removing shirt and pants from the rolling rack, checking the tag on the suit of clothes to the tag on the man's wrist, then ripping both of them off and finished dressing him. Mr. Kulick pulled a pair of what looked like cardboard shoes from a giant box and wiggled them onto his feet. Krista wheeled a casket next to the gurney and together they picked up the ends of the sheet he was on, Mr. Kulick said, "One, two, three," and they heaved him into the casket, yanking the sheet out from under him when he landed. Krista pulled a Bible from a bag that was hanging on the rack, arranged the dead man's hands around it as if he had just closed the book after reading a particularly inspirational passage—and she said, "See, this is why she has to go, Dad. That polish looks awful and she's too stubborn, or something, to change. I think there's something seriously wrong with her," and then all of a sudden the lights dimmed and they were wheeling the casket out of the room through a pair of swinging doors.

I balled up Captain Kirby's sleeping bag and shoved it into the corner then I nudged the door of the broom closet open. The smell of sulfur almost knocked me out. There were two more cadavers in waiting and the place looked definitely creepy with just the safety lights on. I told myself the two bodies were just sleeping, like in a hospital or something because if I heard a sound at that point, I would have fainted.

I pulled out my phone and saw it was four o'clock in the afternoon. If I left now, I might be able to make it to Sunny Vale by eight o'clock on my bike. I remembered what Captain Kirby said about a missing persons report and I wondered if Granny O'Reilly had filed one.

I washed my face and took a drink of water cupping my hands in the sink Mrs. Kirby used, trying not to think of what they washed in there, then I pulled on my backpack, strapped on my Fender and tried the door. It was locked. Of course.

I wanted to call Captain Kirby then remembered she didn't have a phone and called Tim and even though I was holding the phone first up to the ceiling and then by the barred window, I couldn't get any reception.

I hurried past the cadavers through the swinging doors where I saw Krista and Mr. Kulick move the casket. Beyond the doors was a tiny room with an elevator.

"Great!" I cried, then slapped my hand over my mouth and looked around as if someone could actually hear me. I pushed the elevator button and I listened for what seemed like forever while it made old elevator noises until the door finally opened. I stepped inside. It was huge of course because it had to hold caskets. There was only one button, only one floor it went to. I pressed it.

33

The elevator opened into a little foyer. And the only exit was through a viewing that was already in full-swing. A stocky old lady dressed in black was sitting in the first of a row of chairs that lined the wall, sobbing into a handkerchief. A middle-aged woman was consoling her with one arm while her other arm was playing a card game with a ten-year old girl. The middle-aged woman looked up when I came into the room, then went back to her card game when she didn't recognize me. A man, his head in his hands, was kneeling in front of the coffin. A bunch of old ladies in black dresses and running shoes were lined up the side aisle waiting to pay their respects to the widow. When the first one reached her, sitting down next to her and patting her hand, they all burst into tears and started wailing, and truthfully, until that very moment I didn't really think of the guy in the coffin like he was a person, you know? But when I saw how much everyone missed him, I started crying too, remembering that fresh pair of underpants and the chintzy suit that Krista had put on him, and the short sleeve shirt—the kind that Mr. Dow who was cool in every other way, wore—and the polyester tie and those cheap cardboard shoes that Mr. Kulick pushed on his feet, which were covered with a blanket as if he could get a chill. Next to the guest book was a basket of holy cards. I picked one up. It had a picture of St. Michael the Archangel on one side and Michael Croslis' name on the other side like a dance card. I put it to my bosom, sat down in one of the mourner's chairs and started to bawl. The place was filling up and since everyone else was crying, it was easy to let go and honestly, it felt very cathartic and I was crying my eyes out when someone jammed a pointy shoe into my ankle. I opened my eyes. It was Krista Kulick.

"You are such a freak," she said.

"I was just…"

"No no no no no no," she said. "You were in the basement, weren't you? With that other freak, Janet Kirby. I saw you come out of the elevator. You know I can call the police on you, don't you? You're trespassing. I don't think you want me to call the police, not after your mother…."

"Okay, okay. I'll leaving," I said, smarting from being called a freak.

"Are you two living down there or something? This is it for Mrs.

Kirby. She knows the rules: no visitors while she's working. Is she out of her mind? She's already on probation. Are you having drug parties down there? What do you think it would do for business if people knew that there were drug parties going on around their loved ones?"

Krista was getting herself worked up thinking about everyone having drug parties without her or something.

"I don't even drink," I said.

"Don't you? I heard about the parties at your house when The Griffin's there."

"It's all a big mistake, Krista," I said, "I used to walk Mr. Croslis' dog. That's why I came here in the first place, and then I got lost. I was looking for the bathroom. It's not Mrs. Kirby's fault. I don't even know Mrs. Kirby. Like, who is that?"

"Well, you know Janet, don't you?"

"Of course, I know Janet," I said, "She's the drummer in my band."

"Yeah, I saw your poster," Krista said. She looked wistful. "I wanted to try out. I play. But I don't have any time for things that don't support my goals."

Mr. Kulick was beckoning to Krista from the back of the room.

"I have to get back to work," Krista said.

Although, truthfully, it seemed like getting back to work was the last thing she wanted to do. "Are you going to do this after you graduate, Krista?" I asked her. "Is working in here like one of your goals?"

"Of course!" she said, scowling and scratching her arm. "It's a recession-proof business. You never run out of customers. I already have a built-in clientele who have had family members' funerals with us. And, like, look at you. You came here because you walked Mr. Croslis' dog and the next time you need funeral services, you'll think of us. Right?"

Mr. Kulick was coming down the aisle.

Krista whispered to me. "Now get out of here, before I tell my father that you were trespassing."

"You're not going to fire Mrs. Kirby are you?" I asked.

"What do you care? I thought you didn't know her," Krista said.

"I don't actually know her, but it would be a shame to blame her just because I was looking for a bathroom."

"I don't know. I think she's off, you know what I mean?" Krista said, looking unsure of herself.

"Well I heard she used to do celebrities' make-up in Hollywood. That's just what I heard."

"I just don't like her," Krista said.

Mr. Kulick came up to us, and Krista said, "Dad, this is Mercy O'Reilly. Her mother's the teacher who had sex with the student."

I felt like someone punched me in the stomach.

I picked up my Fender and backpack, not waiting for Mr. Kulick to kick me out.

"You can't stay here," Mr. Kulick said. "This is a private service."

"I don't want to stay here. I have a home," I said. "It's in Texas."

"You can't stay here," Mr. Kulick said, calling after me.

As if I were dying to stay.

I pushed my way through Mr. Michael Croslis's mourners. The Croslis family was big and dark haired and their voices were really loud. It was so obvious they were all related, probably like you could tell Jane and me and Granny O'Reilly were a family when we were together.

On the way out I signed the condolences book. Now that I saw how much people missed him, I really did feel sorry that Mr.Croslis was dead. He wasn't just a body with a suit he probably only wore at Easter, he was somebody who made some people happy and more likely pissed a lot of people off with his loud mouth. The truth is, I got the feeling he would have annoyed me and I probably wouldn't have liked him if I had known him when he was alive. Or maybe I would have. Maybe he could tell great stories about his boyhood in Greece. I've heard that some grandfathers were very good at that. So, liked him, not liked him. Maybe both. It's like, I could have sworn that Krista Kulick thought I was cool. And she probably did when she thought of my band and The Griffin, because that stuff was undeniably cool and she even wanted to be in my band. But me hanging around dead people in her basement was definitely not cool. As Mr. Rajeet's son said, two things can be possible at the same time.

34

I definitely was sorry that Captain Kirby had sold the Fezzari because after a few miles on my three gear Sears Huffy—I think Granny O'Reilly owned it when she was a girl—I felt like a hamster on a treadmill that powered a carousel.

This was the first time I had ridden my bike anywhere except to school or Dunkin Donuts or had even been in the country by myself. Certainly Jane and I never thought to park and hike a trail when we found ourselves driving around after Sunday dinner at Ruby Tuesdays. "I don't know why everyone gets so excited about the great outdoors," Jane would say. "You can hardly ever get comfortable on the ground and there are ants and wasps and mosquitoes and bug spray makes you feel like you're the bug and leaning against a tree like they do in the movies hurts your back—they're just acting—and anyway," she would say, delivering the death sentence to any desire I had to visit the woods, "anyone with a water bottle can be outdoorsy. It's so unoriginal."

When I got off of potholed Old Route 22 the road got gravelly and then turned into dirt. I knew I was in Amish farmland—we'd studied the Amish in American history class, although I'd never been this far out of Milltown—when a black horse drawn buggy passed me. The man with the whip had a beard and was wearing a black coat and a straw hat. Two girls riding on the seat behind him, his daughters I assumed, were dressed in sun bonnets and calico dresses. They looked like extras in a 1950s Technicolor musical about Oklahoma.

I was watching for a sign that said "Sunny Vale Mill"—Kirby told me you could go right by the entrance a dozen times without seeing it—but every farm sign had a name like Yoder or Zook, and I was starting to think I might have passed it.

Green shoots had broken through the ground all the way to the horizon, and when I squinted the fields looked like graceful lime green line drawings, and there were these long gray one-story buildings back off the road with fans in the walls that gave off a low hypnotic thrumming and I knew they were mushroom houses because they didn't have windows. There was something soothing about all of this, and I might have enjoyed it if I didn't have the feeling I was being followed. Every time I turned around, though, I saw nothing but an empty dirt road. I think I wanted someone to be following me because I felt so lonely, and, I have to admit, a little scared. I really missed Tim. Captain Kirby, too.

Plus it was getting dark, and the sinking sun was turning everything including me on my bike into long spooky shadows. My bike didn't have lights and the road was narrow and curvy. I jumped off my bike to walk a little, keeping to the side of the road in case another buggy came by. I tied my sweater around my waist, I was hot and sweaty from pedaling, but, as soon as I did, a couple of flies landed on me. Then even more, and then they started biting.

"Hey, get off of me!" I started swatting myself. Hundreds of them with green heads like in a science fiction movie swarmed me. I thought maybe they could smell the funeral home on me.

I got back on the bike and started down the road, trying to lose the flies, but each time I slowed down, they would catch up and land on me. In about a quarter of a mile—and I smelled it before I saw it—I almost ran over a dead deer. Its belly was wide open and crawling with flies. Its legs were unnaturally spread and it looked like it was going to explode.

"Yuk," I yelled, pedaling as fast as I could to get past it. The road followed a stream and I was thinking about jumping into it to get rid of the flies when I saw a faded wooden sign that said "The Mill at Sunny Vale." I hopped off my bike and walked it into a dirt car track that went into the woods. Bringing a swarm of biting flies with me wouldn't make a good first impression, and I dropped my bike and was hitting the back of my neck like a crazy person, my eyes scrunched shut, when suddenly somebody pinned my arms to my sides.

"Stop!" a voice said. "Stop moving."

It was Tim. I tried to wrench away to keep swatting.

"Make them leave me alone," I pleaded.

"The more frantic you get the more they like it. They love heat. Stay still for a minute and you'll cool off."

In the five minutes he held onto me, the sun set and the air got chilly and the flies flew home, wherever that was.

"Where did you come from?" I sounded annoyed, but I was never happier to see anyone in my life.

"I couldn't let you just run off by yourself."

"You don't think I can take care of myself? I can take care of myself," I said.

"I was worried you might run into something you didn't know anything about, like a dead deer and biting flies."

Tim knew a lot about being in the woods because his father and grandfather were always taking him on survivalist grocery expeditions—first a rousing game of paintball, then off to kill a deer, then going to a farm where they slaughtered hogs, bringing home enough bacon and meat to last them a year.

"Were you like behind me or what?"

"I was a mile ahead of you the whole way. I would stop and wait for you to catch up a little before I went on."

"Why didn't you just wait for me?"

"Because I wanted you to know you could do it yourself."

I wasn't sure it actually counted as doing it yourself when someone was watching out for you, and I was going to argue some bullet points about this when a pickup truck that looked like a beat-up old toaster came up behind us. The driver hit his brights, cut the engine—it backfired twice—and hopped out. He had blond beard stubble and was wearing overalls, a flannel shirt, and a baseball cap that he took off to scratch a completely shaved head. He looked maybe Jane's age.

"You guys okay?" he asked.

"There's a dead deer back down the road," Tim said.

"Did you hit it?"

"Of course we didn't hit it. We're on bicycles."

"Right," the man said. He stuck out his hand. "I'm Jonah Weil. But everybody calls me JW. It's easier."

We looked at him blankly for a few seconds. It was obvious that he expected us to know who he was and then I remembered he was the guy Captain Kirby was always talking about.

"The JW?" I finally found the wit to ask.

"Yes. Yes!" he said. He was obviously delighted to be him. And why not? He was famous, right up there in Captain Kirby's trophy case alongside Michael Pollan. She was always blabbing about how he was living an authentic hip lifestyle and quoting his sayings like other kids quoted Bible verses.

"My friend is a big fan of yours," I said. "Me, too, obviously."

"Great. Thank you. It's been a great year for authentic living, hasn't it?"

I nodded, trying to remember one of Captain Kirby's authentic living sayings, but I came up blank.

"But we have a lot more work to do. Lots more," he said.

I had no idea what he was talking about, but I said, "Right. I totally agree."

After taking in our bikes and guitars, he asked, "Are you lost?"

"We're here for the cooking camp."

"It doesn't start until day after tomorrow."

"Our friend said it would be okay," Tim said, "That you wouldn't mind if we came early. To get oriented."

"It's not my decision. You'll have to talk to Zina, she's my business head. She likes to interview applicants in advance, make sure everyone is simpatico with each other and the program. Is that all you brought?"

I held up my backpack.

"Did you bring your knives?"

"How stupid of me," I said, "I left in a hurry."

"I was very specific on the website: Bring your knives."

Tim dug in his cargo pocket and brought out his Boker hunting knife.

"Whoa, partner," Jonah said. "Cooking knives."

"I use this for everything," Tim said. "Tying off entrails and stuff."

"Yeah? You hunt?" Jonah asked. "We'll talk later," And to me he said, "I don't know how you're going to cook without your knives."

"I'm really good at mixing things. And opening cans." In fact, I thought, I probably could get a degree in mixing and opening, just based on life experience.

"Half of cooking is preparing the food. You need precision instruments to make a concise cut."

"I totally agree."

"And yet you have no knives."

"I can borrow yours."

"You can't borrow knives. It's like borrowing someone's baseball glove. It conforms to your hand. You can't just give it back as if nothing happened."

"I can improvise," I said. "I'm very original."

"Originality is not the point. Any clown can be original. They think they're authentic but they're not. Improvisation is never authentic." He sighed. "Well, you made the pilgrimage. If Zina approves of you I'll buy you some knives on the web and you can pay me back."

We were out here in the middle of freakin' nowhere with a cuckoo knife philosopher with a probably imaginary friend named Zina and it was all my fault. I was about to whisper to Tim that we should drop our bikes and run when Jonah said: "Throw your bikes in the back and I'll drive you to the mill. Come on. Here." He picked up my bike and threw it in the back of the pickup. Tim, who actually seemed to like Jonah, threw his bike in the back and climbed in the cab. I squeezed in next to him.

As he maneuvered the pickup over ruts, Jonah lectured us about the authenticity of fresh air and growing your own food and using locally grown produce.

"But you know that," Jonah said to Tim, "You hunt. That's as authentic as you can get."

"Yeah, but he uses a rifle," I said. "I don't think that's authentic, do you? Maybe if he wrestled the deer..." I was getting peeved that I could find no way into the authenticity inner circle.

On either side of the car track I could make out neat fields which I thought must be part of Sunny Vale's field to yield—or was it stable to table?—philosophy that he yammered on about the whole way in.

"Yeah, my friend said you knew everything about food," I said, trying to show some enthusiasm.

"And lifestyle," he added. "And sound. Sound is fundamental to living authentically."

"I agree absolutely," Tim said. "I'm working on building my setup now."

He seemed to forget that he abandoned that setup when he followed me.

"Well, I build tube speakers," Jonah said. "You cannot get a better sound in the world. I don't understand this digital fixation. It's like listening to a recording of a recording. So what if you hear some crackles and pops on vinyl. Those are the sounds of real life. You are the first generation that has experienced a loss of fidelity. I pity you."

"Captain Kirby didn't say you were into music," I said.

He pulled on the emergency brake in front of an old stone water mill.

The mill looked like a restoration project. The wall facing us was half re-pointed. An open second story double door glowed orange in the blackness. An iron pole jutted out above it. A thick rope with a noose at the end hung down from the pole. It made me think of The Rocky Horror Picture Show: Cue lightning and howling wind.

Jonah saw me looking at it with my mouth open. "It's a message from Zina that she's depressed. I don't think she'll be in the mood to talk to you tonight."

"Is that how you communicate?" I asked. "What does she put out when she's happy?"

"But you can stay," Jonah said. Obviously I didn't exist for him. "You're over there." He pointed to a barn with a metal roof outlined by the glow from the mill window. "That's where the students are billeted." He pulled my bike out of the back of the truck. "It's the dorm, as it were."

Without the pickup's engine belching and without Jonah's talking, everything was quieter than I'd ever imagined quiet could be. I grabbed Tim's hand—he was used to this, right?—and we walked to the barn.

"Everything you need's in there," Jonah shouted after us. "See you bright and early."

35

The unused barn where the students slept wasn't very fancy: dirt floor with a carpet of straw. Ten single cots with mosquito net hoods, stripped, with folded bedding on top.

Tim and I bounced around on a couple of them before we decided they were all equally uncomfortable and finally pushed two together and lay down, not bothering to put on the sheets. We put our hands under our heads and looked up at the red metal ceiling.

"Are you sure this is the place?" I asked Tim.

Tim laughed. "Captain Kirby was pretty specific. Jonah Weil at Sunny Vale."

"I can't believe Captain Kirby worships this guy. Jeez, he's weird."

"So's Captain Kirby."

We both started laughing and I realized we were hysterical with tiredness.

"Tim?"

"Yeah?"

"I'm glad you came."

He rolled over on his side. "Me, too."

I rolled over to face him. "Aren't you going to get in trouble? What's your Dad going to do? Won't he try to find you?"

"Nah. One less mouth to feed. That's what he said when Mike left. I don't think he gave a damn. We were starting to fight every time we talked, anyway." He pulled at a loose string on the mattress. "I went to your house, Mercy."

"Yeah?"

"Your grandmother left."

"Yeah?"

"Yeah."

"Your mother is all over the news and blogs and stuff again."

I rolled onto my back. "I know." She would be stuck in jail until her trial. I wondered if they let her keep her cell phone.

"Is anybody following me?" I asked. "I mean, does anybody actually care that I'm gone? What about school?"

"Mr. Dow was pissed that you didn't take the exam. He cornered me after class to tell me you were jeopardizing your future."

Jeopardizing your future was like a theme song of guidance counselors and teachers. They seemed oblivious to the fact that sometimes you had to address an immediate pain before you could think about your future.

"I mean, I'm not like a missing person or anything, am I?" I asked, picturing myself on the side of a milk carton.

"Nah, you're just a runaway. Captain Kirby knows I'm with you and said to tell you not to worry. Even if your grandmother reported you missing she said your name just goes into a computer system, and if you don't do something wrong it won't come up. She suggested we use fake names. Just for now."

"Oh."

I told myself, this is what I wanted. I wanted to be on my own, writing songs. I thought that once I wasn't trying to live Jane's version of cool that songs would come pouring out of me. But I was scared. And even though I hated her, I was scared for Jane. I couldn't imagine how she would manage without me. And what were they doing to her in jail? I couldn't let myself think about it.

"Mrs. Kirby got fired from her job at Kulick's," Tim said.

"What!" I sat up. "What a bitch. Over some finger nail polish. Jesus, so what's Mrs. Kirby supposed to do? Do people ever think of that? What's she supposed to do?"

"Actually," Tim said, "She's living at your house. House sitting, she said. She answered the door when I went by."

"How did she....?"

"Captain Kirby said you wouldn't mind. For safe keeping, she said."

I had 300 dollars from Kirby in my backpack. I'd consider it a month's security and rent and not try to figure out how she got into our house. What did it matter anyway? No one was living there, so why not? But, boy, it certainly didn't take long for your footprints to be erased.

"So what are we going to do?" Tim asked. "What's our plan?"

"I have to find The Griffin," I said, "I want to live with him." Was that too much to ask from the universe? Was that too much to ask from him?

Our eyes had adjusted to the darkness. I could make out individual stars in the sky through the holes in the barn and a kind of icy light was coming through the open barn doors and the chinks in the barn's siding and roof.

Tim took his guitar out of its case and began to play around with chords. Without an amp, an electric guitar has a tinny sound. Tim hummed over it and the effect was like a kid fooling around on a toy piano.

"I'm working on a new song," he said. "On the way up here, it kept going through my head."

Of course, I thought, that's what a real musician would do. He would be working on a new song on a twelve mile bike ride. He wouldn't be worrying about things that go bump in the night, like me.

"Show me the chords." I uncased my own guitar and plucked out the progression.

Tim's tenor stretched over the notes:

The night is dark
But I can see
A path lit up
In front of me

I sang, improvising:

I'm lost and sad
I'm out of time
I'm scared to death
My light won't shine

36

Tim and I fell asleep without taking our clothes off. I was in the middle of a pleasant dream for a change. I was on a stage, the lead singer in a spotlight, my band blacked out behind me. I couldn't see them but knew it was Tim and Captain Kirby, but when I opened my mouth to sing instead of it being me a rooster started crowing and his two-note song cued other creatures in his band to start screeching, moaning, yowling, and kicking, all of this coming from underneath my cot—the barn had a lower level below "the dorm." I dragged myself awake and turned on my phone. It was 4:30 in the morning. So much for the peaceful countryside. As Jane would say, nature was way overrated.

Tim was already gone. I checked my messages. Nothing from Jane or Granny O'Reilly. Nothing from The Griffin. I read the Morning Clarion's account of how Jane had tracked down and stalked her innocent victim—"assaulted" him was how Rob's mother put it—and how her bail had been revoked.

I stuffed the phone into my backpack and groped my way toward the mill looking for Tim and hoping for coffee and almost tripped over a brown hen and her sisters who were pecking in the scrubby grass outside the barn. A sliver of sun appeared, like the top of an orange. Behind the house was a little building with opaque plastic windows that looked like a greenhouse. Black hens and white hens stalked the grass around it. I supposed that's where they all lived when they weren't enjoying the authentic free range lifestyle.

I knocked on a giant wooden door on the first floor of the mill then pushed it open. To the left was a huge room with a hole dug in the ground—it looked like someone was building a swimming pool and ran out of money—a walk-in stainless freezer was humming on the right and in front of me was a narrow steep wooden stairway without a railing.

As soon as I opened the door at the top of the stairs, Bob Dylan's tonsilly voice ambushed me, coming from every direction. Four six-feet-tall speakers, one in each corner of a high ceilinged room criss-crossed with giant support beams, were blaring out the sound. A cat was walking across a beam above my head that went into an open kitchen where Jonah and Tim were sitting at an island drinking coffee and smoking fat brown cigarettes. Everything in the kitchen—the island counter which looked like

111

a slab from a three hundred year old tree, the stools that could've been in Madame Curie's lab, the wooden and enamel utensils—looked antiquey. It was like I walked into a time machine and came out a hundred years ago.

"Good morning, Darcy," Jonah said.

"Hi, Darcy," Tim added and I remembered that as of last night we had new names.

"Since when do you smoke?" I asked, not knowing what to call him.

"These are American Spirit cigarettes," Jonah said. "Pure tobacco, nothing else. I'm initiating Karl in the Lenape Indian way. Want to try one?"

Tim, I mean Karl, grinned at me. "They aren't half-bad."

I shook my head. "I need some formaldehyde to get me going."

Jonah took a blue enamel cup off a wall hook. "Some coffee, Darcy?"

"Thank you, yes." It was interesting having a new name. I felt like I could act the way I wanted to act a lot of times but didn't because people get used to you being one way and when you try on a new hat they ask you why you're acting fake. Yes, Darcy will take two sugars with her coffee, brown sugar if you please, and yes, if that's stone ground oatmeal on the stove—or steel cut, or whatever authentic oatmeal is—I'll have a bowl.

"It occurred to us last night that you might be hungry," Jonah said. "But when we came to get you, you were sound asleep."

"We had a long day," I said.

"By the way," Jonah said, "You snore."

"I do not!" I felt myself turn red.

Tim was laughing.

"I'm only kidding, Darcy," Jonah said. "I thought some humor would break the ice between us. Karl told me you two are studying music in college."

Wow, we were in college already.

"I knew you were musicians without him telling me."

"Really? How?"

"You were still holding your guitars in your sleep."

So much for destiny being written across your face.

Jonah went into the living room and shuffled through some LPs. I followed him in and flipped through a stack until I came across, Jump Naked, from The Griffin's Too Hot Handle tour with Aerosmith in the nineties.

"I love this song, don't you?" I asked, dying to tell him I was related to the composer. "How did you get it on vinyl?"

"It's bootleg," Jonah said. "There's an underworld of authenticity out there. A good friend gave it to me and I promised I'd listen to it even though she knows I dislike metal. Heavy is a hammer. It's not music. As soon as I finish my book on Tube Sonamics I'm going to go through my album collection and purge every record I don't absolutely love. A person should do that with everything in their life. Everything you own blares out who you are. Why would anyone want things they don't absolutely love defining their space?"

It was one of those obvious statements that adults were always making as if they just heard a drum roll and God handed them the meaning of life written on a scroll, but I had to admit that there was a ring of truth to it. I thought of poor Mr. Croslis in his coffin wearing that funny, too-small suit his father probably bought for him before he stopped growing, and about his big loud family and how they still defined him even though he was dead. And worse, what Jonah was saying made me think about me. About the Two Cool Society, which was mine only in name. And about The Griffin. I was his in name only too. Both of them defined me, but I had no say whatsoever about them.

"We have a busy day ahead of us," Jonah said. "You need to eat something."

"I'm not hungry."

He handed me a wire basket. "Go get some eggs and I'll make you an egg white omelet. Guaranteed to put you in a good mood. Get a dozen. Zina does her hair and skin with egg whites. The coop is behind the mill."

"Yeah, I saw it. Aren't you coming with me?" I asked Tim.

"Karl and I are right in the middle of a discussion about sound," Jonah said.

I waited for Tim to gallantly join me but he just waved. I went out the kitchen door and down a flight of steps to the back yard. An old metal glider behind the hen house was covered with light brown birds with weird combs. I brushed two of them aside to make room for me—I felt dejected and hungry, my stomach was spazzing. As soon as I sat down I heard the screeching that woke me up this morning. A peacock with its tail fanned out in you-are-really-pissing-me-off mode was making a beeline for me. Apparently, the brown birds were his harem.

"Okay! Okay!" I said and ran to the chicken coop. The closest I had been to chickens before this morning was at Kentucky Fried. But how hard could collecting eggs be? You just scoop them out of the nests, right?

Different colored hens pecked at the ground in front of the coop. When I stepped inside, I was confronted by a white rooster whose head came to above my waist. He wouldn't get out of my way and countered when I stepped left or right to get around him.

"Come on," I said. I waved the basket at him and he puffed himself up and pecked my arm.

I was definitely not in the mood for this. I put the basket down, got up on my toes and flapped my arms and shouted "Stop It! Stop It!" until he backed down.

The coop was a straw filled smelly room with shelves three high along the walls. Hens sat in their nests on the shelves, facing out. I approached the closest one and lifted her to one side to collect her egg. She bit me. "Ouch!" I said. She followed me with her little yellow eyes, head bobbing. I reached under her from the other side and she bit me again. Maybe this was a particularly mean chicken. I walked down the row a couple of hens and got bitten again. On the bottom shelf were two blue eggs in an empty nest. That's probably how you did it. You waited until they went outside to go to the bathroom. I bent to pick them up and the rooster jumped on my back, taking vicious bites of my neck. I screamed, shook him off, kicked hens that were swarming at my feet out of the way and ran back to the house with two blue eggs in my basket.

I showed Jonah where the hens bit me. "Your chickens are mean!"

"Why didn't you wear the gloves?" he asked.

The gloves?

"I only got two," I said, sheepishly.

"Don't worry. Zina is meaner than any chicken." He laughed. "She'll get them later."

Jonah cracked the eggs into a bowl. "There's nothing like free range eggs. Wait till you taste this omelet."

Too Hot to Handle was blaring from the living room. I wondered who Jonah's metal head friend was and I thought how The Griffin would laugh if he could see me. Wait till I told him!

"I love this group," I said.

"Not crazy about The Griffin," Jonah said.

"Well, I think The Griffin is really hot." I knew I sounded like a punk girl but I had to say something.

Jonah laughed. "You don't look like a metal head. Personally, I think he's a clown."

"A clown!"

"Prancing around in that stupid outfit. Jesus, how old is he?"

"Old is Neil Young," Tim said.

"He's a perfect example of what I was talking about. If you spend three quarters of your life in a silly clown suit, you're a clown, aren't you?"

"He's a performer," Tim said. "I don't like metal that much either"— surprise to me—"but he's one of the best at it and his bass player is as good as anyone in rock."

"Perhaps," Jonah said. "We'll talk more later. Both of you finish your breakfast. It's past seven. We've got a busy day ahead of us."

I knew he didn't mean to be insulting. He thought I was eighteen-year old Darcy Somebody, but almost-sixteen-year-old Mercy O'Reilly could barely swallow a bite of egg.

37

I quickly found out what "having a busy day ahead of us" meant.

The reclusive Zina made her entrance into the kitchen. She was six feet tall and a size two at most with long curly blond hair bound in a scrunchy at the top of her head, every tumbling tendril looking as if it lay precisely as planned on a blueprint. The glare of her blue-eyed blondness made me squint. She was wearing a Japanese robe barely closed because, I mean, why bother tying it? I could hardly look at her I was so envious. Tim, I noticed, wasn't having the same problem.

Jonah told us she was a Ukrainian ex-model who had left that business to do something meaningful with her life, which ended up being investing in him. She took care of the finances, so Tim and I would have to talk to her about paying for the cooking school. "I'm the artistic side, she's the business side" he said, pointing heart to head.

"I'll take care of this... Karl," I said.

"You sure? Because I don't mind doing the logistics," Tim said.

I had the hundred from Kirby. "I'm paying. Remember?" I said. Tim was mesmerized but snapped out of it and followed Jonah out of the kitchen, leaving me alone with Zina who ignored me as she pinched some brown twigs into a tea pot and poured hot water over them.

"We didn't sign up on the web or anything," I said. "But I have the tuition."

Zina poured her tea as deliberately as if she were performing a private tea ceremony. "At this late date we only take cash," she said, finally looking at me. She licked her front teeth, took a sip, fixed her incredible blue eyes on me then said, "How old are you anyway?"

"Eighteen."

"Bullshit." She had a deep voice with an accent.

"No, really...." I could feel the air leaving my body.

"I don't give a damn, mind you," she said. "As long as you're not running from something. We get that sometimes. I don't want the school implicated in anything illegal, cause then immigration starts swarming all over the place, asking for papers and all that bullshit."

"Okay."

"So, are you? Implicated in anything illegal?"

"I don't think so. Not that I know of." She was like kryptonite. The skin of eighteen year old Darcy peeled off like a snake's and went slithering under the stove. "I mean, my mother...."

"Your mother what?"

"She's in trouble."

"Drugs?"

I paused, considering. "Yes. How did you know?"

"And you?"

"Of course not! It's why I ran away."

"I can deal with that. I ran away from a bad situation, too."

"No kidding." Zina looked like the type who caused bad situations then walked away from them without cleaning up the mess. Like someone else I knew.

She finished her cup of tea, rubbing her finger over the fine blond hairs on her upper lip.

"And exactly how are you going to pay?" she asked. "The tuition is five hundred dollars each person a week."

"For what?"

"It's a business, not the county home for orphans."

Which made me wince.

"Look," I said, "I can do dishes or clean the… hen house," although I actually couldn't see that happening, "And wait, I'm good at doing laundry. I'm practically a professional at that."

She frowned.

"Captain Kirby said sometimes you let girls do that."

"Captain Kirby is your friend? Okay, we'll try you out in the berry patch."

Which is how I ended up weeding rows of strawberries and getting a sunburn. Here's the thing about organic farms—they don't use pesticides or fungicides or herbicides or bug zappers or anything that's not authentic, so they have lots of weeds not to mention half of the leaves and fruit are eaten by birds and bugs and ground hogs. It was definitely not the tidy rows of whatever I saw growing on the way in yesterday. Zina told me those were Amish farms.

"They look authentic but they pour the same crap on their crops the corporate farms do," she said disdainfully. "I don't know how anyone can eat that garbage." I pretended to agree, although the truth was that the Amish fields looked a heck of a lot better than Jonah's. She and Kirby must meet for tea regularly.

"Their filthy chemicals leach into our garden." She made a face. "It can't be helped."

Not enough of them, in my humble opinion.

A ground hog followed me all morning, eating the fruit which I thoughtfully exposed for him plucking weeds. When Jonah came out to the field to check on me I pointed to the ground hog who was lazing a half dozen rows away waiting for a fifth breakfast. Jonah trotted back to the mill and returned with a chunk of cantaloupe which he handed me, telling me not to eat it. He went to a tool shed and returned with a contraption called a Havahart Trap. He explained that he'd been forced to trap ground hogs because a reporter from Organic Matters Magazine was sitting interviewing Zina on the kitchen porch when he dispatched a groundhog with a shot to its head from his 22. rifle. The reporter freaked, and since then for PR purposes he would trap the pests, drive them a few miles away and release them. He even filmed himself doing this and sent the video to the Organic Matters reporter who then wrote a feature piece about Jonah's quest for perfect authenticity. He put the Havahart on the ground, put the cantaloupe in the back of it, and we retreated to the kitchen porch to watch. After ten minutes of poaching strawberries and suspicious sniffing the ground hog went through the trap door which snapped shut behind it.

"Just like The Hotel California," Jonah said. "Want to come along for the ride?"

"Sure."

"I'll stop in Kutztown on the way back—for supplies—so it won't be a total waste of time."

I stumbled on the way out of the field. "Give me your hand," he said and led me to his pickup. He threw the trap in the back and motioned for me to hop in. I saw Zina watching us from the porch.

"Where's…my boyfriend?" I asked loudly.

"Karl's milking the goats."

"Yuck," I said.

"Are you kidding? Goat milk molecules are easier to digest than mother's milk." He waved to Zina and off we went, Jonah spouting the glories of goat milk.

We dumped the ground hog a mile away, drove to Kutztown, and were back in less than an hour. So much for playing hooky. But instead of exiling me to the strawberry field, Jonah came with me and showed me how to dig in with a pitch fork to get the weeds by the roots so they wouldn't grow back and explained the obvious, which was that strawberries ready to pick were a deep lipstick red. He ate some as we worked, telling me to do the same. "That's what they're here for," he said.

We worked in tandem for a couple of hours and I relaxed into the pace he set, and after we filled a 25 pound bucket he got a dipper of water from the rain barrel which he shared with me.

"This feels pretty good, you know?" I said surprised.

"I wouldn't be doing this if it didn't," he said.

The sun was hot but the air was still spring cool. My body hurt from the bending and lifting, but it was a good hurt. I hadn't felt the compulsion to update my boxes since Tim saved me from the greenhead flies. Was that just last night? So much was happening right now. Strawberries and weeds and ground hogs and blue sky, hot sun and cool rain water. Everything was new, not the same old same old.

After we filled another bucket, Jonah stuck my pitch fork in the ground and we walked back to the mill for lunch. Another ground hog ran past the hen house and into the strawberry patch.

"You think he found his way back here already?" I said.

"Not the same guy," he said. "Younger. Maybe one of his children. I'll deal with him later."

"You must waste a lot of gas taking them for rides," I said.

"The people who make me famous live in cities and think nature is like a Disney movie and I do what I have to do to keep them happy." He made an angelic face and I laughed.

"Thank you for letting us stay, Jonah," I said as we were washing up at a trough under the porch.

"I had to leave a kind of bad situation in a hurry."

"I figured." He held out his hand and pulled me up the stairs. "You kids'll work it out. And call me JW. It's easier." I smiled at him. I was definitely wrong about him. I liked him and I felt really sorry that Tim and I had lied about who we were because you couldn't start a friendship with lies. And I thought now that I could probably learn stuff from him like from Mr. Dow. A thousand questions were churning in my head, like for instance whether gimmicks like the berets I wanted Have Mercy to wear or The Griffin's costume meant you couldn't be authentic. But before I could ask anything, we were facing Zina on the porch and she didn't look happy.

Jonah dropped my hand, pecked Zina on the cheek and went into the kitchen, whistling.

Zina stuck her foot in front of me.

A sucker-punch happens to you when you're so dazzled with your shiny self that you don't see a smack-down coming.

"What is it, Zina? Is something wrong?"

"I saw you two out in the field."

"Yeah. You told me to weed the strawberries. Jonah was teaching me how to do it."

"There's only one thing I don't tolerate around here," Zina said. "I don't care about your druggie mommy or that asinine friend of yours who came into the mill three times this morning so he could moon at me."

"Hey!" I said.

"I just better not hear you're hot for teacher."

38

Six other students arrived late in the afternoon. While they were in the barn getting unpacked, I helped Jonah get a tray of sandwiches together which Tim delivered. After we sent the sandwiches over, Jonah made us something he called "amuse bouche" from leftovers in the refrigerator and Zina went to bed with a migraine. Jonah and Tim were arguing about what was more important the woofers or the guitar connected to them, and I was looking at the surrounding landscape through Zina's noose when Captain Kirby pulled up in front of the mill in her mother's van. I ran down to meet her.

"I am so so so so so glad to see you," I said, hugging her.

"I couldn't leave right away, sorry Mercy," Captain Kirby said. "I got here as fast as I could."

We went upstairs. Jonah and Tim had put on head phones. They both waved at Captain Kirby.

"Doesn't your mom need the van?" I asked.

"Naw. She's staying at your house, by the way. I knew you'd be cool with it. An empty house should never go to waste, don't you think? I'll clear her out before your mom gets back. Don't worry."

Before Jane gets back. I had been calling the court house from my window seat all afternoon. All I got was a confusing vectoring system and voice mail boxes that I'm sure no one ever retrieved messages from, although I left messages on all of them, saying I was Jane's sister in case someone was looking for me so I wouldn't leave a trail. At the end of two hours of calls, I had no idea what Jane's status was, when her trial was going to be, or anything.

"I'm Darcy now, by the way," I told Kirby.

"Got it. Who's he?" She pointed to Tim.

"Karl."

"That was smart," she said. "I got caught once because I used my real name."

One of the new students, a girl as tall as Zina, joined us in the living room. Her jet dyed hair had a giant blue streak in it and was pulled into two braids that reached her waist. She wore a short calico cotton dress that showed her long legs and white anklet socks under patent leather Mary Janes. I don't get women who dress like little girls as if girlhood was this precious time, not a stage in your life to be gotten through as quickly as possible. Or maybe it was supposed to be ironic or something to be a six foot tall woman pretending she hasn't reached puberty. Anyway, she had a proprietary air like she'd been at the mill before. She plopped down next to Jonah. He lifted off his headphones long enough to give her a kiss on the cheek and tug a braid. No wonder Zina got migraines.

Satisfied that she had staked her claim to Jonah, she turned her attention to us.

"Hi Janet," she said to Captain Kirby.

Captain Kirby grunted.

"I'm Clarisse," she said to me.

"Clarisse?" I couldn't help blurting out. Why did groupies always have odd names?

Captain Kirby laughed.

The girl squinted at me. "Do I know you?"

"I can't imagine from where," I said.

"No, really. I know you. You live in Milltown, don't you?"

"I'm from Akron. It's in Ohio."

"Okay."

Bored with me, Clarisse went to the turntable, removed what was playing, put on a new record and started playing with the controls.

"Jesus," Jonah yelled, yanking off his headphones. "Turn it down, Clarisse."

Clarisse unplugged Jonah's headphones and Jump Naked was suddenly bouncing off the walls. She shimmied toward Jonah and stuck her tongue out at him. He shook his head and laughed. So this was his metal head friend. I could see an evening stretching out in front of us where we had to watch Clarisse dance, watch Clarisse be cute, just watch Clarisse.

I walked over to Tim and whispered in his ear. "I want to go to bed. I'm tired from all that weeding and stuff."

"You sure?" he asked. "It's still early."

"It's all this fresh air, you know?" I put my hands on my hips and leaned backwards to stretch my back. The truth was that I was worried that Clarisse recognized me, because I definitely recognized her. She was in the Trap when The Griffin came last week. I faked a giant yawn and shook my head like a wet dog.

"I'll see you later. I'm not ready to turn in yet," Tim said.

"Sure."

I wandered over to the barn kind of enjoying the end of day sky. Yeah, there were bugs, and snakes were probably just waiting for dark, but if you didn't obsess about things that could bite you, if you just let your skin tingle from the cool air kissing it and watched the sun sneak away to China or wherever, you saw that Jonah was definitely on to something. I was thinking that every time I pictured Milltown I saw a black and white photograph when a tap on my shoulder made me jump.

"Hey," Captain Kirby said.

"Oh, hey."

"I couldn't take the Clarisse show any more either," she said. "I know her from last year. People who need that much attention make my head hurt, you know?"

"Yeah, what's with the little girl play clothes?" I asked.

"She's trying to fool us so we don't notice her vampire fangs. She knows I don't like her so she makes a point of vamping when I'm looking."

I laughed. "So, does she want to be a chef, or what?"

"Naw. Being around JW gets her off because he's famous. That's the way she gets her nachas."

"Nachas?"

"Jewish slang for pleasure."

"You're Jewish?" There were maybe four or five Jewish families in Milltown and the kids had a club at the high school called a Hillel that met in the library once a month, plotting to get extra holidays off, I always thought.

"On my dad's side," she said.

"Oh."

"When I was little I would sit on his lap on holidays while he and my uncles argued about the meaning of life and whose wife made the best borsht and which one of them was the alpha mensch."

I wasn't sure what to ask. Is your dad dead? "Sounds cool," I said.

"My dad's a pretty big deal television producer. Like mom's Vanna White gig was one of his shows. He walked out on us when he realized mom was mental."

"Do you ever see him?" I asked.

"Not if I can help it, yeh sometimes, you know how it is, he's my dad," she said and laughed. "But a mensch means a stand-up guy which my dad definitely isn't."

We had come into the barn. Half unpacked suitcases and clothes were draped over all the cots. "Which one did you take?" I asked.

"Over there," Kirby said.

"Let's drag it next to me and Tim." Which we did. We tucked the mosquito netting under our mattresses and lay down on our backs looking up through the holes in the barn roof.

"It was my idea that we leave California," Captain Kirby said. "After my mom was fired."

"By Vanna White," I said.

"Yeah, Vanna White. What a bitch. After mom was fired she was done for. It's the same for makeup artists as it is for movie stars. You get a bum reputation and all of a sudden no one knows you. At least my dad had nothing to do with her being fired. Mom managed that on her own. My dad's remarried. His fourth. Mom's still pretending they're just taking a time out."

"You picked a swell place to start over."

"We were on our way to New York. Milltown was a stop off. Mom said she had friends here."

"Do you?"

"I haven't met them yet."

One day, I knew, I was going to hear The Entire True Life Story of Captain Janet Kirby—when Have Mercy was a famous band and I could take charge of my life the way Kirby took charge of hers. Like making sure her mom didn't walk in front of a truck, or something worse. A sour taste came up my throat. I had actually been feeling sorry for Captain Kirby. I was projecting.

The other students were trickling into the barn. Tim was walking with Clarisse, heads together. He broke away when he felt me staring.

"Jonah is so awesome," Tim said.

"I knew you would like him," Captain Kirby said. "Did he tell you that he and Zina are going to let me be like the sous chef when they put together his pilot for the Food Network? Talk about getting creds!"

I nodded approvingly while I wondered if Captain Kirby's television producer father had anything to do with it. I was being cynical, one of the things Mr. Dow had told us to be on the lookout for in ourselves. "You're not thinking for yourself when you're cynical. You're at the mercy of what someone else is making you think." Mr. Dow. I wondered what he would say if he could see me now.

"Jonah has the most incredible sound set-up," Tim said. "I want to use his amps tomorrow and jam. We'll sound awesome. You guys up for it?"

"Hey," Captain Kirby said, "Maybe we can convince them to use Have Mercy as the official band of their television show. You know, Jonah can banter with us and we can play his theme song before commercials."

"It can totally work," Tim said.

"We can't think about that until after I see The Griffin," I said.

"Yeah, of course," Captain Kirby said.

"No question," Tim said.

I felt kind of ashamed turning a jet of cold air on them. I could see they felt it. But I couldn't help myself. What I'd been for almost 16 years was over and all I was left with was me and that didn't feel like much of anything.

"I have to get some things squared away first. You know what I mean, right? Then we'll do it, okay?"

"Not a problem," Captain Kirby said.

"We got your back," Tim said. "Listen to this." He bowed his head to his guitar and picked out a tune. "It's more jazz than rock, but I think it will fit the show."

Clarisse had been sitting a few cots away. She came over and touched Tim's arm. "You're very good," she said to him. "Think about what I told you."

"I will," he said and smiled.

I made a face at Kirby that she didn't seem to notice.

"We'll need a signature drum roll for when Jonah wants to take a break," Tim said to Kirby. She pulled out her sticks and banged out a riff on the metal frame of the cot.

I pulled the blanket over my head. Tim and Kirby were sprouting wings and I wanted to feel good for them. But I didn't.

39

The rooster woke everyone up at four thirty. Nobody complained, though. They just picked up big metal cage-like baskets that had appeared by everyone's cots during the night and headed to the chicken coop like in a zombie movie.

Tim and I followed, thinking we had missed some key programming somewhere along the way. No sign of Captain Kirby.

"So that's what these baskets are for," Tim said. "I thought they were weird hats or something." He put one in front of his face like a catchers' mask.

Everyone put on long suede work gloves that were hanging on pegs at the entrance of the chicken coop and immediately began confronting the yellow-eyed devil birds sitting on the shelves. I watched as one girl moved a hen aside with one gloved hand while gathering the eggs beneath the hen and gently placing them in her cage basket with the other. The hen was pecking her the entire time, but she couldn't feel it through the suede.

"So that's how they do it," I said.

"Look," Captain Kirby came running up to me holding her basket which was already full.

"I didn't even see you," I said.

"I was up for a while and got a head start. This is so cool."

I stood in front of a chicken who I swear to God was glaring at me.

"Do you want some help?" Captain Kirby asked.

"Do they make us do this every day?"

"There's no better thing to wake up to than fresh eggs," she said.

She expertly maneuvered my chicken then the three chickens next to it off their broods, making a clucking sound that made them seem to like her, and put their eggs in my basket. Across the coop, Tim held up his full basket and headed outside.

"I find this soothing, don't you?" Captain Kirby asked as we joined the parade to the mill's kitchen.

Jonah had already made coffee in a giant samovar, which I had to admit smelled pretty good, and there were six cast iron frying pans on his six-burner stove.

"Who's up?" Jonah asked cheerfully.

A couple of people jumped to claim a frying pan.

"Not you?" I asked Captain Kirby.

"Nah, I've made a zillion omelets. Let someone else have a chance."

"Did you get the wild chives, Janet?" Jonah asked. Kirby pulled out a fistful of pungent smelling greens from her overall's pocket and put them on the chopping block table. "Here you go, kids," she said.

"Someone chop those," Jonah commanded and six knives came out of sheathes and people got to work on the spring bulbs.

Jonah gave a short demo on making a fool-proof omelet, cracking three eggs into a big clay bowl and tossing away the shells with one hand. He was wearing a white chef's jacket and a white cap. He tossed a big glob of butter into a pan, turned the gas up to the max, fast stirred his eggs, poured them into his pan while with his free hand he cracked three more eggs into the bowl. I was looking at a born performer.

"Lots and lots of butter in the very hot pan, eggs ferociously whipped, and... " He sprinkled some of Captain Kirby's chopped chives in the middle of the eggs, wiggled the pan while scraping the egg from the sides with a wooden spatula. "Hurry up, fold it, fold it, and voilà!" He slid the omelet onto my plate. Kirby slapped two fat slices of olive bread she'd toasted on a four sided tin contraption that fit over one of the burners next to my omelet and slapped hands with Jonah.

Everyone applauded and one of the students stepped up to the stove to try to replicate Jonah's performance.

"Great, huh?" Captain Kirby said, taking a bite of my toast.

Out of the corner of my eye, I saw Clarisse talking earnestly to Tim. "Unbelievable when you think about it," I said.

"I called my dad this morning," Captain Kirby said. "On Jonah's phone. I woke him up. About the pilot. I think my dad's going to go for it. This is a huge opportunity for me. For us, if Zina decides to include Have Mercy. Which I haven't told her about yet. But I think she'll dig the idea."

"They know about your dad?" I asked. "Who he is?"

"Of course they know. How do you think things happen?"

"They happen because you're good at what you do. Cream rises to the top, etcetera, right?"

Captain Kirby looked at me as if I were an alien. "My dad and what he can do for Jonah and Zina is a big bargaining chip to get me included. That doesn't mean I'm not good at what I do. You think Have Mercy would get a shot if your dad wasn't The Griffin? There are thousands of good garage bands out there."

"Eight million," I said.

"Okay, eight million. You wouldn't even be thinking about it. And you know it. You're his kid. His name gives you creds. It opens doors. "

"That's not true!" I said and then realized everyone was looking at me because I'd shouted.

Captain Kirby pulled me by the shirt out of the kitchen, down the stairs and outside. "Then why," she asked me, "are you in such a big hurry to get to Houston to see him?"

"Because he's my father. I have a right to see my father."

"Excuse me for noticing this, but you don't even know the guy."

"I know enough. We're both musicians." I thought for a second. "We both know Jane."

"Yeah, Jane has a lot of influence with The Griffin. As soon as he hears Jane is in trouble he pulls up stakes and moves the wagon train out of town."

"You don't know anything."

"You don't even know if he thinks you're a good musician."

I stared at her, horrified.

"But, he's still willing to help you, isn't he? That's what dads do. They have no choice. Especially if they've been pricks."

"The Griffin is not a prick," I said.

"Yeah, right," Captain Kirby said. "He knows he's been a bastard and deserted his little girl, and like my dad he'll jump at the chance to make it right, professionally anyway, because he can't do what you really want him to do."

"And what do you think I really want The Griffin to do?" I asked

"You want him to be a part of your life. Not be a drive-by father."

I thought of The Griffin's home in Texas which I was allowed to visit only on Google Earth and the Wikipedia entry where I wasn't even a link, no matter how talented and special our family was.

"All this pure stuff, all this authentic stuff, it's all just bullshit, isn't it?" I asked. "It's just a way to get on a television show."

"So what? Getting on a television show would be a way out for me and my mom. It could restart her career and give me one. Can't you see that?"

"But what about your real self? Are you a chef or are you a TV wannabe?"

"What does it matter? Whichever one works."

"Don't you have to find yourself? Isn't that what Jonah's always harping on? Finding your authentic self."

"You don't find yourself. You create yourself. And you can put anything in the stew you please. What? You think you can keep all the different parts of your life closed up in like little boxes or something?"

As a matter of fact, that's exactly what I thought.

"Everything that's ever happened to me, and everything that's been done to me that I didn't have a say in, and every stupid thing I've ever done to myself, I know it will all keep happening, all of it, and I don't give a shit

126

because that's who I am. I'll keep on being me and walk through any door that's open to find out what's on the other side."

I felt like crying. Keeping everything separate was the only thing that let me keep me under control. "Listen," I told Captain Kirby, barely able to talk. "I'm not like you. You can be in my band, but from now on I want you to keep your nose out of my business."

40

Captain Kirby spent the rest of the day chopping and dicing with the paying students, the students with full knife sets, while I was sent to milk goats with Tim in the far barn. Milking goats wasn't as hard as milking cows—something I actually did once at a county fair when I was 10— mostly because goats are smaller. I filled a pail with milk then dumped it into a huge stainless vat, over and over, feeling like Mickey Mouse in the Sorcerer's Apprentice, and it wasn't even eleven o'clock yet.

"So," Tim said, "Clarisse thinks we should go to Nashville to make a demo. So we don't go empty-handed to The Griffin. And then, if Jonah and Zina decide they want a band for the show, we have it for that too."

Ever since Tim started talking to Clarisse all he could talk about was making a demo. I looked on-line, and even a bargain basement studio setup in Nashville—where all the demos in America seemed to be made —cost at least two thousand dollars.

"Well, maybe Clarisse would like to chip in," I said snidely. "You can't just go to Nashville and announce you're here and expect people to just do it for nothing."

"Actually, she says she knows people there who would do it for her as a favor. She says she can arrange it so they wait for their money till we hit something."

"If we make a demo don't we want it to be ours? We buy the studio time and the mix. Nothing owed later. No one else involved." Was that wanting to keep everything in little boxes? I asked Captain Kirby in my head. I knew the answer of course.

"Anyway, how does Clarisse know so much about it?" I asked. "Is she like a musician or a groupie or what? What is she?"

"She has money, that's all I know," Tim said. "I think she's a trust fund kid. She said she was backing Jonah's show, too. Part of it anyway."

No wonder Zina didn't kick Clarisse out for having the hots for teacher. "And I guess she's planning to back you, too."

"Not me," Tim said. "Us. Have Mercy."

"Well, why isn't she talking to me, then? Have Mercy is my band." I laughed sarcastically and peered under my goat's belly at Tim, who stopped pulling on his goat's udder and looked back at me thoughtfully.

"I think we should play tonight," he said. "We need to play. When a band doesn't play together for a while it falls apart."

Captain Kirby wasn't at lunch, which was kind of a relief. I didn't know what to say to her. She wasn't at dinner either, which was five fabulous courses. I had never tasted food so delicious and I was sorry she missed it. One of the other students served everyone—including Jonah and Zina. We were sitting on hard benches at a long wooden slab table. Jonah kept up a running commentary on each course, how it was prepared, how he tasted little adjustments the chef had made in the recipes, and he was raving about the strawberry puree with chocolate sauce and whipped cream when Captain Kirby came out of the kitchen, took off her apron and took a bow to enthusiastic applause.

"Captain Kirby's an amazing person," Clarisse said to Tim. She was sitting on the other side of him. "I don't know why she doesn't like me."

"You know," Tim turned to me. "Kirby told me she only drummed one time with a cousin before the night she auditioned with us in the Trap."

I didn't know any such thing but kept quiet.

"She says you have to try everything when you get the chance because you never know how it's going to end up," Tim said. "That's really cool, don't you think?"

"Where's it gotten her so far?" I snorted.

"Are you kidding? She's Have Mercy's drummer. She's going to be in a cable network food show. She's captain of a champion hockey team. And she's only going to be a senior. I think you can learn a lot from her."

"I can learn a lot from her?"

"No, not just you. I mean, anyone can. I can."

The other students were clearing the table to get ready for an evening of music. Jonah was putting a record on the turntable when Tim said, "JW, can we plug our guitars in? Can we?"

Jonah shrugged. "Why not?"

"Wanna?" he said to me.

"That would be awesome," Captain Kirby said, appearing out of nowhere and looking around for something to drum on while Tim ran to the barn to get our guitars.

"You guys are a band?" Jonah said to me. "That's cool. Why didn't you tell me?"

"Can I use these?" Kirby asked Jonah, fingering a row of glass tubes suspended from the ceiling by wires that I guess were supposed to be a sculpture.

Clarisse saw me looking at them and whispered, "Bertoia."

"Bertoia? What's that supposed to mean?"

"Bertoia is the artist who made them. B-e-r-t-o-i-a," she whispered again, pronouncing each letter like she was helping me cheat on an exam.

Captain Kirby went into the kitchen and came back with two

oversized wooden spatulas. She tapped the tubes. "This will work. We just need mikes."

Which Jonah had, of course. While he was setting that up and Captain Kirby was plinking the glass tubes, Tim brought up our guitars, hooked them up to the speakers and we started going through our repertoire.

It's a funny thing about music. Once we started playing I didn't feel down anymore. Captain Kirby made the glass tubes sing like bells and I was thinking that she'd invented a whole new vocabulary in sound that we could take on the road that would make us famous and was for real and not a gimmick. Tim was answering Kirby's vibes and I was following Tim.

Jonah was smiling at us appreciatively, Zina had recovered from her migraine and was sitting on the loft stairway, and the other students were sitting on the window ledges and floor.

Captain Kirby yelled, "Come on, let's do Hole in the Sky!" It was her favorite song in our repertoire.

Tim gave the key, E flat, and played through it once. I took the mike and began to sing, intoxicated with my own voice. I gave Tim a we're smokin' look, then I looked at Kirby. She grinned and nodded back at me. I looked around the room at the faces that were digging us until I came to Clarisse. I stopped singing and dropped the mike. Tim and Captain Kirby stopped.

"You okay, Mercy?" Tim said.

"I know who you are," Clarisse said, unwinding herself from her window seat perch. "You do live in Milltown, don't you?"

"No. Akron. I told you. Sometimes Texas, though, I'm on my way there now..."

"No, you're The Griffin's daughter." She came up and stared into my face then turned around to address the little audience. "You were playing this song the night The Griffin came to Milltown, weren't you? In the garage? I was there. It was you," she nodded at Tim, "and you," she walked up to Captain Kirby and poked her in the chest—Kirby looked like she was about to punch her—"and you." Her face lit up. "That was the night your mother….."

I closed my eyes. Here, in the middle of nowhere, in some New Yorker's fantasy of farm life, with chickens that laid blue eggs and perfect omelets and peacocks with hen harems and goats whose milk was better than your mother's and ground hogs who freeloaded, and stuff that was authentic just because it was old, in this place where nothing was really real, at least not real the way I understood real, Jane and The Griffin—even though they didn't give enough of a shit about me to even answer my phone calls or give me a ride out of town like Jonah gave his ground hogs—had managed to reclaim me and make me pay for the only thing I couldn't help being, their daughter.

Everyone was looking at me. It was like that day at school—could it only have been three days ago?—but even worse because in front of this tiny audience what was happening felt even more personal. You Can Run but You Can't Hide, the Girl Thing song was playing in my head and I was crying.

Clarisse was giving Jonah an up close and personal. "The night her mother" she was saying looking over her shoulder at me when Zina grabbed her by the braid. "Shut up, you slut," she said and tugged her across the room to me.

"And you, you little lying twit. I knew your name wasn't Darcy. And what about you, Karl? Who are you? This is a culinary arts school not a hostel for trash. All of you, out of here. Right now."

"Whoa, Zina," Jonah stood up.

"I'm tired of it, Jonah," Zina screamed. "I'm tired of it. It's your sycophants or me." She ran up the steps to the loft, her perfect face all red and twisted, and believe it or not what I was thinking was how cool it was that I hadn't paid her yet.

Jonah sank back on the sofa, spread his hands apart, made a face at us and shrugged.

Tim blasted a chord through the speakers. He hummed a couple of bars through his mike. It was the song we'd started the night before and he sang:

The night is dark, But I can see
A path lit up in front of me

I moved in to share the mike:

I'm lost and sad, I'm out of time.
I'm scared to death, my light won't shine

Tim answered:

Then, my sweet friend, You'll borrow mine

41

We unplugged our guitars, cased them, waded through the other students who didn't offer to help and tossed them with our stuff from the dorm into the back of Captain Kirby's van. Zina was watching, arms crossed, from the mill's open window. I was kind of hoping that Jonah would come down to say goodbye. I don't know what I would say to him but I was feeling a little guilty that it was like a door had slammed in his face because of me. But then how come he didn't realize that Zina's noose maybe was about him, you know?

Captain Kirby was the last one out of the mill. She was wearing her chef hat, I think to make us laugh. She started the engine and we were bouncing onto the car track when someone pounded on the side of the van. Captain Kirby braked and rolled down the window.

"Can I catch a ride with you?" Clarisse asked, out of breath. "I hitched a ride here with one of the other students."

Captain Kirby started to roll the window up.

"Let her in," Tim said.

Captain Kirby looked at me. I shrugged.

"Get in," Kirby said, pointing to the back. "Where are you going?"

"I haven't decided," she said. She heaved her backpack in the back and sat on the floor next to it. "Where are you guys going?" she said. "Back to Milltown?"

Going back to Milltown was not actually an option.

"You know," Clarisse said, "Zina's such a bitch because she's scared immigration is going to deport her. She doesn't have a green card. She doesn't even have a visa anymore. I don't know why Jonah puts up with her. She'd better give me my money back, that's all I can say. What a bitch, throwing me out like that. You guys too." She settled down and looked around the van. "Hey, is this your band bus? Cool."

We rode down Sunny Vale's car track—a couple of times it felt like the van was going to tip over, which made us laugh, and out onto the dirt road. Captain Kirby sped up and soon we were at a stop sign by Route 22. At a crossroads. Left to Milltown, right to Houston.

"I'm sorry I screwed up culinary camp," I said to Captain Kirby. "And everything else, too."

"Not a problem," Captain Kirby said. "I'm the one who wanted Hole in the Sky."

"I shouldn't have played it," Tim said.

"That's a seriously cool song," Clarisse said. "That's why I remembered it. But you've got to cut a demo. Or you're just another guy with a song that anyone can rip off."

"Raymond said I should cut a demo," Tim said.

"The Raymon?" Clarisse said. She made a fake squealing noise.

"Yeah."

"Well, you can't do it in Milltown. You need to go to Nashville. That's where everyone goes to cut demos and I told you I can help with that."

Clarisse was in her twenties and she wasn't so much pretty, as, I don't know, confident. She didn't constantly apologize for her existence like a lot of girls my age did. Like, not a word about getting us thrown out of the mill. It was an irresistible quality and I felt a twinge of jealousy because Tim wasn't trying too hard to resist it.

"Actually," I interrupted. "We're on our way to Houston. To see The Griffin."

"Well," Clarisse said, switching her attention from Tim to me. "You want to have a demo in your hand when you see him. That's how it's done."

"Maybe we should go to Nashville, Mercy," Tim said. "It'll only take a couple of days to cut a demo. Right?" he asked Clarisse.

"Couple of days," she said. "Then, you're not just this guy hanging around, you're a guy with a demo, a group with a demo, I mean. My dad's in the business. Or he was. Before Napster took all the fun out of it for him."

"That would make it really worthwhile, Mercy," Tim said. "Like she said, then I'll have a demo to give Raymond and you'll have a demo to play for The Griffin."

Was I supposed to say no to a guy who had left his family to rescue me? "It's up to Captain Kirby," I said. "She's the driver."

"Isn't this a band bus?" Clarisse asked. "Shouldn't the whole band decide?"

All four of us looked through the windshield at the sign with an arrow pointing east to Milltown and an arrow pointing west—to Nashville...and beyond. Houston. Any hope of me ever becoming a real musician lay to the west. Any hope of me belonging to a real family lay in that direction too. Go west, young woman! Well, southwest, actually.

"You can drop me off in Roanoke at my aunt's house," Clarisse said. "I'll set things up for you from there."

I was about to say, "What do you think, Captain Kirby?" but before I could, Captain Kirby released the emergency brake, put the van in gear and turned west.

42

After four hours of driving through Pennsylvania, some of it right into the sunset, we crossed into Virginia. Captain Kirby relinquished the wheel to Tim and sat in the back with me. Clarisse moved up to the passenger seat because she knew some shortcuts along the way, "I think I can remember them," she said. "Although, I was pretty messed up back in those days." She tossed her black and blue braids, leaving us to guess what she meant.

We stopped at the Bristol welcome center one mile into Virginia and everyone was taking a bathroom break and buying tasteless lukewarm coffee from vending machines. Tim had come back from the Information Center with a map and spread it open over the steering wheel to figure out our route while he drank some coffee.

"I am so beat," Captain Kirby said. She moved the bikes then opened up a sleeping bag and squirmed into it.

"I am so sorry about everything," I whispered to her. I didn't want Clarisse to hear me. "Especially the television show."

"I told you, no big deal," she said.

"Well, it is a big deal. You want to be a chef—or a television star or something—and this was going to give you creds, like you said, and now, because of me..."

"Cut it out. It's not the end of the world," she said, "It was a nice-to-have, not a necessity. Anyway, I got my money back."

Clarisse who apparently had bat ears shrieked, "You got your money back? From Zina? From her? How did you manage that?"

"Zina is a rational person," Captain Kirby said. "And she has a well-founded, I would say, fear of immigration."

"You knew about that? I thought I was the only one Jonah told. So did you blackmail her? How did you do that!?"

"I reasoned with her," Captain Kirby said and yawned. "Plan B will now kick in. One thing you learn playing hockey is always have a backup plan of attack."

"But what if you don't get to be a chef now?" I moaned.

"Or what if I get to be a chef some other way? Or, what if I get to do something else which is even more awesome?"

Captain Kirby was sounding an awful lot like Mr. Rajeet's son. I didn't get how they could stand it that two things were possible at the same time.

"And now," Kirby said, pulling the sleeping bag up to her chin, "I am going to catch some well-deserved zzz's. Wake me when we're close to Nashville."

"You're going to drop me in Roanoke first," Clarisse said.

"No we're not. You're going to Nashville with us unless you can't do what you say you can do. Or you can hitch a ride with a trucker. I saw a bunch of trucks idling in the lot when we pulled in. They sleep in the cabs. Bang on a door. They won't get pissed 'cause you're a girl, but they'll expect you to pay, one way or another."

"Why don't you like me?"

"I'll take you back to Roanoke after you get us set up."

I was going to protest that it would mean more time getting to Houston, but I'd screwed up so much already that instead I pulled out my phone and called The Griffin. My call went to voice mail. Well, of course, I thought, it was like one thirty in the morning. He wouldn't be awake.

"Captain Kirby?" I said.

"Ummm…"

"You said your Plan B is kicking in. So, what is your Plan B?"

"My Plan B is to figure out what Plan B is after I take a nap."

43

We were on the road for about fifteen minutes when a clunking sound made the three of us say in unison, "What the...." And woke Captain Kirby.

She sat up and listened for a second then yelled, "Pull over! Pull over! We got a flat."

"There's no room to pull over!" Tim yelled back at her. "Everyone's going 90 miles an hour."

"You're ruining my rims!" Captain Kirby said. "Oh my god, they don't make rims for this car anymore."

Tim lurched into the right lane, the van limping, us swaying, and I thought for a horrible minute that it was going to tip over. When he got to the shoulder, he tried to slow down and almost lost it trying to keep the van under control. Finally, we ground to a halt, the back swinging out into a field.

We exhaled then got out to look at the damage.

"Shit," Captain Kirby said.

"Where's your spare?" Tim asked.

Clarisse looked up at the sky and stretched. "It's a glorious evening, isn't it? It's kind of nice to be stopped next to a field. I wish we had a picnic. We could have like a candlelight picnic."

The traffic was whizzing by at 90 miles an hour.

"Your spare?" Tim asked.

Captain Kirby's face was stone. "I wasn't expecting to go on a road trip."

"You don't have a spare?" Tim asked.

"Well, technically, I do. But it's as flat as this one. I never got it fixed from the last time."

"So now what?" I whined.

Captain Kirby and Tim stared at the flat tire as if wishing could inflate it. I kicked it and hurt my toe. Clarisse came back from twirling in the field and said, "So, who called Triple A? When are they coming?"

"I don't have Triple A," Captain Kirby said. "I didn't need it."

"That's the stupidest thing I ever heard," Tim said.

"Hey, hey, hey," Clarisse said. She reached in her wallet and pulled out a gold plastic card. "Voila! Clarisse will arrange everything."

She called Triple A, giving them her number and our location while we looked at her glumly. If there was anything worse than being stuck on a superhighway in the middle of nowhere with a flat tire and no spare, it was being grateful to Clarisse. She would take over our whole trip. My whole trip.

"Look," she said, "It could be winter, but it's not, it's June! We won't freeze to death or anything and the tow man said he would be here in fifteen minutes." She started dancing again and we were forced to look at her because she saved us. We sat down on the ground while the traffic roared past us.

"Let's get in the field and wait," Tim said, "It's safer. Even if it's only fifteen minutes."

Everyone but Clarisse followed Tim into the field. She wanted to be able to flag the tow truck down, she said, although it would be pretty obvious to anyone driving by that we were the party in distress. I didn't think anyone was going to be able to see her in the dark anyway.

I was sitting next to Captain Kirby. "I'm sorry about this," I said. "It's more than a car, I know."

"Shut up," Captain Kirby said. "We'll fix it and move on."

"With what kind of money?" I asked. "Clarisse can get us towed, but we're going to need at least one new tire and..."

"I said, shut up," she said.

"We already spent seventy-five bucks on gas."

"Okay!" she said, biting her fingernails.

Tim went back out to the side of the road and was talking to Clarisse. Laughing.

I was miserable. There seemed to be no way I was ever getting to Houston. The exhaust from the traffic was sickening. I thought I would probably die out here. I coughed in case anyone was interested, then I got up, shook the grass off my jeans and walked over to Tim and Clarisse.

"It has to be more than fifteen minutes already," I said.

"Well, it's not like a precise science," Clarisse said. "It's two o'clock in the morning and I'm sure we're not the only emergency he has to deal with. Come on, dance with us!"

I walked back to Captain Kirby.

"Is she on drugs, or what?" I asked.

"What time is it?" Captain Kirby asked.

"Almost two."

"Yeah."

We waited silently in the field for another hour—watching Clarisse dance to the light of the oncoming traffic. I was miserable and there was nobody to complain to. I actually missed Jane. If nothing else, she always listened to me. I fingered my phone.

Finally some blinking yellow lights on top of a tow truck came slowly down the highway. Tim and Clarisse had stopped goofing around, but the guy found us anyway. He hopped out of his truck to access the damage, his mood as sour as ours. A giant cigar was in the middle of his mouth, the tip glowing red.

"Where's your spare?" he asked. "I could just change it instead of towing you all the way to Hagerstown."

"It doesn't work, we already tried it," Clarisse said, trying to charm the man.

"Irresponsible kids," the tow man said. "It's the middle of the night."

"Technically it's morning," Captain Kirby said. "We called you hours ago when it was the middle of the night."

"You want a tow or don't you?" the tow man asked. "I don't need lip from a bunch of irresponsible kids. Who has the card?"

He took down Clarisse's information, who had given Tim a twenty to give to the tow man to sweeten his mood, then hooked the van to his tow. We squeezed into the cab with him, me sitting on Tim's lap, Captain Kirby next to us with Clarisse on her lap.

"Ugh," Captain Kirby said. "I hope this isn't a long ride."

The tow truck driver continued smoking his cigar, not even asking if any of us minded, which I did.

Tim stroked my hair. "You okay?"

I breathed deeply and let myself relax into him, putting my arms around him and my head on his shoulder. It was amazing how physical contact with Tim made me feel better even though the stupid driver was smoking his head off and Clarisse was trying to get Tim's attention and Captain Kirby was biting her nails and was, for the first time ever, silent. "I am now."

44

It was five o'clock in the morning by the time we got to Park's Auto Shop in Hagerstown. We got out of the cab and stretched while the tow truck driver unhitched the van. The parking lot of the garage was jammed with cars.

I looked at the shop. It was closed and a sign on the door said they opened at eight o'clock.

"What are we supposed to do until eight o'clock?" I asked.

"You can do whatever you want," the tow man said, and with that he got in his truck and drove away, leaving us to sit on the step waiting for the mechanic to show up.

"I got to get some coffee," Clarisse said. "Anybody want to walk with me? It looks like town is that-a-way."

Nobody did, so she took off while Tim examined the van in the morning sunlight. "All of your tires are as bald as a baby's ass," he said.

"No kidding," Captain Kirby said.

"We should probably get four new tires before we try driving all the way to Nashville."

"Houston," I corrected them, in case they forgot.

"I meant Houston," Tim said.

The owner of the shop, Jin-ho Park, a middle-aged Korean man, arrived at seven. A cute Korean boy about our age followed him out of his SUV.

"Triple A called that you were here," Jin-ho said. "So I thought I'd come. Tires, no problem. I got lots of tires. New."

He put the van on the lift and he and Tim and Captain Kirby discussed the fact that it needed a tune-up, an oil-change and as Tim said, four new tires.

While they were dickering about how long this was going to take and if Clarisse—who had come back with a carrying tray of coffees and a bag of bagels—could be persuaded to front us the money so we could continue, the Korean boy came over to me.

"This sucks," he said. "The flat."

"Yeah." His hands had black grease in the creases just like his father's. "You work here too?"

"Supposedly. I'm supposed to be learning mostly."

140

"Learning what? Mechanics?"

"No, I'm supposed to be learning how hard he has it so I'll want to go to college. But I mostly get people coffee and lunch because he doesn't trust me to work on the cars, which I can actually do but he doesn't know it. I mean, I'm here every summer. Doesn't he think I learned anything?"

"Don't you want to go to college?"

"He wants me to." He jerked a thumb towards the garage where his father was explaining why he had other jobs which had to be done before he got to Captain Kirby's van. "Doesn't your father want you to go to college?"

He had me there. The Griffin and I had never had a conversation where we discussed my future. "I'm going to be a rock and roll star. So, it's irrelevant."

"Is your dad going to let you do that?"

"Well, he's a rock and roll star." It bothered me now that The Griffin never told me what he thought I should be, what I should do. I felt aggrieved. Wasn't that part of his job?

The boy sighed. "I'm supposed to be the first Korean president of the United States."

I burst out laughing then the boy did too.

"It's ridiculous, isn't it? Do I look like a president of the United States?" He looked off into the distance, his thumb and forefinger pinching his chin.

"It's not that you don't look like a president," I said, "It's just pretty obvious that you don't want to be."

"Well, then maybe I will be," he said. "See how screwed up I am? Just because you don't think I want to be, I'll say I want to be. I don't even know what I want. It's all his fault."

"Seong-min!" the elder Korean yelled. "Get us coffee!"

"See ya," Seong-min said.

"Yeah."

Jin-ho Park had to work on a Hummer and an Audi and a Lexus SUV, take a coffee break and do some inspections and then have lunch before he changed our tires, oil and tuned the engine. It was three o'clock in the afternoon by the time he was finished. Clarisse worked it out with Tim that she would pay for the repairs on our "band bus" but that Tim would owe her as soon as we made a hit.

"This stinks," Captain Kirby said, "But Jin-ho said we wouldn't make it to Nashville, let alone Houston, without the repairs."

"I know," I said. At least we were getting back on the van and heading towards Nashville which was en route to Houston. God, it seemed an eternity away.

I looked for Seong-min to say goodbye. He was behind the garage smoking a cigarette, fiddling with a couple of bolts on a rectangular object with holes for cylinders. He was totally engrossed in what he was doing and looked up only when I kicked a piece of glass. "Look, it's an old gasket head," he said. "I found it in the junk yard the other day. They don't have them on cars anymore. They have a computer chip instead. Isn't this cool?" He held it out to me to inspect. "The old ones were way cool."

"Goodbye Mr. President," I said.

He got up and bowed his head. "Goodbye rock and roll star."

45

Clarisse decided to ride all the way to Nashville with us—I mean, Captain Kirby decided for her—and we arrived on the Nashville ring road just before midnight.

"Go straight to the Hyatt," Clarisse said. "That's where Bilbo holds court on Friday nights."

Bilbo was the person who was going to help us cut the demo, at least I guessed that was the plan because I had slept for most of the nine hours it took us to get there to avoid having to deal with the fact that I had totally lost control of the trip.

"Can't we just find a motel first?" I asked. "I really need a shower."

"We can get a room after we meet Bilbo," Tim said self-assuredly. His self-assurance had been swelling up since Clarisse handed him the cash to tip the tow guy. It was really annoying how much he was enjoying being a kept man.

Tim pulled the van under the Hyatt overhang and a valet with a mane of glossed black hair combed straight back in a pompadour appeared. He walked around the van then signaled Tim to roll down the window. "You're kidding, right bro? The bathrooms are for guests." Clarisse leaned over Tim and stuck her head out the window. "Oh, Miss Davenport," the valet said. "I didn't see you."

Clarisse got out and walked around the van. "Good evening, Robert," she said, handing him the keys and tucking a twenty into his vest pocket. "This is a band bus. We're filming tomorrow."

"Got it, Miss Davenport," the valet said. "Whatever you need."

Tim got out of the van and stuck out his hand. "Tim Coles," he said.

` "Sorry, I didn't recognize you," the valet said.

I looked at Captain Kirby with a this-has-gone-far-enough-please-help look. Kirby had exhumed herself from her sleeping bag and was watching all this with a giant grin on her face—it registered with me that this was her kind of game. She pulled open the sliding door and jumped out. "Let's check out the party," she said to me.

Clarisse led Tim through the lobby ahead of us into the hotel club, Mangoes. A not-bad band was playing and a stage hand was having a lot of fun with the stage lights, flicking them red, then blue, then bright white in rapid succession.

"There's Bilbo!" Clarisse said, waving then moving through the dancers on the floor.

"Who's Bilbo again?" I asked Tim.

"He's going to arrange our demo."

"Oh."

"It'll only take a couple of days, Mercy," Tim said. "In a couple of days you'll have a demo you can hand The Griffin. It'll be really cool to walk into his dressing room with a demo."

I didn't answer.

"I know you want to get right to Houston," Tim said. "But Clarisse is doing us a real solid you know?"

I didn't know. Not really. I mean, what was the point of making a demo of a song I didn't write?

"You think it's a good idea, don't you?" he asked.

"Yes, of course. A great idea."

Clarisse came back. "Bilbo's over there. He's one of the most powerful men in Nashville." She pointed at the smallest person at the crowded bar who raised a glass in our direction. He was sitting on a high bar stool with his legs dangling just above the foot rest. The other people at the bar had on jackets and ties. Bilbo was wearing a black leather vest open to his navel. Tons of gold gleamed on his chest and on his fingers. He was bald on top and bushy above the ears. Clarisse grabbed Tim by the sleeve. "Come on! He's dying to meet you."

"He actually looks like a hobbit, don't you think?" I said, laughing over my shoulder to where Captain Kirby had been standing.

I looked around and saw her engrossed in conversation by the kitchen door with a petite female security guard who was fiddling with her gun belt as she and Kirby talked. When Kirby felt me watching them she smiled and waved me over.

The closer I got, it became obvious the security guard looked like a beautiful doll. Everything about her was in perfect miniature proportion. She gave me a jealous once-over as I crossed the room then the expression on her face changed from suspicious to relieved. Her metal nametag said "C. Reina-Navarre." She stuck out her hand, "Carmen. But call me Carmencita. Everyone does because I'm so small." She gave me a dazzling smile.

It was the first time in my life I didn't feel like the little shrimp. "Hi," I said. "Mercy."

"Hey, guys," she said, "I'm still on duty and have to do rounds again in five. We can meet for breakfast when my shift is over. Meet me at the *Cocina Salvadoreña* at six, okay? It's right in the building." She grabbed a cocktail napkin and drew a map, underlining her cell phone number twice. "In case you get lost," she said, smoothing her jet hair. "They do amazing *huevos rancheros* 24/7. *Hasta luego,*" she said, touching Kirby's hand and smiling.

The air was so thick with pheromones that I fanned myself to get some oxygen. Carmencita patted her holster and walked away, looking back once to give Captain Kirby a final dazzling smile.

I snapped my fingers in front of Kirby's face as she watched the elevator door close on Carmen.

"Come back to planet earth," I said.

"I like it much better on this planet," Captain Kirby said. "Is she the coolest or what?"

"How would you know? You just met her."

"I gotta learn Spanish right away. Damn. I should have taken Spanish instead of shop. You're taking Spanish, aren't you?"

"Yeah, well, I can read it better than I can speak it."

"We gotta do a brain transfer between now and breakfast." She kept looking at the elevator which had whisked Carmencita out of sight. "She has five brothers and sisters. Her whole life revolves around her family."

"She's beautiful," I said.

"And funny!" Captain Kirby said. "I feel like I've known her all my life. But I've only known her for an hour. She's going to night school. She wants to get her bachelor's degree in police science and become a forensic specialist or something and put her brothers and sisters through college. I really admire that."

"Fifteen," I said.

"Fifteen what?"

"You've known her for fifteen minutes. Not an hour."

"Well, I haven't felt this way about a girl since… since never. I think I'm in love."

"Captain Kirby, I hope you don't mind me pointing out that Carmen has told you she plans to go into law enforcement, is in fact already a cop, and you're, well, you have a talent for crime you have to admit." I was being really snarky, hoping to bring back the derisive Captain Kirby who would take my head off for being a jerk. But Kirby was in a trance and didn't notice.

"Crime is just one of my talents. I can reform. I want to reform! Say something in Spanish," she commanded.

Captain Kirby had been hit by the thunder bolt, which I knew a little about because of my feelings for Tim. Everything I knew about Captain Kirby up to now included me. I didn't know how to have a relationship with her where I wasn't on the first team. And anyway, the idea that she could be in awe of someone was mind boggling. The lid of Kirby's box exploded off and blew away with a woosh. I closed my eyes and tried to will it back like it was a boomerang or something but it was gone.

Kirby shook my arm. "Tell me how to say 'What should I order for breakfast?'"

"Carmen said *huevos rancheros* are a specialty where you're going to meet her. So say, "*Me gusta huevos rancheros*'. That will impress her," I said and looked away.

Tim was engrossed in conversation with Clarisse and Bilbo. He felt my eyes boring into his neck because he massaged it and turned around, saw me and waved me over. I waved back but didn't budge.

Up until right then I hadn't let myself consider whether Tim was falling in love with Clarisse. Maybe you fall in love with people who can do things for you. Maybe I fell in love with Tim because he kept saving me. Maybe Carmen would save Captain Kirby. I could see that. Maybe you fall hardest for a person who knows like absolutely nothing at all about who you've been up till right then. Maybe I should find out where the lady's room was because I wasn't feeling so hot. My stomach was spazzing like crazy.

"*He perdido ambos mis amigos*," I said.

"Hey, that sounds great. Say it again."

"That actually doesn't have anything to do with your breakfast date. It just came out."

"Come on, Mercy. Help me out here!"

"Okay. Okay. How about: I want something spicy. *Quiero algo picante*."

"*Quiero algo picante*. I want something spicy. That's perfect." Captain Kirby put her head back and laughed then repeated the phrase a couple of times.

"*He perdido ambos mis amigos. Quiero irme al aeropuerto*."

"Should I learn that too?" Captain Kirby asked earnestly.

"No, I was just thinking aloud." I have lost both my friends. I want to go to the airport.

46

Captain Kirby finally stopped staring at the elevator like a dog waiting for its master to take it for a walk and we wandered toward the bar where Bilbo had his arm around Tim talking to Clarisse's phone which she was holding up in front of them like she was taking a video. Bilbo said something to Tim who nodded in agreement and said something back. "Louder, both of you," Clarisse said and they repeated whatever it was they'd said. "Got it," Clarisse said, looking at her phone's screen. Bilbo shook Tim's hand, pecked Clarisse on the cheek and walked up to me and Captain Kirby. "You're the bass player and the drummer, right? See you tomorrow afternoon."

Clarisse said she had some friends she wanted to see. She congratulated Tim, nodded goodbye to me and Captain Kirby and left.

"What was that about, with the iPhone I mean?"

"I made a contract for us with Bilbo. He fronts the demo and gets paid when the band hits it. No papers to sign. Pretty cool, don't you think?"

The Griffin had told me that novice musicians should never sign anything without an entertainment lawyer being in on it because by the time they wise up it's too late. They're already slaves. Well, too late had just happened.

"I gotta turn in," Tim said, yawning. "I'm beat from the drive. Let's get some sleep before breakfast." The three of us drifted towards the registration desk.

"Listen," I said, halting the procession. "I'm going to leave."

"What are you talking about?" Captain Kirby said, "Why do you want to leave?"

I was too tired to explain the urgency I felt. My head was bobbing, but no actual words were coming out of my mouth. All I knew was that if I didn't leave for Houston right now I was never going to go. Something would always get in the way. A flat tire. A demo.

"We need you," Tim said, "or how do we do the demo?"

"It's your song, Tim. You don't need me."

"It's our song," he said.

"I'm not going to argue with you," I said. "You'll get a studio musician to sing and play bass, probably better than I do." I looked from

Tim to Kirby. It was the truth. It hurt but I was finally saying it.

"Look, it's three o'clock in the morning." Tim said. "Clarisse paid for a suite for us. We'll get some sleep and you'll feel different in the morning."

"I just need to borrow some money from you guys."

I still had the three hundred dollars that Captain Kirby gave me in the basement of Kulick's. A plane ticket to Houston had to cost at least that and I still had to get to The Griffin's house.

"You don't have any ID," Captain Kirby said. "How are you going to get on a plane?"

"I have my driver's permit," I said. "I'll tell them my faithful dog is dying or something."

"If you just wait a couple of days, we'll drive down together," Tim said. But he was already reaching in his wallet. He handed me two hundred dollar bills. "It's half of what I saved from work."

Captain Kirby went to a chair, sat down and took off her left shoe. "Here," she said, handing me two hundred dollars after she put her shoe back on. "It's half my refund from Zina. She owed me five hundred but four was as far as she would go, immigration or not. Look, I would leave with you tonight, they have studio drummers too, but I gotta stay and see what happens." She jerked her head towards the elevator and I knew she meant Carmencita. "You understand, right?"

"Absolutely," I said and hugged her.

"We'll be right down as soon as we do the demo," Tim said. "I just don't understand why you're leaving."

"You're doing what you have to do. So am I," I said. I kissed him and held him for a minute. "I gotta get my backpack and guitar out of the van. Then I'll have the valet call me a cab."

I'd never felt more alone in my life but I felt elated, too, almost like I was going to faint. I was finally on my way to Houston and my real life.

47

I know it sounds funny, but the cab to the Nashville airport was the first cab I ever took. We only had one cab in Milltown, called the Quikcab, which Mr. Dow said was the very definition of irony in case any of us wanted to know. The owner of Quikcab, Mr. Hefflefinger, was a little off, endlessly cruising the streets of Milltown after his soldier daughter was killed in Iraq, forgetting to pick passengers up and forgetting to let them off.

Anyway, the driver of the cab in Nashville had a beard with like a hair net over it and wore a giant white scarf wrapped around his head. I'd never seen that. When I tried to be sophisticated and make polite conversation and ask him where he was from, he got testy.

"I am a Sikh," he said, and when I asked him what that was, he said, "Google it."

But I didn't let his bad mood get me down. Nothing could get me down.

The highway out of Nashville was empty, probably because it was only four in the morning. As we sped toward the airport I saw a highway information sign ahead of us that made me rub my fists into my eyes. I pressed the down button, stuck my head out the window, and looked up at the sign as we whizzed under it. The sign said in white letters like twenty feet high: JOHN C. TUNE AIRPORT, exit, 2 ½ miles, use right lane. A tune airport? It was obviously a sign.

Anyway, the back seat had no seat belts and the driver sped over every pothole—I think he aimed at them—and I wasn't heavy enough to anchor myself to the seat so I kept bouncing up, almost to the roof of the cab and I was definitely getting carsick.

"Hey!" I said, and was going to complain when the driver pulled up at the entrance to US Airways without him even asking me where I was going. He glared at me in the rearview mirror and pointed to the meter which said forty dollars. I handed a hundred dollar bill to him.

"You don't have anything smaller?" he asked.

I shook my head.

"I have to get change," he said, snatching it out of my hand and going into the terminal. He came back with five twenties which probably meant that I was supposed to give him a twenty dollar tip which I considered for about a millionth of a second before I jumped out of the cab, shouldered my backpack and guitar and walked through the terminal doors without looking back while he shouted at me in Sikheze.

According to the giant departure and arrival billboard US Airways flew to Houston. The terminal was quiet. A girl janitor was slopping water onto the floor. A bored looking attendant was manning the US Air counter. I wound my way to him through a belted maze like they have at movies on Saturday nights.

"Checking in?" he asked.

"I want to go to Houston," I said.

"On which flight?"

"Whichever one is next."

He looked at me for the first time.

I gave him a big smile.

"Do you have identification?"

"I have money," I said, pulling out the hundreds.

"I need to see some identification."

I pushed my driver's permit across the counter and he examined it and me, then pulled out a clipboard and slid his finger down the page.

"I have a six o'five to Houston."

"Great. Sign me up!"

"Are you traveling alone?"

"Yep."

"What kind of credit card will you be using?"

"Money."

I pushed my bills towards him and he looked at them like they were monopoly money. He picked up the hundreds, making a face. "We don't take cash, miss. Just a minute, please." He disappeared through a door and after what felt like a long time he came back with a security guard right behind him. The attendant handed the guard the clipboard, and after he read it the guard was talking into his cell phone and I was thinking that maybe Granny O'Reilly had put my name on a special deportation list.

The terminal was beginning to fill up and five or six people had appeared in line behind me. One of them pushed up next to me at the counter. He was tall and dressed like a businessman except for his thick gray hair which was tied back in a ponytail.

He gestured to my guitar and smiled at me. "You a musician?"

I nodded.

"You going to a gig?" he asked.

That was a good question. "Yes, I am."

"It's a tough life, being a musician. Your parents know what you're up to?"

I thought about it for a minute, then laughed. "No. They have no idea practically."

He laughed, too.

"You remind me of myself when I was a kid."

The attendant was talking into his cell phone, conferring with the security guard and looking at me.

"Is there a problem with your credit card?" the man asked me.

"The problem is, I don't have a credit card," I said.

When the airline attendant came back, the man said to him, "Excuse me, this is my niece. I was supposed to meet her earlier." He turned to me. "Hello, dear. Sorry I'm late. Put her ticket on my card." He handed a credit card to the attendant who looked at the security guard who made some let-me-think-about-it grunting noises then nodded okay, and in a minute the attendant was handing me a ticket, a boarding pass, and my three hundred dollar bills. "Your flight departs from Gate 25, Miss O'Reilly," he said. "Have a pleasant journey."

"Let me help you with that," my rescuer said, picking up my guitar which I'd been resting on my foot while all this was going on. As he walked me away from the counter, you can imagine, I didn't know whether to kiss him or run. But since he had my guitar the second option was out. The mystified look on my face made him laugh and his laugh was nice so I laughed too.

"I'm Tom Borden, Miss O'Reilly."

"Mercy," I said.

"Nice to meet you, Mercy," he said and handed back my guitar. "I have to admit, I laughed when I saw the man at the airline counter giving you a hard time. Musicians are suspicious characters."

He made a sinister face and I laughed.

"I'm going to Houston, to join my dad's band. Although, actually, he doesn't know it, yet."

"And who is your dad?"

"The Griffin."

"The Griffin? No kidding!"

"Do you know him?"

"I lived in Detroit for a while in the 1970s and I was friends with Fred Smith. You know him? Sonic Smith, MC5, Patti Smith's husband?"

"Are you kidding? I have a poster of Patti Smith on my practice room wall! Although," I could see it now, "That's not the same as knowing someone personally. Did you play with him?"

"Yeah. I did."

"Then why…" Why are you wearing that business suit? I wanted to ask.

"I didn't want it badly enough," he said.

"You mean you weren't good enough?"

"No, I was plenty good. I just didn't want it badly enough."

I could only stare at him like an idiot and Mr. Borden laughed again. "So you're going to be playing in your dad's band?"

"Well, not exactly," I managed. "I have a band of my own."

"Very cool," he said.

"But it's complicated at the moment."

"It always is."

We had been walking the whole while he was talking and we'd arrived on auto pilot at the check-in to my parting gate. Mr. Borden looked at his watch. "Well, Miss O'Reilly," he said. "This is where we part." He pointed at the first class lounge.

"Hey, I owe you money," I said. "For my ticket."

"Right." He looked at the bills I pulled out of my pocket, then looked at me.

"You know what? I don't have change. Pay me back when you're a famous rock and roll star."

I was emboldened by his friendliness and blurted out, "Mr. Borden, do you really think I'm going to be a famous rock and roll star? Or did you just say that as a joke?" I needed to know what he saw when he looked at me. Did he see that something special that says I'm going to make it as a rock and roll star or did he see someone who was kidding themselves? I mean, what if it was just some weird fantasy that I cooked up? I closed my eyes. "I mean, what do you think honestly?"

When I opened my eyes, Mr. Borden was staring at me, then he smiled. He touched his brow in a salute, said, "If you're going to be a rock and roll star, Miss O'Reilly, I can't stop you," and turned to walk towards the first class security check.

"Miss, hello, Miss," a security guy was tapping me on the shoulder. "Your boarding pass, please."

"Yeah, sorry," I said. I was watching Mr. Borden disappear.

The guard stamped my pass and handed it back to me and I joined a line of people who were taking off their shoes and emptying their pockets and putting their stuff in bins that looked like what busboys use to clear dishes in restaurants and pushing them onto a carousel that went into a tunnel of some kind so I did the same, pushing through my guitar and backpack and putting my cell phone and shoes in a bin.

A female guard signaled me to walk through an archway and when I walked through it an alarm sounded. "Step forward," the guard said. She ran a wand up my legs and between my legs and around my torso and shoulders. "Do you have any metal in your body?" she asked.

"Just the metal plate in my head," I said, thinking of Captain Kirby, then giggled.

"This isn't a game, girlfriend," the guard said. "You wanna miss your flight? It's probably your belt buckle. Go back, take your belt off, put it in a bin, and walk to me again." Which I did and no alarm went off this time. "Next," the guard said.

I retrieved my backpack and guitar, my cell phone and belt, and put on my shoes and walked down a long busy corridor toward the Gate 25.

There are hassles on the yellow brick road I said to myself.

I stopped at a food stand and bought ham and eggs, toast and coffee, and took them to a table by a window which I looked out of as I ate them—they were awful and made me think of my perfect omelet at the mill—and I watched the faces in the windows of a plane that was taxiing by hoping that Mr. Borden's would be one of them.

I opened my cell phone to call The Griffin, I knew this time he would answer, but before I could press his number my phone rang. The screen showed a Milltown exchange I didn't recognize. I stared at it for a minute then I touched answer and gave a very quiet, "Hello?"

"Mercy O'Reilly?"

"Who's asking?" I said, thinking I would hear Mrs. Valliere's voice.

"This is Specialist Dutton from Lehigh County Prison. I have someone who wants to talk to you."

Before it registered what was happening, a familiar voice came on the phone, "Mercedes? It's me. It's Jane."

48

"Jane!" I screamed. So much had happened since we got thrown out of the Mill, that how much I missed talking to her came rolling over me like a giant wave. "Are you okay? Where are you? Why didn't you answer my calls? When can I see you? What are they doing to you?"

"I'm fine, honey," Jane said. "Well, not really fine. I'm in jail."

"Are you getting out?"

"They moved up my trial, I mean I'm not having a trial, I pleaded guilty so this stupid shit wouldn't drag out. In a couple more weeks they'll sentence me, probably to community service or something, it's complicated."

"Can I see you?"

"Dutton lent me her cell phone so I could call you. She's a guard. They confiscated my cell phone. That's why you couldn't reach me. I'm not supposed to have contact with minors."

"I'm not a minor, I'm your daughter," I said.

"I know," Jane said, "But you're only fifteen."

"Almost sixteen."

"It doesn't matter. They won't let me see you right now but we'll fix that after I get out." She paused and I could hear her lighting up a cigarette.

"I thought you would quit smoking in jail."

She laughed. "There's nothing else to do here. I smoke more now than I ever did."

"Isn't there a gym or something where you could work out?"

"Mercedes, what's all that noise? Where are you?"

I looked around at the people waiting to board. Cowboys and cowgirls in pastel skirted business suits—a Texas dress code Principal Thwaite would definitely approve of—were talking loudly to one another.

"I'm at the airport."

"In Philly?"

"Nashville, actually."

"Nashville? What are you doing in Nashville? Is my mother with you?"

"I'm going to Houston. To see The Griffin."

"The Griffin? Honey, he's probably getting ready for his tour. He's not going to have time to see you."

"If I show up, he'll have to make time to see me."

"Mercedes, I don't think it's a good idea. I'll be off in a minute, Dutton. Dutton needs me to get off the phone, Mercedes. The shift is changing. Mercedes, tell Granny O'Reilly to take you back to Milltown. What the hell is she thinking? Let me speak to her."

"She went to the bathroom."

"I'm almost finished, Dutton. Listen, Mercedes. I'll be out of here in a couple of weeks then we'll go see The Griffin together. I promise. We'll go see his show. I know you always wanted to do that. Tell Granny O'Reilly what I told you. Okay?"

"Okay."

"I love you, Mercedes. Do you love me, Mercedes?"

"Yes I love you. You're my mom. How could I not love you?"

"I've been doing some thinking in here. We'll do things differently when I get out, okay?"

Whatever Jane was planning to do differently when she got out I wasn't going to be there to do it with her.

"Okay," I said.

She sighed. "At school? The teachers and stuff? What are they saying about me?"

The loudspeaker was announcing my flight.

"I gotta go, Jane."

"You're going home, Mercedes, right? Promise me."

"I promise, Jane. I'm going home."

155

49

It was a crowded flight and I curled up to the window to see out. A yellow skirted cowgirl business woman stowed her suitcase in the overhead and plopped down in the seat next to me.

"Good morning," she hollered. I think if I was sitting up she would have thumped me on the back she was so enthusiastic about meeting me.

"Hi," I said.

"Is that your guitar up there?" she asked. "My daughter Vera plays guitar in a band. Do you play in a band?"

I nodded.

"Well, I told Vera I approved of her doing it on the side but not to make music her life. What kind of a life does a musician have? They never settle down. It's degenerate."

"Not always," I said.

"Always," she said. "I said she could join the lawyers' orchestra. Houston has a quite good lawyer's orchestra. So does Austin. Your mother isn't letting you run wild with a band, is she?"

"Of course not."

"And I hope you ate breakfast because they don't give you anything to eat on this flight. Not even a bag of pretzels. It takes less than an hour but I mean, really."

"That's okay," I said. "I'm fine."

I looked around. Thankfully nobody was listening. It was embarrassing that this woman thought I needed someone to mind me. I hugged the dinky little pillow the steward gave me and snuggled up closer to the window.

"You look like you're freezing. Do you want my blanket? I'm not going to use it."

It seemed easier to just accept the blanket than to say no thank you. I covered myself with it and closed my eyes so she'd get the picture that I wasn't a big conversationalist.

Finally we took off and the cowgirl businesswoman buried her head in the airline magazine that sold junk like matching saunas for your dog and cat, and I was left alone to look down at the clouds. The pilot announced we would be cruising at 34,000 feet. I quickly did the math in my head. We were more than six miles up. Mr. Dow had told us about how Neil Armstrong's life had turned inside out when he looked out of his moon capsule and saw the earth shrunk to the size of a baseball below him. He became a poet, Mr. Dow said, because being up that high he was able to get a completely new perspective on everything. That's what poets do, he told us. They see things that the rest of us can't. We weren't up high enough for the earth to look like a baseball, but you did get a completely new perspective than from when you were walking down Walnut Street. Everything seemed to fit together like an endless jigsaw—the houses were connected to backyards which were connected to driveways which were connected to streets which became roads which went out into the country where rivers and streams were the roads etcetera instead of everything being like a muddled mess when you were in the middle of it trying to punch your way out to something new. From up here I could see how putting things in boxes that I kept separate from each other might be all wrong. If the boxes didn't connect, what was there to write songs about? Nothing. I thought about how Mr. Rajeet's son didn't seem to mind that two things could be possible at once. I would have loved to talk to him about that now because from up here it looked like twenty things or a hundred things were possible all at the same time—depending on how you connected them—so that even though you were north of something that didn't necessarily mean you were in the north. It just meant you had a northern perspective and your perspective could change all the time. I was still in this mind loop when the captain announced that according to his perspective we were preparing to land.

My cowgirl businesswoman seatmate smiled at me.

"This is your first time in Texas, isn't it?" she said.

"How did you know?"

"Texan girls love to fix up their hair." She made a tsunami motion over her own hair which was poufy and blond and matched her yellow business suit.

"We don't do that so much in Pennsylvania," I told her. "There's not enough sun."

I didn't know what I meant by that, but she laughed and I did too.

"Who's picking you up?"

Why did she think I was a kid who had to be escorted around? Didn't I just come all the way from Milltown, Pennsylvania basically by myself?

"My dad," I said.

"What part of Houston does he live in?" she asked.

I didn't actually know. All I had was the address I glommed from the net. I pointed out the window. "Look! What's that building?"

The building was the airport and in a second we were on the ground and Mrs. Big Hair Yellow Suit was standing in the aisle giving me instructions on how to navigate the airport because of course I didn't know that it was the tenth busiest in the whole country and was constantly under construction so it could get even bigger—this was Texas after all!—until I turned on my cell phone and pretended to be texting people and she finally left saying, "Now don't forget," and I sat back down until I was the only one left on the plane.

A stewardess was picking up magazines and garbage from people's seats and putting them in a plastic bag.

"Take everything with you," she said.

"Got it," I said. I unfolded myself and retrieved my guitar and backpack from the overhead and walked slowly down the narrow aisle out of the plane, across the jet way, and into the terminal which was frantic with activity and announcements on loud speakers. Everyone was walking with purpose and I started walking fast too so I wouldn't stand out. But the fact was, I didn't know how to find The Griffin now that I was here. The flow of people was going in one direction so I followed them—catching a ride on a moving sidewalk—hoping to find the exit and finding myself instead at the baggage carousel where Mrs. Big Hair was reading her phone and waiting with other passengers from the flight for the bags to be unloaded. I quickly turned and started walking in the other direction and found a line of people outside the building waiting for cabs. I joined it. A concierge was stewarding people into cabs, asking them where they were going. I practiced saying the address "17644 Hockenberry Road" that I had never said aloud to anyone but myself. Just saying it made me feel good. 17644 Hockenberry Road. It's where The Griffin lived with Marjewel. It's where my half-brother Isak lived. I would be living there soon too. Why hadn't I done this sooner? I didn't need to get permission to live with my father. How laughable an idea was that? We would celebrate my homecoming by entering my name as a resident of 17644 Hockenberry Road in Wikipedia and telling the folks at People Search that I was a person connected to The Griffin and please enter that. I put my head back and laughed. The man in front of me in line turned around and smiled because I was grinning from ear to ear. I never felt happier in my life. When I finally reached the front of the line, I asked the concierge how much he thought it would cost for a cab to take me to 17644 Hockenberry Road.

"Hockenberry Road?" He thought for a minute. "That's in The Oaks, isn't it?"

"It's a big house with a swimming pool," I said, realizing immediately what a stupid thing it was to say.

"A hundred fifty, hundred seventy-five max," he said. "The Oaks is pretty big."

"A hundred and fifty dollars?"

He pointed to a line of beat-up cars on the other side of the traffic island. Several drivers were leaning against their cars, smoking. "You can negotiate with one of them if you want. They're not licensed hacks, but they'll get you where you're going a little cheaper than these. If one of them asks you for payment in advance try another one." And with that he swooshed me aside and put the next person in line into a cab.

I crossed the street to talk to the driver of the first car in line, a beat-up red Honda Civic like Jane used to drive. The driver was listening to Spanish music on an iPhone.

"Hello," I said and showed him the piece of paper with The Griffin's address on it. "How much?"

He squinted at it, then at me, and it occurred to me he might not even know where Hockenberry Road was.

"Two hundred fifty," he said.

"Two hundred and fifty!"

"How much you wanna pay?" he asked.

I started to explain my situation to him, how I was all alone and was there a bus or something I could take when a yellow sleeve came out of nowhere and yanked me away.

"I knew your father wasn't picking you up," Mrs. Big Hair Yellow Suit said. "Now tell me the truth. Are you a runaway? I had a feeling you're a runaway. Are you?"

"No! I'm going to my father's. He just texted me that he's in a meeting and can't pick me up."

"No responsible father would leave his underage daughter alone at the Houston Airport," she said. "Where are you going?"

"Okay, look," I said, looking around to see if anyone was listening to us. "The truth is my dad doesn't know I'm coming. I'm surprising him. He'll probably be home by the time I get there."

"Which is where?"

I gave her the piece of paper. "That's in The Oaks, I think anyway. That's what he said." I gestured towards the concierge.

"My my." She gave me a funny look. "That's where the Bushes live."

"He has a swimming pool," I said.

"Everyone in Houston has a swimming pool, honey. You would expire here without one."

She was pulling a suitcase on rollers and she handed the handle to me without letting go of my sleeve to get me moving. "You pull this thing. I'll take you there."

"I don't want to make you go out of your way," I said.

"It is way out of my way, but I have a daughter, too, and I would want someone to give her a lift if she was stupid enough to land in a strange big city without a clue of what she was doing. Where's your mother, by the way?"

She glanced back and saw that I was groping for an appropriate answer. "It doesn't matter," she said. "Come on."

50

Mrs. Yellow Hair said Houston was in the middle of a terrible drought and that's why everything was brown and crackly looking and when I put down my window to feel the air, Mrs. Yellow Hair overrode me with her own controls and put it back up saying, "Mosquitoes."

What I never could have imagined was that driving from one side of Houston where the airport was to Hockenberry Road would take two hours. But it did. The neighborhoods fanning out from the inner city to the airport were distinct developments. Nearest to the airport were cracker box track homes that could use a coat of paint and had pieces of furniture and other stuff piled on the curb for the garbage men or the neighbors to pick through. Then came middle class homes, a lot of them pretty big ranchers in developments with gates around them, and furthest out, where Mrs. Yellow Hair in her giant black SUV was taking me were immaculately landscaped acres dotted with humongous McMansions that you could only glimpse from the highway because they were encircled by high stone walls and had guard houses in front of gates that looked like they were copied from castles. Mrs. Yellow Hair pulled into one of these.

"Give me that paper," she commanded.

I gave her the slip of paper with the address on it and she handed it to the security guard, who came out of his shack and peered in the window to get a good look at us.

"I'm giving this young lady a ride," Mrs. Yellow Hair said. "She's visiting her father who lives here."

"What's your name, miss?" he asked, then went back into his command post and looked at a list.

"Who is your daddy?" Mrs. Yellow Hair asked. "This is a very expensive neighborhood."

"He's a musician. The Griffin," I said.

"The Griffin?" she said. She got a dreamy look on her face then laughed. "I used to have the biggest crush on him. He was so handsome. That was a long time ago, though. Jesus, he must be, how old?"

"He's at the Toyota Center this week. The show's sold out." I felt proud saying that, even though I didn't know if it was true.

"Well, you might actually have a shot at making it as a musician," she said. "Not like my Vera. My husband's a banker. It's all who you know."

The guard came out of the guard shack again. "What's your name, again?" he asked me, and when I told him he went back in and picked up a phone.

"I could just walk in. How far can it be from here? I only have this to carry," I said, holding up my backpack and guitar.

"They don't let you just walk into a place like this," Mrs. Yellow hair told me. "There are security guards with dogs in the back of jeeps patrolling the streets and you'd be stopped before you were out of sight of the gate."

The gate guard was on the phone for a long time and the awful thought occurred to me that The Griffin was home and he was telling the guard he didn't want me let in. Finally, the guard came out, walked to the back of the SUV, wrote down the license plate number, and handed me form on a clipboard for me to sign, write where I was going and what time I'd gotten there. He pressed a button by the gate and it opened and we were winding our way past the greenest lawns I'd ever seen and shiny explosions of flowering trees and gardeners wheeling barrels of mulch and sprinklers were on everywhere which seemed really piggy considering that outside the gates there was a terrible drought.

Mrs. Yellow Hair stopped in the circular driveway of a giant mansion which I recognized was the house I'd looked at a thousand times on Google Earth—although the fact was that all the mansions in the neighborhood looked kind of the same.

"Do you want some cash for gas?" I asked. "I have money."

"Save your money in case of an emergency," she said.

"You can go now," I said. "I'm okay." I didn't want The Griffin to see Mrs. Cowgirl. He would split a side laughing at her yellow suit and big hair and she would probably blush because she used to have a crush on him.

"I'll wait to make sure you're okay."

"I'm okay," I said.

And there I was. In a giant circular driveway, looking at The Griffin's house, as if I had entered the Emerald City and had an appointment with Oz the Great and Powerful.

There was another driveway that shot straight back off the circle down the side of the house. I saw the band bus parked nose out halfway down it. I put my guitar and backpack down on the lawn, my lawn, right? and walked back to look at it. A guy in white pants and no shirt was polishing the grill. There was Bang on the front grill, and Raymond sneering his Cheshire cat sneer under one of The Griffin's wings, and then there was a third figure leaning familiarly under The Griffin's other wing. I walked opposite it and stood back so I could see it whole. It was a young boy in black leather pants and open vest. The boy's hair was painted black as a crow's and was braided down his back. I was looking at it for a really long

162

time I guess because I heard a horn honking. Mrs. Yellow Hair wondering where I was. I knew who the new figure on the bus had to be without even having to think. It was Isak.

I came back out on the lawn and waved to Mrs. Yellow hair to stop honking and I turned around just as the door opened and a boy was standing in it, a guitar dangling off his shoulders and earplugs on his neck.

"You're lucky. I almost didn't hear the phone," the boy said. "I was practicing."

I had known Isak existed, forever of course. I had him stored in one of the smallest boxes in my collection. His hair was even blacker than on the side of the bus and his face was broader and had stronger features than the painted face. He had the same fuzzy hair on his cheeks and chin that Tim had.

I walked back to the SUV and Mrs. Yellow Hair opened the window. "I'm okay," I said. "Thank you for giving me a ride."

"Who is that boy?" she asked.

I said the words in my head to see how they sounded before I said them aloud: "That's my brother, Isak."

I walked back to where I'd put them down and picked up my guitar and backpack and stood for a minute staring up at Isak, thinking it was probably as curious for him to have a sister as it was for me to have a brother I'd never met. Unless, he didn't even know I existed. But then, he sent me that text message when Jane was in trouble. But how could he know what I looked like? I walked up the steps and stopped in front of him.

"I'm Mercy O'Reilly," I said. "The Griffin is…."

"I know who you are," Isak said, stepping out of the way. "Come on in."

51

The house was sparsely furnished, not in the way Jane's and mine was sparsely furnished because we couldn't afford much, but in a way that looked deliberate. The floors were marble and shiny as an ice skating rink. Isak led me through a couple of large rooms that didn't look as if anyone ever used them to the kitchen.

"Are you hungry?" he said, opening the refrigerator and staring into it. "I'm starved. I've been playing all morning."

"Yeah, I guess I am." I put my Fender and backpack on the floor and climbed onto a stool at a giant granite island in the middle of the kitchen. I hadn't eaten much of the egg breakfast I'd bought at Nashville and before that nothing since our pit stop in Hagerstown.

" I guess you're a vegetarian too," Isak said.

"No, but whatever you have is fine. Anything." I could've eaten an entire side of beef—isn't that what they grew in Texas? Isak microwaved a giant plate of rice and beans and put it steaming in front of me. "Napkins and forks," he said, going to heat up his own plate and pointing to a floor to ceiling wall of drawers. "Third and fourth ones."

"I didn't know The Griffin was a vegetarian," I said. "It's always pepperoni pizza and Chinese take-out when he's at our house."

"You're kidding? He's the one who insists on it. I didn't like it at first but I'm used to it now."

He pulled up a stool next to me. "Do you like my Fender?" he asked.

"What do you mean, your Fender?" I said.

"Was mine," he said. "I like my Martins better. I've been working out on my D-28. Got it as a present from Raymond. Great resonance. Ever tour their factory? I did. Last year. It's a trip."

Did The Griffin actually give me Isak's hand-me-down guitar? And how come exactly did my half-brother come to the part of the country I live in to tour the Martin factory without me knowing about it? I wondered if Jane knew? The Griffin probably dropped him at the Philly airport on his way to Milltown.

"I mean, the Fender's a perfectly good guitar, but I said it was okay to move it along. So it's not like I'm going to confiscate it or anything."

"What wonderful news," I said.

"I'm only kidding you," he said. "You don't have a sense of humor, do you?"

Didn't I? Here, I always thought I was a laugh riot.

"But I'm not kidding about the Fender. It was mine. I'm just not going to confiscate it."

"Okay! Okay!"

Now that I had something to eat I didn't feel so spacey. I looked around the kitchen for signs of The Griffin. I couldn't picture him living here. Actually, the only place I could picture him living was in his band bus parked in our driveway in Milltown.

"He isn't here," Isak said, reading my mind. "He's at work."

"What do you mean, he's at work?"

"I assume that's why you're here. To see him. The thing is I don't know when he'll be home. He's like, getting ready for the tour. They have a shitload of new songs he sprung on the guys at the last minute and they don't have them down yet, plus he's working out with a personal trainer. He let himself get really out of shape. He's an old dude, you know, and he can't spring back like he used to."

An old dude? We were talking about The Griffin here.

"So, where does he practice?"

"In town."

"He has to come home sometime. I can wait here,"

"I guess so. But my mom will be back soon."

"So?"

"Where are you staying? It might be better if you wait there."

"I'm staying here," I said, surprised that he wasn't taking that for granted.

"I personally don't care," Isak said, "But my mom doesn't like surprises."

"So, call her and tell her I'm here. Or give me her phone number and I will."

"You don't get subtlety, do you? My mother doesn't like you."

"What do you mean she doesn't like me? How can she not like me? I never did anything to her. She doesn't even know me."

He shrugged. "You want to see my set-up? Maybe jam? On my Fender?"

"Possession is nine tenths of the law."

"Maybe you do have a sense of humor," he said.

We picked up our guitars and headed downstairs to what seemed like a whole other house. I saw that it was actually the first floor and that the main entrance to the house was on the second floor. Anyway, it was nothing like the musty old basement stairs that led into the Trap. Isak turned on a bunch of lights.

"Yeah, anyway," he said, gesturing for me to go first. "Why do you call him The Griffin?"

"Isn't that his name? What do you call him?"

"Dad?"

52

We entered a glassed-in room which housed electric guitars on stands, microphones, music stands, amps and speakers. It was like a professional recording studio and I felt foolish, thinking how I had bequeathed the make-shift amps and speakers in the Trap to Tim as if it were some big deal. Next to this stuff it was just a lot of junk.

"You have a sound board," I said. I had never actually worked one, but it was high on my list of things I wanted to learn as soon as my real life started, which I guess was right now.

"For a good mix, it's essential." He plugged his guitar into an amp. "And for when we record."

"You record down here?" Tim could've just made his demo here.

"Well, you have to wear headphones for everything because the neighbors bitch." He tossed a set to me. "Even though it's soundproof. Or as soundproof as you can make it when you're surrounded by houses. That's why Dad does metal in town."

"We have bitchy neighbors, too," I said, thinking of Mrs. Tudesco and her yapping Pomeranians. "One of them's always calling the cops on us."

"They wouldn't call the cops. They would throw us out," Isak said.

"They can throw you out of your own house?"

"Technically they can. It's like a condo association, but Mom would never let it get to that. She would be mortified. 'I am so mortified.'" He made his voice go soprano.

I laughed, but if that's what Marjewel was like I was in big trouble. Jane practically made a habit of mortifying people. It's what we did.

We both put on our headphones. Isak switched on a microphone in front of him and gestured for me to do the same.

"Hey," he said through the mike, "You might know this one."

He ran through the head, a stanza, and the bridge of Hole in the Sky.

I felt my face get white. "Hey. That's my song. Our song."

"Don't have a fit," Isak said. "I'm just fooling with you. Dad was singing your boyfriend's praises. No one's going to rip you off. It's your boyfriend's song, isn't it? What's his name?"

I strummed the bridge. "Tim."

"Well, how about this?" Isak started playing. "It's one of mine." It was like he was meandering through a field of wildflowers, going nowhere in particular but enjoying the trip. He started singing. I joined in on the bass. It was a love song to the desert. To water holes and poppies and sage and naked mountains. It wasn't anything like any relationship song I'd ever heard. It was like a revelation. Captain Kirby had said "Mom is not a people person," when I met her at Kulick's. Maybe you didn't have to just write about people. It was so cool to think about having a brother I could explore with. I had been defined against just Jane and The Griffin for my whole life and it had never occurred to me that that wasn't the only way to know myself. I could define myself, like right now, against a brother to whom I didn't have anything to prove. I could see what having a real home had made of Isak. He wasn't in awe of The Griffin. He didn't have anything to prove like Jane did—saying she'd show The Griffin by doing something so unbelievably stupid that didn't even make her happy. Isak was at home with himself.

When he finished his song I smiled at him and started the head to the new song that Tim and I had been working on at Sunny Vale.

I close my eyes when I play and I did now too. When I got to the end of where we'd gotten so far I looked at Isak. He nodded. "How about this," he said and played a new bridge between the stanzas and kicked in with a stanza of his own.

We toodled around with his bridge and more words came shooting out of his mouth just like they did out of Tim's and I could see that he was even better than Tim. But how could he not be? Tim had gotten more confident just jamming with Raymond and Bang in the Trap. Isak lived full time with The Griffin for Pete's sake. That's why I wanted to be here. That's why I was here.

Isak segued into a Latin riff, made it rock and finished with some lyrics in Spanish that I didn't understand.

"That's for my mom," he said. "That's the part of me that's a Latino rocker."

"What do you mean you're a Latino rocker?"

"My mother is Mexican," he said.

And before I could ask him more about his mother and his Mexican heritage, Marjewel was knocking on the glass wall and smiling at Isak, her smile turning to disbelief, then anger when she saw me.

53

If Isak inhabited real space in my mind, Marjewel had been like an incomplete drawing, a menacing figure without a face who kept The Griffin from being with me and Jane.

Isak pulled off his headphones and opened the door, then went back to the music stand and plugged back in.

"Turn it off," Marjewel commanded. She was staring at me. "Who's your friend?"

"Mom, this is...'

"I know who it is," she screamed.

Isak scratched a couple of high Cs that mimicked a screech.

"Stop it and plug in your the headphones," Marjewel said. "You know you're not supposed to do that."

Marjewel had Isak's face and jet hair. She was neat and polished like a car that had just gotten detailed: glossy highlighted hair, buffed skin, fingernail and toenails that shone with new paint. She obviously was returning from a "day of beauty," one of those things Jane and I were always saving up for but never quite got to because her car or some appliance broke down just as we were on the verge.

"Why are you here," she asked.

"I'm waiting for The Griffin."

"What do you want to see him for?"

"Do I need a reason to see my father?"

"My husband is preparing for a tour. We don't need the media crawling all over us because you've shown up. Wouldn't they just love this." The look on her face changed from rage to derision. "So tell me," she said, "how is your mother enjoying jail?"

Isak pulled off his headphones. "Mom, cut it out. Chill out, will you. Mercy is my guest. Okay? We're just jamming."

"How did she get in my house?"

"I let her in."

"*Querido*," she said. "You shouldn't have." She ran out of the room. Isak put his head down and picked on his guitar, adjusting the strings, ignoring his mother's exit, ignoring me.

I was breathing really fast. I could hardly hold the pick in my fingers I was shaking so hard.

"Thank you, Isak," I said into the microphone. I knew he heard me because he nodded his head, even though his eyes were closed.

I closed mine too. All I had to do was hang in long enough for The Griffin to get home. I pictured him flying into the room, picking me up with his lion's claws and carrying me away to a place where we could be father and daughter together. If only I could wait that long.

54

Isak and I jammed for another hour—I knew he was doing it to soothe me—then he told me he had to go to The Griffin's studio downtown and did I want to come?

"I'm playing with them," Isak said. "You know Dad broke off with Aerosmith, don't you? This concert is all his. Righteous Anger."

"Righteous Anger?"

"The name of the tour. Dad wants me to join him on the tour. I've been thinking more and more about Latin rock, I want to develop a sound of my own, but I'll just do this tour and see how it goes. Can't hurt to see what it's like on the road. Last chance. Wanna come with me?"

"I think I'll wait here," I said. I knew if I left the house Marjewel would change the locks or alert security to not let me back in. It was really lucky that Isak was home by himself when I arrived.

"I have a tune that I want to work on," I lied.

"You're more than welcome to it, but Mom is going to come down as soon as I leave. She's a badger when she's angry. Dad and I are used to it. I don't know if you can take it."

"I'll be alright," I said. If Isak knew what I had been through lately he would have known I could take care of myself, that I couldn't be bullied by Marjewel or anyone.

"Show me this," I said, pointing to the sound board. "Then I won't bother you anymore."

Isak walked me through how to record a CD and edit it on the software program on his Apple. "You can't break it," he said. "Believe me. I did all kinds of dumb shit on it when I started and it's still here. At your service. Indestructible. So don't be afraid to experiment. Just keep this backup tape in the tape player so you don't lose your work in case you screw up." He slipped a small thick cassette in the tape player. "That's the big mistake I always make, not backing my shit up. I'm leaving it on. You're ready to go." He cased his guitar and pointed to the glass door and smiled. "I'm not going upstairs," he said. "Have fun."

"Hey, Isak?"

"Yeah?"

"Thanks for that message when Jane got in trouble."

He nodded.

"Does it feel weird to have me here?" I asked. "I mean, to find out you have a sister?"

"Dad always talked about you. So not really. I feel like I've always known you."

"He did? The Griffin talked about me?"

"Sure. He doesn't say anything to mom after he visits you and your mother, but he tells me. I think he feels really bad about how things are."

"Really?"

"Yeah. He said how you were this funny little kid who was always showing him charts and graphs to explain things that were going on in your life. He thinks that's hilarious."

I felt my face get hot. I thought it had made me seem rational and grown-up, like Mr. Dow. It never occurred to me that I was being ridiculous. "Well, it's not so funny when you get to talk to your father like five minutes a year."

"Yeah, I guess."

"He never talked about you," I said.

"We're tight," Isak said, ignoring my dig.

"Did he ever say anything about…" I closed my eyes and made a wish. "Anything about my music?"

"Just that you wanted a guitar. So I said you could have my Fender."

55

The sound board was amazingly simple to work and I engrossed myself in figuring out the different channels and sound levels because I wasn't feeling so hot about myself, and I was thinking whether I should call Tim to come down immediately, that he could do a demo right here, when I saw Marjewel standing on the other side of the glass wall of the studio staring in at me. She must have heard Isak leaving. She pushed on the door and when it didn't open she gestured at me to let her in.

"I thought I'd wait here for The Griffin," I said, talking really fast. "Isak said it was okay. I was just playing around on the board. Isak said it was unbreakable. I've been keeping my head phones on."

Part of me didn't think I owed her any explanation, but part of me knew that I was basically a trespasser.

"He might not be home for a long time," Marjewel said. She pulled up a stool and sat down, tugging down her skirt. "I find musicians to be unreliable," she said, talking in a quiet tone that was scarier than the anger I expected. "They tell time by a different clock. They are always, always late when they show up at all. They are narcissists and live without any thought of consequences of their actions and leave messes for other people to clean up. Don't you find that to be true?"

I knew she was laying a trap for me. "I only know the members of my band and they're always on time," I said. "They're more on time than I am. And responsible? Ha! Tim? Captain Kirby? I wouldn't be here right now if it weren't for them."

"Oh really? You have a band? You're a musician too?" she asked.

I knew that any answer I gave was the wrong answer. "I'm trying to be a musician."

"But they are charming, don't you think? Your mother thought so. She was so charmed by my husband she thought she would take him away from me."

"My mother didn't take anybody," I said. "Jane and The Griffin were in love."

"She said that?" Marjewel asked.

Of course they were in love. I knew they just tried to act casual when it was time for The Griffin to leave to spare my feelings, so I wouldn't be so sad when he left. Because he always left. It was the most reliable thing The

Griffin did: leave.

"Well, they had me," I said and laughed nervously.

"The Griffin is my husband," Marjewel said. "Isak was already here when you were born and your mother was riding in the bus, pretending that my son and I didn't matter. I knew he was with other women when he was on the road. But my husband having a child with someone else? How do you think that made me feel?"

"It was special with Jane," I said. "The Griffin and Jane and me, we're a special and talented family. We have our own rules."

"Is that what your mother tells you?" Marjewel laughed sadly. "You insist on waiting here till The Griffin comes? When The Griffin comes home to his house, my house, our house, you can ask him if he thinks you are part of a special and talented family or if you are just the daughter of a groupie who was too dumb to use birth control."

I was stunned. "He'll tell you who we are," I said, but even as I said it, I thought of Evelyn, the groupie The Griffin took into the bus that night in Milltown and Evelyn was no different from other groupies over the years. Was it possible that the only difference between Evelyn and Jane was that Jane was unlucky—stupid?—and got pregnant? Was I just some accident caused by two careless people who never considered that what they were doing would have consequences for others, like, for me? That thought got caught in my head and I couldn't dislodge it and it was crowding out everything else in there and my head was getting all misshapen, and it was knocking over the piles of boxes I had so neatly stored in perfect rows and they were splitting wide open, messy contents spilling everywhere. Jane's stuff was mixing with stuff from Isak's box which was mixing with stuff from Tim's and Clarisse was in Tim's, how did she get in there? Everything was out of control because my giant head was beginning to shake like an earthquake, smashing boxes open, and Captain Kirby burst out of her box riding the Fezzari, and Mrs. Tudesco looked at me knowingly, shielding her Pomeranians eyes, and all the neat little divisions I had positioned so diligently to keep the boxes segregated in their own quadrants were suddenly growing legs and marching around on their own.

I was breathing so fast I thought I was going to pass out.

"It's so not true," I said in a raspy voice that sounded like I'd been yelling. "What you're saying...Jane and The Griffin...."

But there it was. Something deep inside of me must have always known the truth because why else could I never bring myself to call my parents Mom and Dad like every other kid on the planet?

Marjewel smiled slightly. "So maybe, being a narcissistic musician yourself, is the reason you can't see how your presence here, in my home, would have the consequence of enormous pain for me."

"I have a right to see The Griffin," I said. "He's my father."

"He has a responsibility to you, of course, and I make sure he does what's right—yes, I make sure of it—but I wouldn't call someone who sees you twice a year a father, actually, would you?"

Every pronouncement she made she turned into a question she acted like I should answer.

"How do I know how many times a year you have to see a person to call him your father?" I screamed. "See, I want to fix that. I want to see him more than twice a year."

"Are you saying that you think you're going to stay here? In my house?" Marjewel asked.

"It's not your house, it's The Griffin's."

Marjewel burst out laughing and kept laughing so long I thought she was going crazy.

"Why don't you ask The Griffin about that, too, as long as you're going to have a big heart-to-heart conversation with him?"

For some reason I can't explain, I thought of the frog Krista Kulick and I dissected in biology class to analyze what was inside it, but I was the frog being cut apart—with Marjewel making sure The Griffin did the bare minimum and me with my charts and graphs and PowerPoint presentations that The Griffin couldn't wait to tell Isak about as soon as he got home so they could have a good laugh about how ridiculous I was. Hahahaha. And I gave him copies of some of those charts. How could I ever look at him again? And this house where I always imagined I really belonged was what? I was always able to bear that Jane was a substandard mother because I was certain my supersized father with eagle wings and lion's haunches would one day pluck me up and take me to his castle where we would truly be a special and extraordinary family. How could I be so dumb? My whole life had been such a ridiculous lie that I couldn't believe I was still breathing. I was alone in the world. My mother was in jail for having sex with an underage student and my father, my father wasn't a superhero. The only reason he even came to see me was because Marjewel made him. He was nothing but a bunch of feathers and crepe paper, a giant gimmick held together by a glue gun and staples.

I felt cold and I slumped to the floor and curled up in a little ball, sobbing, gagging. I felt Marjewel stroke my hair, saying "There, there, *niña*. You are almost a grown woman," she said. "Maybe it's a good thing you came here, so you can see the truth for yourself."

"I didn't do anything wrong," I said. "It's not my fault."

"No," Marjewel said. "But that doesn't change anything. And that is part of knowing the truth."

56

I guess I fell asleep because it was dark outside when I got up off the floor. Low wattage emergency lights illuminated the studio. I had no idea if I was alone or not because the studio was sound-proof so I knew I couldn't hear if anyone was upstairs in the house. The Griffin might not be home for hours, maybe days. Based on my own experiences with him he showed up whenever he pleased and left when things got real. And honestly, I didn't know what I had to say to him anymore.

I counted my money. I could get to the airport and throw myself on the mercy of the airlines and hope they would just stick me on a flight home to get rid of me as some kind of pathetic charity case—isn't that what I was? Or I could ask Isak for a ride to the airport and fly as far as four hundred bucks would get me.

I picked up my guitar and plugged it in, turned on the sound board and put a blank CD in the player, and when I did the lights came on. I thought I would record something to show Tim—if I ever saw him again— how easy it was to do it.

I did my usual warm-up with some scales, then struck a chord, an E flat—my key—and was astounded at the violence that came out as I played every note in the chord: E flat, F, G, A flat, B flat, C and D. Then I turned on the microphone, prepared to sing my usual la-la-la-la-la-di-da but instead a wordless sound came rolling up through my body and exploded out of my mouth—louder than anything I ever sang, truer than any sound I ever made—a scream. It was bigger than my body seemed able to produce and I didn't recognize it as me, and it went on and on louder and louder and I couldn't stop it and it felt like my eardrums would burst in the headphones. It was crystal clear and if I had been a soprano I would've broken the studio's glass walls. When I finally ran out of breath, I inhaled, thinking that whatever had happened was over, but it wasn't and words started pouring out of me. Like the scream, the words were coming from inside my body but I had no control over them.

I'm all alone
But I don't cry
I'm free as lightning in the sky
I come and go and do my dance

I'll light you up
Give me a chance
World's finest partner
Me with Me
I am my own best company

I burst into tears then I screamed again. I'm a very good screamer, it turns out. I played a bridge and more came pouring out. For the first time in my life I started a song that wouldn't stop. There was more inside and I savored the taste of the words in my mouth and let them come out in their own time, which they did.

There's you and me
Which one's more free?
You can't stop me
Being me

That's your best shot?
That's all you've got?
My lightning shows
It ain't a lot

Gonna leave me?
Make me cry?
Try to hurt me?
I don't die

Cause I'll still be
With me and me
I am the world's best company

I fiddled with the chords and the rhythm and when I thought I had it right, I put another blank CD in the player and recorded it. Then I played it back again and again. And I laughed and laughed. I stood up and did a dance. I had always felt self-conscious dancing, but now I thought I would definitely incorporate dancing into my stage routine if I ever got the chance. I popped the CD out of the player, found a Sharpie and wrote on the CD: Mercy... Me! and I put the CD in my backpack. I was smiling. Jane was right, I never smiled. Now I couldn't stop.

The soundboard had a date and time counter which came up after I stopped recording. It was five o'clock in the morning. I had been working non-stop for almost twelve hours and it was the most alive I ever felt. I gathered my stuff together to go up to the kitchen to get a cup of coffee and leave, when I saw three figures coming down the steps to the studio. Captain Kirby waved, Tim smiled at me, and Raymond flashed me his usual devilish grin.

57

Tim dropped his guitar and backpack and held me in his arms. He smoothed my hair—which probably looked like a tornado carved a path through it—and kissed me. "You look tired but you look really good."

"Sorry it took us so long," Captain Kirby said. "Traffic on 440 was stop and go."

"That's bullshit," Tim said, "I had to drag her away from Carmen."

Was Captain Kirby blushing? I hugged her and pushed the bangs out of her eyes.

"We had a moment," she said.

"Or three," Tim said.

"Are you going back to Nashville?" I asked.

"Isak told us you were downstairs," Kirby said, avoiding the question. "He's a cool dude."

Raymond had been circling me. I tried to avoid looking at him. "Sometheeng is different, *vrai*? Do you see it?" he said to Tim. "You have taken a lover, no?"

"I had a growth spurt," I said.

"Oui?" He squinted at me. "Yes, that is it! You are taller."

Tim held up a CD. "We nailed it, Mercy. Hole in the Sky. We rock!"

"How did you know where I was?" I asked him.

"I called Raymond," Tim said.

Right. I had forgotten they were buds.

"They're in freaked-out mode getting ready for the tour," Tim said. "Righteous Anger. Isn't that a cool name? A gofer borrowed Isak's jeep. They're already ferrying stuff to the Center to set up. Kirby loaned them the van. They have a tractor trailer full of equipment too. It's awesome. The Griffin asked Raymond to bring Isak home and we hitched a ride."

So he knows I'm here and can't even take a break to come see me. Probably because Marjewel didn't tell him he had to.

"We open tomorrow night," Raymond said.

"But after that, we got to get back to Milltown," Captain Kirby said.

"Milltown? Didn't we just escape?" I said. "What happened to 'Milltown is not an option'?"

"I talked to my mom yesterday," Captain Kirby said.

I braced myself. Like had Mrs. Kirby burned down the house?

179

"And?"

"Your mom's trial is set for next week. Not trial. She pleaded guilty and they're going to sentence her."

"It's all over the net again," Tim said. "It's a circus."

"You'll probably want to be there," Captain Kirby said.

How I spent my summer vacation. I waited for my stomach to start spazzing and when it didn't I realized that I wasn't feeling forgiving exactly, but I didn't feel resentful either. I just felt really sad that Jane had gotten herself into a mess she finally couldn't ignore her way out of. I couldn't fix it, but I could show up.

"Yeah," I said. "I probably do."

58

Sometimes you get so pissed that you can't stay angry or you'll burst. Maybe that's what had happened with Marjewel. Or maybe she was waiting to see if what she said had gotten through to me because she said that me and Captain Kirby and Tim could stay until after the concert. But then, she told Tim, "I've having the house painted so you'll all have to leave right away." Which was totally lame-o because the house looked as detailed as she did.

Isak reported that The Griffin could hardly button his chaps and was so out of breath after an hour that he was working double sessions with his trainer and dietician to get him into as good shape as was possible in less than 24 hours—"or it's Spanx," Isak said and laughed.

"That's why he couldn't come home to see you," Isak told me. I knew it was bullshit, that Isak was playing older brother, but it made me like him even more.

Isak shooed us aside and moved deliberately around the studio, packing stuff in a padded aluminum case. Then he said the studio was all ours. He was spending the final 24 hours in town with The Griffin, Raymond and Bang.

Tim was blown away by Isak's set-up. He put his demo of Hole in the Sky in the CD player.

"I can't believe how good it sounds, better than it did in Nashville."

"It sounds great," I said.

"I know."

Tim appeared thoughtful, like he was hoping I would say I'd give the demo to The Griffin. He couldn't know that The Griffin had bragged on him to Isak and had taught Isak the basics of Hole in the Sky and that Isak had sprung them on me. The truth was Tim probably had more pull with The Griffin than I did.

"Why don't you give it to Raymond? He's already a fan of yours."

"Yeah, I know," Tim smiled. "Actually, he already heard it and he likes it. Anyway, he told me he's thinking of leaving the band. We already talked to Bilbo. Actually, I introduced them." Tim seemed really pleased with himself. "Bilbo's flying down to talk to Raymond about representing him."

"What?"

"Yeah. Since Isak joined them Raymond says it's not fun anymore. The Griffin is working solos in for Isak like he's a better guitar player and he isn't. Raymond's the best, but it's The Griffin's call not Raymond's because The Griffin writes the songs."

Tell me about it.

"Does The Griffin know?"

"Raymond told me he's been thinking about leaving to start his own thing for a while. I think he wants me to come with him."

I nodded, trying to comprehend what this meant for everyone. Raymond had a whole fan base of his own separate from The Griffin. Music blogs were always talking about Raymond as one of the great all-time guitarists and his following would undoubtedly go wherever he was.

"You can join us if you want, I'm pretty sure," Tim said. "Raymond really likes you."

I didn't feel like arguing about whether or not Raymond liked me, but joining a group with Raymond as the leader was the last thing in the world I would do especially since they were both going to be under contract to Bilbo. More importantly, now that I had written Mercy…Me! I didn't want to play someone else's songs. I wanted to get to work writing my own.

"We can talk about it later," I said.

Tim grabbed my hand and forced me to look at him. "Mercy, if I go, what's going to happen to us?"

I said, "I don't know," but I actually did.

"I have to take advantage of this thing with Raymond. I mean, it's the best thing that ever happened to me."

He had said that about Have Mercy and me not so long ago.

"I think you need to go where this leads you. You know what Captain Kirby says about going through doors when they open."

"I still want there to be us, Mercy."

I was almost sixteen now and I suspected that the chance of me and Tim being an "us" would disappear once he went on the road with Raymond.

"Are you gonna finish school?" I asked.

"I'm not sure my dad would even let me back in the house. He hung up on me when I called him yesterday."

I wanted to ask him how he felt about Clarisse, but restrained myself. "Let's just get ready for the concert and not even think about…things…until it's over. Okay?"

"Yes, that's great, but look, Mercy," Tim said, "About the concert. I think Raymond is going to ask The Griffin to let me do Hole in the Sky."

"What makes you think that?"

"He kind of said he would."

"On stage?"

"If you mind, I won't do it, I swear."

My dream had always been to be at a Griffin concert, get the nod, and have him pull me up on stage to sing with him. Now it was going to happen, the dream was coming true, but I wasn't in it.

I felt my throat get tight and I forced myself to ask, "Does The Griffin know?"

"Actually, he thought it was a great idea. Bilbo called him. He's my manager now, you know. Raymond played the demo for him. He loves the song."

"He took time out to hear the demo?"

"So, is it okay?"

If you couldn't make someone love you, you certainly couldn't convince them you were talented if they didn't think so in the first place. Like, I had to let go of the idea that I would ever be anything to The Griffin but his "funny little kid."

"It's okay, Tim. I wouldn't have come this far without you, you know that don't you?"

"I couldn't do it if it made you mad."

Yes, you could.

"I wouldn't be here at all if I wasn't in Have Mercy."

I had wondered back in Milltown whether Tim cared for me because I was me or because I was The Griffin's daughter. He had made me think it was me. But now it didn't seem to matter if I had been wrong. It only mattered that he was leaving. I was going to really really miss him.

"I want you to do it, Tim. I really do. Of course, I do." I forced a smile. "I'm glad I'm going to be here to see it. On stage? With The Griffin? No one deserves it more."

"I'm glad you're my friend, Mercy."

"Friends of course," I said, "Always!" It sounded an awful, like being The Griffin's "favorite girl."

"Oh, hey, by the way," he said, really excited. "Clarisse and Bilbo are both coming down for the concert. It's like my first paid gig and Bilbo wants to check it out."

"Naturally."

59

I was so exhausted, I slept the entire next day until three o'clock in the afternoon when I was awakened by women's laughter coming from the kitchen. Marjewel was teaching Captain Kirby Spanish.

"No, no, no, Janet, that's not how you pronounce it. Not moo-jar! Like this: moo-hair. Moo-hair. Say Moo and Hair"

Captain Kirby puckered her mouth and said it over and over. "Moo-hair, moo-hair, moo-hair."

"What does that mean?" I asked.

"*Mujer* means woman," Marjewel said, glancing at me. Now that she had a definite date when I was leaving she seemed willing to accept my presence. She even smiled at me when I parked myself on a stool at the island.

"Janet is fixing something to eat before the concert," Marjewel said. "This is scrumptious, Janet." She held up a piece of goat cheese wrapped in arugula and handed it to me.

"Splendiferous," I said.

"We had a cook growing up so I never learned how," Marjewel said. "She would throw me out of the kitchen when I wanted to watch. But Maria comes in twice a week so Isak doesn't starve."

"What do you mean you had a cook?" I asked.

Captain Kirby gave me one of her come-on-already looks. "She doesn't mean she had a restaurant, Mercy."

Marjewel laughed. "My father was very wealthy," she said. "My mother was very spoiled. Me, too."

It didn't seem fair that Marjewel grew up with a cook and a father who spoiled her while Jane grew up with Granny O'Reilly. For that matter, it didn't seem fair that Isak had a mother who worried about him starving to death while my own mother paid so little attention to the stove she never noticed that the clock on it was six hours off.

"The bus will pick us up at seven then go to the studio and pick up the band," Marjewel said. "Can you *mujeres* be ready?"

"The bus is picking us up? The band bus?"

"The Griffin thinks it's *muy dramatico* to enter with an entourage," Marjewel said. "*Muy* means very, Janet. The vowels are everything in Spanish. If you get those right people forgive the consonants. I am sure there are courses on the internet. Ask Isak. He will know. You have a very cute accent. Carmen will find it *muy adorable*."

Captain Kirby had certainly charmed Marjewel into thinking she was *muy adorable*.

"Hey," Captain Kirby asked me, "Are you going to put something cool on for the concert?"

"Isn't this cool?" I asked, pinching the sides of my dirty jeans and curtseying. "Since it's formal, I might put my bra on. How about you?"

Captain Kirby looked down at her black chinos and black tee shirt. "I want to stay in character. I think it's important for your brand to have a consistent look."

"So you're a brand now?"

"Did I say brand? I meant band."

Captain Kirby was on the exit ramp, on her way to another adventure. I could see her tail lights. We would have school together next year, but things would never be the same. Captain Kirby was right: you can never go back. Maybe I would have to start having my own adventures.

"I can loan you girls some clothes, if you want," Marjewel said.

We checked out her silk shirts and designer jeans and high-heeled sandals—they were in a walk-in closet that was as big as my bedroom—and said, "No!" at the same time.

"Thank you, though," Captain Kirby said. "Ma'm."

"Suit yourselves. Seven o'clock," Marjewel said, shooing us out of her closet. "At least make yourself presentable. You look awful. Use the bathroom off the kitchen. Just make sure you leave things as you found them." She forced herself to give me a little nod and the teensiest of smiles.

The bathroom was like a spa. We showered and put on some clean clothes before heading back to the kitchen to finish off the rest of the food that Kirby made.

"She's not so bad," Captain Kirby said, "For a step-mother."

"I suppose you've had worse?"

"What do you mean by that?"

"Everything that happens to me, you've already gone through it. It's kind of boring."

"Is that how I sound?" Kirby actually looked hurt. I'd never seen her be anything but cool before. Being in love was making her sensitive.

"I'm sorry. It's just that Marjewel doesn't consider me a step-child. She considers me an accident."

Captain Kirby gathered up the dirty dishes and put them in the sink. I started washing them. Just like home.

"You know, Mercy, I'm gonna check this thing out with Carmen. See if I, if we, can make it stick."

I held a dish up for inspection. "The prep is as important as the cooking, right?'

"Like, how many times do you find love in a lifetime?" Kirby asked.

"You haven't had a lifetime yet. You're only seventeen," I said.

"Almost eighteen."

"Do you think it's possible to find the someone who's going to be right for you forever at eighteen? What if at twenty someone better comes along?" I asked her.

"The odds are that someone else will come along. If not for you, for your partner. I don't really know. All I know is, I never felt like this before and I have to see where it goes."

"People change," I said, thinking of Tim. Was I in love with him? He had changed. How would he feel when he saw that I had changed?

"What if you finish growing up and you're so changed that Carmen doesn't like what you've become?"

"I'll deal with that when it happens. But, hey! You never know, maybe me and Carmen will be one of those couples who stay together forever."

"You never know," I said.

"I have a very strong loyalty streak in me."

"I know, Captain Kirby."

"And anyway, wherever this takes me it's not like you and I won't be friends anymore. We'll always be friends. And school next year." She laughed her low "hehehehe" laugh.

It sounded like a demotion. Kirby and Tim were the first friends I ever really had and I had to let them both go. Now I saw what happens when you let people out of their boxes. They run away.

Captain Kirby frowned. "I just hope Carmen feels the same way. She is so together. And I have a lot of loose ends."

It was the first time I ever heard Captain Kirby express any self-doubt. "How could she not love you?" I asked. "You charmed Marjewel, you charmed Mrs. Valliere. Granny O'Reilly said you were street smart and I never heard her say anything nice about anyone. Everyone loves you. Even I love you...as a friend, of course. So what's your problem?

"I didn't start out completely honest with Carmen, and I'm worried she'll think I'm a complete bullshit artist when I tell her the truth, and I'll have to sooner or later, and maybe she'll never trust me."

Kirby was the most up front person I'd ever met so I couldn't imagine that it was anything game-changing. "So, what did you lie about?"

"I told her my name was Janet Kirby and that me and my ma were on our way to New York when we stopped in Milltown to visit some friends and she got a great job as a make-up artist and that's why we stayed."

I repeated what she said in my head. "So, which part is..."

"A lie?"

I nodded.

"Most of it."

"But your mother is a make-up artist…"

"Was."

"And you do live in Milltown…"

"But we didn't stop there to visit anyone. You know that. We stopped there because my mother kidnapped me. The court said she was an unfit mother and gave me to my father. I mean, it's ridiculous because he didn't want me. I bought us phony ID from some Mexicans I knew in East L.A.—boy are they good—and we changed our name to Kirby."

"So your name isn't …."

"No. I mean my dad doesn't care, which is the funny part. But we're both in the system, and if I used my real name the FBI would be all over us and my mother would end up in jail. Technically, she abducted me, even though it was my idea. I just have to stay hidden till I turn eighteen."

We sat on the island stools for a long time.

"So, did you actually call your father about Jonah's and Zina's TV show…?"

"Oh, yeah, that was real. He's real. He was totally on board with it. He wished me luck with my new life and said I could count on him for help. Pretty funny, huh? It's kind of too bad that Zina screwed that up, but I'll find something else. You will, too. There's always something else."

"So," I said, "What am I supposed to call you?"

"Look, Mercy, can you forgive me? I didn't know I'd get so involved in your life or I would have been straight with you from the beginning. It was a mistake and I know it. And I made it with Carmen too. I never had any real friends before. No one but you knows that me and my mom lived in a freaking funeral home. You're more like me than anyone I ever met. I mean, your mom is a nut job and your dad likes you as long as you don't come within a thousand miles of him. I knew I could trust you. I was going to keep it just me and my mom until I turned 18. I thought I could wait till I was 18 to start being a human being."

It was always just me and Jane, too. We didn't have to lie about our names, but we did about everything else, trying to make people believe we were normal. "Sixteen. Eighteen," I said, "What's the difference, huh? It's a long time to wait to be real."

Marjewel called from the front door, "If you girls don't come out right now, the bus is going to leave without you!"

"Oh my god! It's gotten so late!"

I stood up to go but Captain Kirby pinned my hand on the island under hers.

"So?" she said.

I wriggled my hand out from under hers. "The only thing I couldn't forgive you for is if you made me miss a ride to The Griffin's concert on his band bus."

60

The band bus was parked in the circular driveway with its engine running, speakers on the grill blaring out a song I'd never heard, probably one The Griffin just wrote. The paintings of The Griffin, Bang, Raymond and Isak on the bus's side looked brand new, like they'd just been detailed.

I asked the bus driver about the song as we boarded. "He calls it Plan B Black Hole. The Griffin's on fire. This is a new beginning for him," he said. "He wrote it yesterday."

Tim was already in the back. I sat down on The Griffin's orange Barca Lounger. My heart was pounding so hard I put my hand over it to slow it down. Marjewel gave me a disapproving look as she walked by me.

"I'll get up when he gets on," I said. I wanted to be part of it all by osmosis even if the reality was that I wasn't. I squirmed around in the chair to rub some of The Griffin's mojo off on my pants and shirt, which I knew I would never wash again.

"You having a heart attack or what?" Captain Kirby asked, sitting down on the lounger's arm.

This seat was where The Griffin sang songs to me when I was little and he came to town. This was where The Griffin sat to dole out Christmas presents, even if we didn't get them till February. This was where Jane probably sat on The Griffin's lap while I was growing inside her. It was even maybe where I was conceived.

"Fine. I'm fine," I said.

Tim sat down across from us. He was grinning like an idiot.

"Ready for your close-up, Tim?" Captain Kirby asked him.

"Absolutely."

I could see he wasn't nervous. All the weird shit he'd gone through with his crazy survivalist father and grandfather, somehow it hadn't taken control of him and somehow he hadn't needed to take control of it. He was honest and he wasn't afraid. That was his secret.

"You'll be great," I said.

"You'll get your chance too," he said.

"Maybe."

Was Mercy…Me! a good song? If you measure the worth of a song by its power, the answer was definitely yes. I would get my chance, but I didn't want to jinx it by saying it aloud.

I felt my phone vibrate and I looked at it. It was a phone number from Pennsylvania. Jane!

"Mom?"

"Mercedes! I was hoping you'd pick up. Put it on speaker, I can't hear you, there's a lot of noise in here."

"Is something wrong?" I asked her.

"I was feeling lonely and wanted to hear your voice, that's all. Silly, right? Dutton let me use her cell phone again. She's a really good person."

"You'll be okay, Mom," I said.

"Do you think so, Mercedes? Really?"

"I'm leaving tomorrow. I'll be there for your sentencing, Mom."

"Where are you? What do you mean you're leaving tomorrow? How come you're calling me mom?"

"You'll never believe this. I'm in Houston! I'm on The Griffin's bus! We're going to his concert!"

"How did you get to Houston?"

"It's a long story. It'll have to wait."

"I guess I have no choice. Be careful, honey. You know what happened to me when I was sixteen."

"Don't worry, Mom. I'm cool."

Jane sighed. "You are. You really are. We're the Two Cool Society, right?"

I laughed. I would explain to Jane when we were finally together that the Two Cool Society was disbanded, that you can't go back to how things used to be, like Captain Kirby said. But here's the thing: why would you want to? "I'll record the concert for you on my phone. As much as I can get on it."

"Dutton wants her phone back. I've gotta go. I love you, Mercedes."

Captain Kirby had been listening in. When I paused she kicked my foot.

"I love you too, Mom."

61

On the drive into town—now that I knew I was just an accident he'd decided not to repair and that he thought I was just a little kid with a penchant for geeky charts and graphs—I was thinking that I didn't know how I was going to react when he boarded the bus, but here's what happened, it was exactly the same as always. When he climbed up the stairs into the bus and filled the aisle with his presence, spreading his wings for us to admire him, I didn't see the gimmicky part: the fake feathers, fake tail, the glue holding everything together. I saw The Griffin who was capable of making thousands of people go wild with joy over his music. I knew then that it had been ridiculous to think that he could ever be a regular dad and cut the lawn or pay attention to my insecurities as noted on PowerPoint or buy Jane flowers or even pick up the phone every time I called like other dads did for their kids, because he wasn't like other dads. He was The Griffin, larger than life. He was a crummy dad, but a great Griffin. And knowing that broke my heart, but the fact is my breaking heart gave me my first real song.

Gonna leave me?
Make me cry?
Try to hurt me?
I don't die

Was it a fair trade? I would have to find out.

Everyone fussed over him and he peered out from under his heavy make-up and errant feathers, and looked at me expectantly, and I rushed to him and he enveloped me in his eagle wings, whispering in my ear: "You're my favorite, girl. You've always been my favorite girl." and I looked at him with tears in my eyes and he said, "No crying. This is a big night for me, Mercy. A new start. For you too," and before I could ask him what he meant by that he got involved in a discussion with Tim that I tried unsuccessfully to eavesdrop on.

He was right. It was a new start for me too. As of right now, I was stepping out as a special and talented me—Mercy O'Reilly. Just me. Without the weight of my special and talented family holding me back.

Raymond, Bang and Isak came to the front of the bus and were the first to get off when we pulled through giant garage doors into the back of the Toyota Center. A crowd of groupies was being held back by policemen. The Griffin grabbed my hand as I got off. He walked a few steps toward them, took me in his arms, and covered me with his wings. He really knew how to play the crowd. They went crazy and if it hadn't been for the policemen arms linked holding them back they would have run me over.

"And so it begins," Marjewel said, edging me out of the way to be at the Griffin's side as his entourage made its entrance.

The groupies' screaming bounced off the garage walls. It was like that night at the Trap, but the adoration felt more intense, almost frantic. It was freakin awesome.

The band was already in costume, so there was no need to go into dressing rooms, and we were a half hour late anyway. We walked down a long tunnel under the tiered seats—I'd googled the Center and kind of knew what it looked like and I could see the brightly lit arena at the end of it. As we got near the end of the tunnel lights started flashing like crazy and an announcer was shouting something that I couldn't make out and a throbbing noise began. We came out on the side of the stage. Security guards were waiting there and they escorted me, Tim, Marjewel and Kirby down some steps and into a row of seats right in front of the stage that had been saved for us. The flashing lights were so bright and were flashing so fast that we were all basically half blind and the security guards had to hold our hands or we would have tripped over each other. Bilbo and Clarisse were already seated there and they gathered Tim between them, shouting stuff into one another's ears. The throbbing noise had subsided and was replaced by moans and boos. My eyes began to adjust and I stood up to look around and what I saw was so scary and thrilling that I'll remember it for the rest of my life.

Isak had said he was a little worried that they wouldn't get the numbers if Aerosmith wasn't involved—this was The Griffin's first concert without them in ten years—but he shouldn't have been. I'd told Mrs. Big Hair that the concert was already sold out, and it was. I'd googled the Center's capacity, 18,000 seats and it looked like every one of them was filled.

And then something else began that was more scary than it was thrilling. Bang came on stage and the roar started again then diminished. Then Isak walked on stage to mixed "who is that?" shouts. Then Raymond emerged and a roar turned into loud chants of his name. The three musicians went about the business of checking amps, testing mikes, connecting wires, tuning guitar strings, acting as if they were on the stage alone not in front of 18,000 fans, and the crowd quieted if you can call it that. It was like the in-between of crashing waves when you know another is coming. Raymond looked at Bang and Isak and nodded his head and the group leaped into a jacked up version of Hotter than Hell and 18,000 people began to sing the words and I got caught up in it and Tim and Kirby did too and even Marjewel sang along and we were looking at each other and laughing and even Bilbo and Clarisse were clapping and laughing, then we stopped because a roar went up that was so loud, so deafening, that you didn't just hear it—you felt like it was coming from inside you and would split your skin. The Griffin had come on stage. He walked to the front—apart from the other band members who were looking at him and each other and laughing—letting the crowds' adoration wash over him for what seemed like a very long time but was probably only a minute and I was thinking, how do rock stars feel facing thousands of maniacal worshippers with nothing separating them from the crowd but the stage and a dozen security guards? They were there to make the crowd believe that their awe of them was justified. Only music could do that.

The Griffin spread his wings in such a way that the crowd knew to quiet down. Some girls seated right behind us were screaming out the names of their favorite songs. I turned my phone on to record for Jane.

From the speakers came a faint sound like someone was sobbing, and I felt my pulse race with recognition, then I felt a ripple of anticipation go through the crowd as they strained to give a name to what they were hearing. The sobbing got louder and louder as the sound tech played it in a loop and the sobs went on and on and I heard the girls behind us start crying. Then the sobbing stopped and there was no sound at all coming from the speakers and only a few shouts rippled across the heads of the silenced listeners. But then all of a sudden the speakers emitted a scream that was so heart-broken it was almost unbearable and it went on and on and repeated itself and repeated itself until the audience began to scream and I knew who was screaming. It was me. It was the back-up tape of me from the studio. Isak must have taken it with him when he left and played it for The Griffin. The scream finally stopped and Bang starting banging his drums and Raymond and Isak began playing the chords, my chords, the chords to Mercy...Me! and the audience erupted. And it was for me. I felt the audience's love and I let it envelope me.

The Griffin came to the edge of the stage and pointed at me and two security guards lifted me onto the stage and Isak handed me my Fender which I strapped on. The crowd was going berserk and I felt a new emotion, a feeling of incredible confidence because the crowd was chanting my melody—my melody!—and it created something I had never felt before—the feeling of possibility so big that even this colossal theatre couldn't contain it, the feeling that anything could happen because it was my life now and it felt... wonderful.

I turned to look at The Griffin. He was waiting for me, playing the bridge for me to walk across into my song.

I smiled.
He raised his finger to cue the band, then looked at me and nodded.

ABOUT MADDY WELLS

Maddy Wells is a wife and hopefully one day a mother. Have Mercy is the first book in the Have a Life series. Maddy is working on the second book in the series, Have Faith, while trying to figure out what to name her cat. Ideas about that or just say hi: Maddywells@blueheronbookworks.com

www.ingramcontent.com/pod-product-compliance
Lightning Source LLC
Chambersburg PA
CBHW020623180626
46810CB00007B/2907